The Curse of Purgatory Cove

Pete A. O'Donnell

Visit our website at www.StillwaterPress.com for more information.

First Stillwater River Publications Edition

ISBN-13: 978-1-950339-33-4
ISBN-10: 1-950339-33-5

12345678910

Written and illustrated by Pete A. O'Donnell
Cover art by Christopher Hilaire.
Published by Stillwater River Publications, Pawtucket, RI 02860

Publisher's Cataloging-In-Publication Data
(Prepared by The Donohue Group, Inc.)

Names: O'Donnell, Pete A., 1977- author, illustrator
Title: The curse of Purgatory Cove / Pete A. O'Donnell.
Description: First Stillwater River Publications edition. | Pawtucket, RI, USA :
    Stillwater River Publications, 2019. | Interest age level: 008-012. |
Identifiers: ISBN 9781950339334 | ISBN 1950339335
Subjects: LCSH: Pirates--Juvenile fiction. | Paperboys--Juvenile fiction. |
    Ghosts--Juvenile fiction. | Magic--Juvenile fiction. | CYAC: Pirates--Fiction.
    | Paperboys--Fiction. | Ghosts--Fiction. | Magic--Fiction. | LCGFT: Action
    and adventure fiction.
Classification: LCC PZ7.1.O2295 Cu 2019 | DDC [Fic]--dc23

Dedication

This book is dedicated to the memory of my uncle, Richard Halliday, who sailed on the HMS Rose, a reproduction of an eighteenth-century British tall-ship. I've known no one who loved history more.

It is also dedicated to the memory of my uncle Gerrard Smith who told me the tale of Captain Blood while camping on the coast of Maine. He fired my imagination and created my love of storytelling.

I sailed with them both and I miss them greatly.

Chapter 1

Canine Caper

Tuesday had a 'Monday' feel. Even with summer three weeks away I wanted to pack my things and vanish. I knew it was coming too, that stupid letter, and I'd already worked out my escape plan, sort of. What I hadn't figured on was meeting a crazy old pirate who had the one thing I needed.

I grabbed my house keys and faded Sox cap, pulling it down over my eyes as I headed toward Purgatory Cove.

It was early. I stopped my bike near a pile of newspapers at an old factory building. I rolled them up then rode back and forth across the narrow street. There was no traffic, just a truck full of dead fish at the Harbor Inn. The tide was up, filling the stone parking lots. I wanted to turn around when the road began to rise, but there was one more delivery at the dead-end.

I pedaled slowly up the hill towards a fenced-in yard with a shack and a beaten-up barn in the middle of it. There was no grass, just gravel and nautical garbage thrown everywhere. Like a junkyard for ancient boats, complete with a cranky old dog.

The junkyard's owner didn't tip. He paid in coins counted out precisely, placed in an envelope he stuck in his fence. I'd rather he didn't pay at all.

The guy kept to himself, some sort of 'criminal' or 'dangerous psycho' according to what I hear in town. Some mornings I could see him out near the barn, or out by the broken boats, walking around, but I never got a good look at him, only his bushy white hair blowing like a cotton ball in the wind.

He knew how to use the phone though. I'd only had this job a few weeks when he called to complain to my boss. Apparently, he wasn't getting his papers. That wasn't my fault though.

I had the paper in hand, ready to let it fly from a safe distance, but I stopped across the street shaking my head. There was a small white envelope in the fence. I would have to go over and get it.

What could be in there, a dollar, maybe two? Probably less. *I could pay it out of my own pocket*, I thought, as I sighed and climbed off my bike. I crossed the street, holding the paper like a club.

I knew he was there. I could feel him watching me. The old man's dog had a tail that never wagged, not that I'd seen anyway. Then again I was usually running away from him.

My eyes went over the yard wondering where he'd come from. There were sailboats and motorboats. Near the back, there was even an old tugboat towering above everything.

I was a foot from the envelope, my eyes searching for the dog when something caught my attention. Half-buried beneath a pile of pallets was a small sailboat. Yeah, I know; that's like finding sand at the beach, but this boat was special.

The paint was faded gray, but I could still read a name stenciled on the back, *Caroline*. I reached out and touched the fence. This was my dad's old boat.

I stood with my mouth open wondering how it ended up here. That's when the dog attacked. He sprung out of nowhere, ramming his skull into the chain links. The fence rattled as his head shoved me back. His teeth were bared, yelping and barking.

I fell over clutching the envelope in a slobber-covered hand. The dog pushed his body into the fence, shoving it out, trying to reach me as I scurried across the street. I'm not going to lie; part of my retreat was on my hands and knees. I think that's the definition of scurrying.

When I got to my bike the dog howled a moment longer, then he settled down onto his belly, growling a little, looking content and happy that yet again he'd managed to get me.

"I used to like dogs!" I shouted at him. He bared his teeth and growled a little.

"I gotta deliver this. It's my job." I held up the paper, explaining. It was pointless though, because he was a dog, and also a jerk. He stood up as I came closer. I'd squeezed the paper so hard it looked unreadable.

I was trying to look through the fence towards the boat, but it was too far back and I'd come too close. The dog started gnashing his teeth and barking again.

"Fine, fine you win," I said tossing the paper over the fence. The dog grabbed it out of the air. For a moment I thought he was going to bring it to his owner. I should've known better. He started chewing and tearing, ripping it to shreds, sending pieces in the air like confetti.

"I really hate you." I was sure my boss would be getting another phone call.

Chapter 2

Boarding Schools and Boats

The worst part was the day wasn't done with me yet.

I hung out with my grandmother after school and didn't go home till dinner time. My mom looked up from the kitchen table as I came through the door. "Guess what came in the mail today?" she asked. Legal papers from her office covered the table, not dinner.

"A million dollars," I said. Actually, I was expecting a message from my boss saying not to bother coming back.

"Close, but no. You got a letter from the Beecher Academy. They want to interview you," she said.

"Great…" I responded.

"We discussed this Tom. It's the school your grandfather and your uncle went to. Senator's kids go there."

My grandfather had brought it up months back at breakfast. I remember him saying how good the super-exclusive Connecticut boarding school would be for me.

"That school with all the rich kids?" I asked.

She gathered her papers into a large envelope. I could tell she didn't care for the 'rich kids' comment. She set the envelope down on the edge of the table, tapping it, "This school is very hard to get into. The fact that they're interested in you says a lot. You should feel honored."

I was fairly certain they were more interested in having another Summerlee on their roster. Even if that wasn't my last name I was still part of the Summerlee family, and as my father used to tell me, being in an old family was like being part of an exclusive club.

"But Mom, it's a boarding school. Doesn't that mean I'd have to live there?"

"Well yes, but you'd come home on weekends and holidays. It's not that bad," she answered as she turned back to her work.

'Not that bad,' was she kidding? I felt a ringing in my ears.

"I just want you to get the best education possible," she said, seeing the look on my face.

"But what if I don't want it?"

"You're not ready to decide what you want, at least not in the long run, and not for your future. A place like this will open doors that you can't even imagine."

"But—"

"I don't want to hear it," she said slapping the table. "You have an interview next Wednesday. You're going to it, and you are going to do your best. Is that understood?"

It was pointless to argue. "I'll do my best," I mumbled.

"Good," she said like that was it, period.

I walked back to my room feeling punched in the stomach. I closed my door, careful not to let it slam. I went to my dresser and picked up a picture, looking at it as I sat down on the edge of my bed.

The picture was of my dad and me, down at the park a little over two years ago. We were both smiling. My mom was there too. She was the one who took it. I couldn't remember if she'd been smiling or not.

My father had been gone for a year now. Mom acted like he was dead, but he wasn't, he was just gone. They used to fight all the time, then one day the fighting stopped. He wrote me to say he was sorry. Someday, he hoped, I'd understand. The letter said he was in Key West, trying to start a charter fishing business. It had always been a dream of his.

My father had lots of dreams. This was the first time he'd tried to make one happen. I think I understood that well enough to not be mad at him, instead I just felt lonely.

After he was gone my mom was angry for a month straight. She'd cry at night and yell for no reason. When that was done she started clearing out everything connected to him; his clothes, his tools, eventually even the house went. The worst, though, was when she got rid of his boat. She'd donated it like everything else.

I used to play on it in the yard, pretending it was a pirate ship. I'd only been sailing on it once and we'd barely made it across the cove. My dad wasn't an experienced sailor, so it took him a lot of bailing to figure out that the vessel wasn't actually seaworthy.

I remember being down at the boat launch, pulling it out of the cove and onto its trailer. It had a half-foot of water in it. We were wet and tired, but happy.

"Maybe when you're older, and I have more time, we can fix her up right," he had said.

"When?" I asked, impatient to spend another day trying to sail.

He ran his hand through my hair. "I don't know, but we'll find the time. Right now she's not safe. We don't want to add another wreck to these waters."

I was standing on the trailer, looking out at the cove, watching the sun drop behind the trees, making the water sparkle. "There's a shipwreck out there?" I asked.

"Plenty out in the bay." He'd pointed to the mouth of the cove. "In fact, the *Freedom's Fortune* is said to lay just off the point."

He smiled, leaned in, and lowered his voice. "It was a pirate ship." He left the words hanging in the air like the promise of magic.

"Have you ever heard the story?" he asked.

I shook my head.

"The captain came here to retire after pillaging the high seas." Dad threw a stone out into the cove, making an explosive sound as the rock splashed. "That was a cannon-ball by the way," he said, winking.

He continued, "See, the captain had fallen in love and married a local merchant's daughter. Of course, before leaving the life, he hid his treasure on an island that only he knew the way to.

"His old crew found out about it. They came in the night and kidnapped him. As they sailed away, a freak storm rushed into the bay. It dragged the *Freedom's Fortune* across Spindle rock. Captain and crew went to the bottom."

"So the treasure is still out there?" I asked.

My father nodded. He finished securing our little boat and stepped out of the water. "They say the captain's bride still wanders the shore looking for her lost husband."

A cold breeze blew off the cove, causing both of us to shiver. He laughed and patted me on the shoulder. "Come on," he said as we climbed into his truck to drive home.

I set the picture down, remembering his laugh. Then I reached under my mattress and pulled out a book. It was one of the few things I'd managed to hold onto. It was a simple guide, maybe a hundred pages long, but it described another one of my father's dreams, a trip he wanted to take.

I thought about the boarding school as I opened the cover, looking at the eastern seaboard, seeing a journey charted out on it. It couldn't happen without a boat though.

My dad's was held hostage by that hermit. I wondered how long it'd been sitting out there, right under my nose. Actually, I guess it was under the dog's nose. There were others I could buy, but I wanted his back. I went to the window, slid it open, and climbed out. The day hadn't been great, but now it was going take a turn for the weird.

Chapter 3

Circling Sword

Outside I picked up my bike and looked at the sun getting low in the sky. I really shouldn't do this, I thought, heading back towards town. It wouldn't take me long to get to his yard and maybe by then the dog would be away for the night.

I was only hoping for a look at the boat, or possibly a run-in with the old man to ask him about it. Why not approach a guy who's made it incredibly clear he wants to be left alone?

I was about to turn and head towards the water when I saw something on Main Street, heading south. It was a headful of white cottony hair blowing in the breeze. The old man was out riding his own bike, heading in a hurry out of town.

For some reason, I decided to follow him. He was dashing down the sidewalk around groups of people strolling on Main Street. He went out into the road when it dropped down a big hill. I watched him cut across traffic, taking a left turn, heading out onto Monthaupset, a strip of land that jutted out into the bay. It was a peninsula covered by a state park, a few private homes, and a couple of horse farms. There was only one main road going out to it. It was lined by stone walls and tall trees casting long shadows.

It was easily three miles to the point. And while I wondered why the old man was heading there, I was even more concerned with why I was following him. Mom would eventually come looking for me. She'd knock on my door and find my room empty; let's just say that's not going to go well for me. Somehow that scared me more than following the old hermit.

I was still being careful though, trying to use the curves of the road to hide. Letting him stay ahead and out of view. That's how I lost him. When I passed the entrance to the park he was gone. The road was empty.

I heard a sound, small stones pinging in spokes and bike tires bumping over gravel. A narrow, dark path cut down into the woods across the street. I could hear him ahead as I climbed off my bike and followed. The forest blocked out the setting sun, but there was light ahead.

I carefully approached, coming to the end of the path where the ground dropped away by a small cliff overlooking a rocky beach. The sun was disappearing into the west, and the Atlantic was getting dark. Waves rushed in, breaking and diving beneath the rocks.

He was below, making his way from stone to stone, carrying a leather bundle. He got around pretty good for someone so old. Coming to a wide, flat rock with a tidal pool in the center, he bent down and cleared some of the scum away.

He laid his bundle down, unrolling it, revealing something dark and metal. It was a knife, or maybe a small sword. It looked ancient and tarnished. There was a pattern on it, strange swirls dancing in and out of more swirls.

Old man, weird knife, and I'm there watching all by myself. My mom said I was smart? If she could see me now.

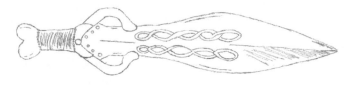

A few rocks crunched out from under my foot and went tumbling down the hill. I looked at the old man to see if he'd heard, but he wasn't facing me so I couldn't tell. I took a few breaths and tried not to panic. There was something strange in the air, an electric feeling.

The sun was creeping slowly down, almost touching the land. The ocean and the sky reflected it with strange colors. The old man took the sword and placed it in the tidal pool.

I expected it to disappear beneath the scum, but it didn't; it floated on the surface. I could see the old man's lips moving. A few of the words reached me, some foreign language, all hard consonants. I didn't understand them, but they echoed in my head, charging the air around me. I held my breath, watching.

In the tidal pool, something started to happen, slowly at first, then speeding up. The sword was spinning! It blurred like the blades of a fan. Then as suddenly as it began, it stopped. It went completely rigid, pointing out towards the ocean. The pool of water was clear and vibrating with energy. It was beyond strange. I wished I wasn't alone so I could ask someone else if they were seeing it too.

The sun was touching the earth as the old man's lips stopped moving. Hurrying, he pulled out a compass, one of those clear plastic ones, from his pocket. He held it over the sword squinting at it, trying to line them up. He took out a pad and scrawled something down.

The compass and the pad disappeared back into his pocket. He reached into the pool trying to lift the sword, but it held to the water. Finally, he yanked it free and fell backward. "Bloody specters!" he cursed.

I'd been in a daze till then, but his voice shook me out of it.

The old man wrapped the sword back in its leather bundle. He'd be coming back up the beach soon. Panic struck me as I realized I needed to get out of there. I turned and hurried away back up the dark trail. I climbed on my bike. The sunlight was fading, making everything look un-real. I had no idea what I'd just seen, but I knew it wasn't normal and I was worried. This guy had a magic sword and I couldn't get his paper to him because of that stupid dog. I think it was a set up.

.

Chapter 4

A Bargain Struck

I got home last night five minutes after my mom came into my room to check on me. She'd already called my grandfather which meant I'd get chewed out by him next. But first came my mom's interrogation. She wanted to know where I'd been. I told her I was out at the point—not a lie.

"What could you possibly have been doing out there at this time of night?" she demanded.

I thought about telling her what I saw. Then I thought about lying to her. I decided on the middle ground. "I was watching the sunset," I answered.

She crossed her arms, waiting for the real answer.

"I figured I better enjoy what I can around here before I get shipped off to Connecticut," I shot at her.

Talk like that could only result in one thing: being sent to your grandparents' house the next day to be 'watched.'

Luckily my grandmother wasn't a very strict jailor. I only had to ask, and I was set free. No one talked about it, but when I went there, it was more so I could keep an eye on her. My grandmother's memory was going, and simple things escaped her. Sometimes she even had trouble recognizing me.

I left their house and went to a small park near the water with a stone monument covered by the names of West Harbor sailors lost at sea. The dates went back to the 1700s. Many of them were Summerlees. Behind the monument, facing out towards the water, were a couple of benches.

Early on a Wednesday afternoon I expected to have it to myself, so I was a little surprised to find someone on my favorite bench, the one closest to the water.

I didn't recognize him at first. I'd never seen him with his hair combed. He was feeding ducks from a bag of stale bread, looking like any other old man. His shoulders were low, and his eyes were far away. There was no leather bundle or magic sword around for me to worry about.

I thought of taking another bench away from him, or leaving the park altogether, but some impulse made me decide to plop down right next to him. I saw this guy doing some really weird stuff last night, creepy chanting, sword spinning. I tried making excuses for what I saw. Maybe the sword was a magnet? Maybe it was battery operated. A prop from the Lord of the Rings, or something? There had to be some explanation.

"Hi," I said. The old man nodded his head before turning his attention back to the ducks.

"I'm Tom," I said.

He looked at me again and asked in a strange accent, "You're the paper boy, aren't you?" I thought of the bizarre words he'd said last night, and wondered again why I was doing this.

I nodded my head, yes.

"You're not very good at your job." He turned back to the ducks.

My mouth hung open. Finally I said, "It's not my fault."

"What?" he asked.

"Your dog keeps taking the papers. He shreds them."

"You're blaming the dog? You ever think of not putting them over the fence? I can walk out the gate you know?"

"Oh," I said, annoyed I hadn't thought of it on my own. "I just, I—"

"It's fine," he said. "The dog is a bit difficult."

19

"And mean," I added, immediately regretting it.

The old man glanced at me, one bushy eyebrow lifted. "A friendly guard dog wouldn't do much good now, would it? You can't keep anything away if you're not mean."

After an awkward pause, I asked, "Are you worried someone will steal your boats?"

"No—I'm not worried about the boats." The old man stared at the water.

"You sure have a lot of them."

He shrugged his shoulders.

"What do you do with them all?"

"Some I fix. Some I don't."

"I think one of them used to belong to my father and me," I said. "A fourteen-foot catboat, all wood. The *Caroline*?"

He took another handful of bread and tossed it. "All my boats are wood, but I think I know the one you're talking about."

"What do you plan on doing with it?"

"Fix it, maybe, or use it for firewood. Depends how bad it is. I haven't taken a good look at it yet." The old man didn't turn his head, but he was glancing at me out of the corner of his eye. He turned the bag over and emptied it.

"You wouldn't really burn it, would you?" I asked.

He smiled a little. It wasn't pleasant. "No, I wouldn't burn it, not if someone were interested in it. I'd fix it up. That's what I do, fix old boats then sell them. It's how I make my living."

"How much could you get for a boat like that?"

He thought about it. "Well she's an antique, probably close to seventy years old, and if I restored her properly, she could catch a fair price."

I was picturing the wad of cash I'd managed to collect under my bed, wondering if it'd be enough.

"I'd probably hope for a couple of grand," Swift added.

"Grand? You mean like thousands?"

"Yeah, maybe two or better if I'm lucky."

I barely had a hundred dollars under my bed. There was no way I could raise that kind of cash in a summer, and I knew I wanted to get the boat before the season was out.

Swift looked at me. He could read the disappointment on my face. "I'll tell you though, if I had someone to help me work on her, I could maybe see my way to letting her go for less."

It took me a moment to realize who he was talking about. "Do you mean me? You want my help?"

He pointed at my chest. "If you're willing to work for it, I'd be willing to let you have it at a fair price."

"Like how much?"

He motioned for me to come closer. Then he lowered his voice. He looked over his shoulder at the water as if making sure we were alone. He said, "I'll ask you to do me a favor. You'll have to take a little trip and retrieve something for me. You do that and I'll give you the boat free and clear. What do you think?"

I was so thrilled I could hardly speak. The words just wouldn't come out. I suppose I should've been more worried about what he was asking, where he wanted me to go and, most importantly, what he wanted me to get.

The old man asked again, "Well Tom, what's your answer?" He put his hand out.

I took the hand and pumped it up and down. "We've got a deal," I said.

"Then we'll start the work Saturday morning."

I let go of his hand. He crumbled up his bread bag. He started to turn and walk away, heading up to his yard. "By the way, my name is Swift, Nathanial Swift," he said over his shoulder.

"Nice to meet you," I said to his back. Then a thought occurred to me. "Hey, how do I get into the yard?"

"Through the gate," he answered.

"No, I mean how do I get past your dog?"

He looked back at me and smiled again. "I'd bring him a bone or something."

"That'll make him like me?" I asked.

He shook his head. "That dog doesn't like anyone, but it might keep him from, you know…"

"Tearing me apart?"

"Yeah, exactly," he said.

Chapter 5

Work Begins

aturday morning I went to Swift's yard with two things. One was the newspaper, he was my last stop after all, and the other was an entire box of dog bones. I went to the gate, stopped, and made sure the box was open. There was no sign of the dog, or the boat for that matter, though I could see the spot where it'd been.

The gate was unlocked. I slowly pushed it aside, wondering where the furry nightmare was hiding. Maybe it was my imagination, but I thought for sure he was watching me.

I leaned my bike against the fence and started to creep in. I could see the barn. That's where Swift told me to go. The doors on either side were wide open, letting sunlight in. I was halfway across the yard when I saw the boat inside. It was sitting in the center of the barn, resting on its curved bottom, and the dog was sitting right in front of it.

He's bigger than I remember, I thought as he turned his head at the sound of my footsteps on the gravel. His lips pulled back, baring his teeth.

I waved to him as my voice went higher, "Hi there."

He growled getting up, slowly coming towards me. I reached into the box of treats and quickly pulled out one of the bones. I held it out for him. "Here boy, see, I'm your friend." His teeth stayed bared as he came closer. I was hoping he wouldn't take my whole hand. He sniffed at the bone then stalked past it.

The box of treats was on my other side, tucked up under my arm. The dog was so close I could smell his breath. He turned his massive head a little and opened his mouth wide. He sunk his teeth in and took the entire box, pulling it from me. "Oh, okay, that's fine," I said as he walked away. He snarled one more time then disappeared into the yard.

"You're welcome," I called behind him as I looked down at the one bone left in my hand. I put it in my pocket, not sure if it'd be enough tomorrow. If I have to buy an entire box every day, then this boat was going to be more than I could afford.

I came into the barn and looked at it. The mast was missing, and weather had turned the decking a dingy yellow. Dark spots covered it, and a few planks were popped loose.

I put my hand on the old boat as a foot came crashing straight up through the deck. The leather boot disappeared, leaving a large, jagged hole. "This whole bloody thing is rotting away. Look at this," another kick came smashing up from inside. "Not an inch of this deck is worth saving," Swift yelled. He was inside lying on his back.

He got up and looked at the holes he'd made. "Is this really the boat you want to fix?"

"It was my dad's."

He stared at me from under those bushy eyebrows.

"Can you do it?" I asked.

He shook his head and got out, walking over to his workbench. "I can. But it's going to be close," he said, pulling up the first page of a calendar.

"I didn't know we had a deadline." I looked over his shoulder. A date was circled at the end of June. We were near the end of May.

"There's probably a lot you don't know." He dropped the page and turned towards me. "That trip you're going to take. It's got to be done on a certain night, the summer solstice."

"Oh," I said, waiting for him to say more.

He didn't though. He pulled out a metal toolbox then dropped it at my feet, kicking it open. "Get any hardware off the boat."

I wasn't sure what he was talking about, and it must've shown on my face.

"Cleats and things like that, anything metal. Take it off and put it in this bucket so we can have it for later." He held a plastic container out to me then took a notebook out of his pocket. The same one he'd had the other night where he'd scribbled a note after that sword stopped spinning.

I glanced over his hand to see if it was still there, but he turned the first page over, looking at me like he knew what I was thinking. "Well, don't just stand there boy, get to work."

I went to the back of the boat to a metal bar just above where the tiller would've been called a traveler. I remember my dad telling me to keep my hand off it so my fingers wouldn't get pinched. I started to remove screws while Swift circled with his little notebook, leaning down and inspecting different spots, then shaking his head. When he came round to the back I had one screw left. I was leaning all my weight on the screwdriver, trying to get it to dig into the metal head, which was almost stripped bare.

"Let me see that," he said, taking the screwdriver and turning it. He pulled the traveler away with large chunks of wood still attached to either end. "No point in being gentle. This decking is going to have to be replaced anyway."

I went back to work pulling off the rest of the hardware. Each screw fought me. "This is harder than I thought it'd be," I said.

Swift looked at me and snorted.

"What?" I asked.

"Nothing, but I wouldn't call what you're doing hard." He reminded me of my grandfather.

"When I was your age, I worked every day, except for Sunday, and it wasn't doing anything this enjoyable." Swift took a crowbar and a hammer and started tearing into the planks that made up the deck.

I felt my face flush. The screws and other fasteners came loose quicker. I threw the last cleat in the bucket and then climbed out of the boat. I found another hammer and crowbar in the toolbox.

"It sounds like you have an accent, but I can't tell where it's from," I said as I pulled a plank away.

"I was born in Cork," he said while hammering down on the crowbar, trying to pop a stubborn piece. "In the south of Ireland, not far from the English Channel."

"You don't sound Irish. My dad's great aunt was from there, and she sounded different," I said.

"I haven't been back in a while." He went to his workbench, telling me over his shoulder to grab a tape measure and mark off the width of the boat at three-foot intervals.

He cut some wood and brought the planks over, placing them close to where I'd measured. Then he made little marks with his pencil.

"I've seen you around with Ed Summerlee. Is he your relation?" He motioned for me to follow him.

"He's my grandfather, my mom's dad," I answered, thinking that was a weird way to ask. Swift darkened the pencil markings, then he took a jigsaw and told me to hold the end of the plank steady.

"So you're part of the Summerlee clan?"

"Yep," I answered.

Swift gave me a funny look. "What's the matter, Tom? You don't like being a Summerlee?" He started the saw before I could answer. The tiny blade on the jig moved up and down, making the board vibrate. I did my best to hold it still while sawdust flew into my face. He cut both ends of the first board and took it over to the boat.

"It's not as bad as all that," Swift said, fitting the piece in as a crossbeam. "The Summerlees are one of the oldest families in this country, pillars of virtue." He laughed a little. I didn't understand.

"Then again, maybe they're not as boring as all that." The piece was snug, and he had to smack it to make it fit.

"What do you mean?" I asked.

He told me to get a hammer of my own and showed me how to tack the boards in, explaining that they were meant to keep the boat from losing its shape. "Do you have any idea how the Summerlees made their fortunes?" he asked.

"My grandfather said it was opening trade routes and building the ships to run them," I answered.

"Oh, they did that," Swift said, "they certainly built ships. Many were used in the Revolution, but the Summerlees are older than this country and their past isn't as pristine as they like people to believe."

"What do you mean?" I asked.

"The British didn't want the colonies to become too independent and the colonists had to do what they could to survive. Even if it meant breaking laws or dealing with pirates."

"Pirates?" I asked.

He nodded.

"You're saying the Summerlees were pirates?"

He'd gone back to his workbench again. His back was turned to me as he answered. "No, they weren't themselves, but they worked with them."

"No way," I said, climbing out of the boat.

"You don't have to take my word for it." He hammered another piece. "The tunnel they used for smuggling is probably still in the wall of your grandfather's basement."

"I've never seen any tunnels down there," I said.

"Have you ever really looked?" he asked.

29

Chapter 6

In the Dark

When I stepped out of Swift's barn, my hands and clothes were covered in dirt. We'd pulled the boat apart and prepped it, but I hadn't gotten Swift to say much else about the tunnel. I wanted to see it for myself.

My grandmother was in the yard, planting. I waved. She looked up but didn't wave back, holding something in her hand, squinting into the sun as she looked at me.

"Can I go inside for a bit?" I asked, pointing up at the big old house.

She nodded her head. "Um, sure Tom, that's fine." She was holding a flower bulb. A freshly dug hole in the dark soil waited in front of her.

"Is it going in that one there?" I asked, pointing.

"That's right," she said, shaking her head. "Good thing you were here."

"Yeah, good thing." I gave her a quick hug and went up the stairs, through the living room, the dining room, and back into the kitchen. I grabbed a flashlight, one of those metal ones that felt like a club. I turned it on in the back hall but it barely glowed, in need of new batteries. "Well that's not great," I said, tapping the side.

The back hall was always cold, even in the summer. It faced away from the sun, and its thin glass windows didn't block the wind at all. It was built directly over the basement stairs, the only part of the house unchanged since colonial times.

The plank doors creaked as I pulled them open. Musty air came up from the darkness. I pointed the flashlight ahead, taking the first few rickety steps, then closing the doors behind me. I didn't want to explain what I was doing if my grandfather came home.

My eyes adjusted while I made my way towards the first light at the bottom of the stairs. I groped around looking for the pull chain at the bottom.

When I was younger, I'd been afraid of my grandparents' house. I was convinced it was haunted. I stopped believing in ghosts, mostly, but in the moment before I pulled the string, I felt the hairs on the back of my neck stand up.

Light flooded the largest room of the basement, leaving purple spots in my eyes. There were cobwebs clinging to the low ceiling, the floor joists, and the thick wooden columns. Boxes and old furniture were stacked along the walls, making the room feel smaller, but it was still too large for the light to reach every corner.

The basement wasn't simply a big open space. Crumbling cement walls and wooden dividers broke it up into smaller rooms. Some of the spaces were only the size of closets. Others looked more like old prison cells, complete with heavy doors. Only a few of the rooms and the main stairwell had lights. But those rooms weren't close to each other. That's the reason I felt much better with the flashlight in my hand, even with its dim glow.

Swift had only given me a suggestion of where the tunnel was: in the southeast corner, under the front parlor. If I walked forward, turning when I reached the far wall, I should find it. Straight ahead, down a dark, narrow hallway…

I walked past the junk piles towards a heavy wooden door held open by a milk crate full of vinyl records. I could see a light dangling from the ceiling halfway down.

Stop being a chicken. I dashed down reaching for the next string like it was a lifeline. I pulled it. The bulb sparked, popped, and died. *Okay, maybe being a chicken wasn't so bad.* I still had my flashlight and a sliver of light coming from the main room. Somehow I stayed.

On either side of the hall were doorways, those little cells I mentioned. Some were open, but I preferred the closed doors. Wondering what was behind them was better than empty shadows. I thought of Swift, how smug he'd been when we were working. I had to see if he was right.

I went to the end of the hall and touched a closed door. The knob twisted, but it wouldn't open. The air was moist, making the wood swell in its frame. I banged my shoulder into it till eventually, it popped open.

There wasn't much inside, just cement walls and boxes. There was no tunnel or even a place a tunnel could've been. Swift must've made the whole thing up. I walked forward and put my light down on one of the boxes. I was curious what was in them, but before I could start pulling at the dried tape, I heard a noise.

Cold air gusted through the room, slamming the door shut and knocking my flashlight to the ground. The light hit the floor with a thud and went out. I was left in complete darkness.

Stay calm, I thought, stooping down and searching. Another cool damp breeze like the one that'd closed the door blew past me.

My hand closed on the rounded metal of the flashlight. I hit the switch, breathing out when it came back on.

I stood and opened the door, sticking one of the boxes in front of it.

I turned towards the others. The breeze felt like it'd come from behind boxes stacked taller than me. I reached my hand over, feeling the air move. I tried to look around the pile with the flashlight, searching for an opening, but all I found was more wall.

There was only one thing to do. I started moving the boxes, pulling them down and stacking them in the hallway. They weren't particularly large or heavy, so it was quick work. With every box I moved, I expected to find a hole, somewhere the air could've come from.

I was almost at the bottom when I saw a small opening just above the level of the ground. The house had a stone foundation held together by mortar. Some of it had fallen away. One stone was missing altogether. It'd fallen back, leaving a dark, empty space. I set my flashlight on the floor and got down on my hands and knees, reaching out to touch it.

It was big enough to pass a softball through. I reached my hand out into the darkness, feeling the air. It smelled stale and salty. My fingers touched wet mud on the other side and felt open space.

The tunnel, just like he said. My heart was the only thing I could hear; it was beating loud and fast. I took the butt of my flashlight, ready to chip away at some of the surrounding stones, but before I did, I listened.

There was noise coming from inside the wall. I could hear water dripping. And the breeze moving, but there was something more. It was soft at first. As I got closer it got louder. I bent down near the floor and put my ear to the opening. There were voices echoing out of the darkness. They were raspy, speaking strangely. Not like Swift's chanting. They spoke English, but with a heavy accent.

They sounded half choked, gurgling with water as they whispered. *"Aye, we'll have him soon,"* someone said. *"Soon, soon, soon...."* more voices answered in a chorus, repeating as the sound came closer, rushing towards me.

Something more than the wind touched the tip of my ear. It felt like insects crawling over my skin. I scurried away, moving so quickly that I left the flashlight behind. I was almost out the door when I looked back for it. The dim beam pointed at the opening. There was dust dancing in its light... Dust, or something else.

I waited, afraid to breathe, feeling detached from reality. Then a noise came from above; a loud crash shook the floor over me. It was the front door closing.

I glanced at the ceiling. At that moment I swear, out of the corner of my eye, I saw something coming towards me, something dark. When I looked down, I sensed it slithering back over the floor, past the stones, and into the hole. I had no idea what it was.

Footsteps sounded above. Someone was in the house. I heard my grandfather's voice call out through the floor, "Tom? Come out here. Where are you?" I dashed forward grabbing the light then turned and dove over the boxes. I ran down the hall, only looking ahead at the stairs. I was tempted to leave the light on, but I sucked down my fear and pulled the string, heading up with the flashlight in front of me. I was lucky not to trip. I came into the back hall, slowing for the first time. I carefully shut the doors with my hands shaking.

I could hear my grandfather in the kitchen. He stuck his head into the hall. "Where were you?" he asked.

"Out back," I answered. He looked at the back door, giving me a chance to drop the flashlight behind a pair of old boots.

"I didn't see you when I pulled up," he said.

"I was helping Grandma pull some weeds. I must have been bent over."

"Were you doing it with your teeth?" He asked. Between the basement and working on the boat, I'd collected a lot of grime. "Anyway, I was going to take you shopping. You've got that interview coming up, and I want you to look your best. I thought I'd buy you a new suit. How's that sound?"

I shrugged my shoulders, "Okay, I guess."

"'Okay, I guess,'" he repeated. "Let me tell you something Tom, there's nothing more important than the way you present yourself. You've got to throw your shoulders back and appear confident. Nothing like a new suit to help with that."

He looked at me for a moment, checking to see if I was listening. "Get upstairs and wash your face. We're going as soon as you're ready." He turned and went back into the house.

"Okay." I looked back at the basement door, quietly wishing there was a lock.

Chapter 1

A Piece of Gold

At church Sunday morning the pastor talked about Jesus walking on water and bringing Saint Peter out. I daydreamed about a catboat and tried not to think about basements. We went to breakfast after. It was always the same place, a little diner on Main Street. We sat in a booth near the back of the room, my grandfather's favorite spot. He'd scowl if anyone took it first.

"I'm going to need someone to drive Tom to Providence," my mom said. "His interview is being held at Brown. Mom, do you think you could do it?"

My grandmother looked up. She hadn't said much the whole morning.

"You know your mother doesn't like to drive in the city," my grandfather interrupted.

"No, it's fine—" my grandmother began to say. He cut her off, placing his hand over hers.

"I'm pretty busy this week, but I think I can find the time," he offered. My grandmother smiled and nodded.

"Tom doesn't seem very excited about it," my mom said without looking up from her eggs.

My grandfather turned towards me, thanks a lot, Mom! I tried disappearing into my plate.

"He didn't seem to mind yesterday when he was getting new clothes out of it," he said. Honestly, only an old person would think a kid could get excited about new clothes, hence Christmas after Christmas of fake smiles when opening a brand-new sweater.

"Is it true Tom, you don't want to go to the academy?" he asked, almost kindly. I knew it was a setup so I just shrugged.

"The Beecher Academy is a Summerlee family tradition," he said. "The last five generations of Summerlee men went there. It's led to distinguished careers for all of them. Why wouldn't you want that?"

I shrugged my shoulders again, keeping my head down and trying to avoid that look.

"Tom, I want an answer."

"I guess I don't want to go away," I muttered.

"Is that all? Well, you don't have to worry. You can come home on weekends, sometimes, and on holidays. The rest of the time you'll be too busy with your studies to miss anyone. It's good for a young man to be away from home, builds character."

Well if that's true, I thought while focusing on my home fries, pushing them around the plate.

They started talking about the extracurricular activities, running through some of the things they thought I'd be interested in. They were talking to each other, but I could tell it was for my benefit.

My mom mentioned the model legislature and the debate team. My grandfather was more interested in the sports. "They don't have hockey. I know you like that game, but they do have lacrosse. It's similar. It's got sticks and goalies," he said.

I didn't know what it was, but it sounded French, and not very fun.

"Do they have a sailing team?" I asked.

Both my mom and grandfather looked a little surprised. He was about to answer when my mom's phone went off.

"Meredith Donavan," she answered. She still had my father's last name, but she said it was only because she started her career with it. It was an almost unbearable mark for her.

"Yes," she said into the receiver. "Okay."

"You've got to be kidding…That's awful…Well, I'd be happy to help in any way I can…Yes, I just have to swing by my office. Then I'll be right over." She dropped the phone into her purse. "I hate to do this, but I've got to go to work for a bit."

"You're kidding!" I said. Surprised by how loud my voice was. I shouldn't have cared. It gave me a chance to get away and work on the boat.

"I'm sorry Tom, but the DA needs my help." She took a twenty out of her purse and placed it on the table. My grandfather tried refusing, as he did week after week. Then he relented, as he did week after week.

We went outside to say our good-byes, and I asked my mom if I could go to a friend's house. "That's fine," she said, "Just be home by dinner." She was already in work mode. I could tell by her voice.

I went to Swift's yard and found the boat lying in two pieces, split right down the middle, like a cracked shell.

"What the—," I started to say in surprise.

"Watch it Tom, no cursing on the Sabbath," Swift interrupted. He was climbing down from the loft, carrying a piece of wood on his shoulder. He moved the plank towards me. "Take this," he said.

I put my shoulder under the wood and nearly fell over. He climbed down from the ladder while still talking. "Sundays are the Lord's day. Not that I've ever been one for keeping the faith. Bring that wood over here before it plants you in the ground."

I dropped the plank onto the workbench. "I didn't picture you being religious," I said.

He laughed a little. "If you've seen what I've seen, there wouldn't be any doubt in your head. I'm sure there's a god, and I know he loves me deeply, it's just most days I don't think he likes me very much." He smiled and gave me a little jab on my sore shoulder. "Can't say as I blame him."

I winced, grabbing my arm. "How come you're in such a good mood?" This was a different Swift than I was used to.

"I found something last night while I was working." He reached into his pocket and pulled out a tarnished piece of metal. "A little reminder of days gone by." He held up a roughly cut thing, barely recognizable as a coin.

"Can I see it?" I asked. In an instant, his mood changed. He looked at me strangely as he passed the coin over. Like the board, it was heavier than it looked. Even though it was black and stained, some of the tarnish had rubbed away. I could see the dull glow of gold. On one side were the remains of a face, and on the other, a cross. "Is this real?" I asked.

"It is," Swift answered, motioning for me to hand it back. There was something in his eyes I didn't like. I tossed it over.

"I thought I'd spent them all," he said, dropping the coin in his pocket. "Imagine how happy I was to find it." He didn't sound happy, not anymore. He quickly changed the subject, pointing at the boat. "The centerboard was cracked, ready to give way. I had to pull it out. I'll make another with that plank."

He rapped on the board with his hand. "This wood is old and hard as steel. It'll make a good keelson, nice and sturdy, able to carry plenty of weight." I noticed how his hand went back to his pocket as he said this. "The transom was rotten as well, but nautical plywood is fine for that."

Swift laid the old keelson on the new plank and made a crude sketch. He cut the plank to length, using a circular saw. The electric tool struggled as it bit into the wood.

"So where did you get that coin?" I asked, holding the board steady.

He looked up from his work and answered, "I took it." Then he motioned for me to go down to the end of the table saw. Swift took a few inches off the plank then checked it against the original. This time he took out a tape measure.

"What do you mean, 'took it?'" I asked.

"It belonged to someone else. I wanted it, so I took it. Now it's mine." He was staring down at his measurements.

He clamped the piece down on the workbench and took out a router, a small tool with handles on either side.

He checked a mushroom-shaped bit against the side of the old keelson then started to cut a deep indent along the new piece. "I'm going to set up a steam-box and a jig tonight to shape this board a bit."

I had no idea what he was talking about. I was still thinking about the coin. "Are you saying you stole it?" I asked.

He shook his head. "As far as I'm concerned it was stolen already."

I stared at him waiting for a better explanation. He sighed. "Look, Tom, there are laws made to protect things like this for the rich and powerful, but who writes those laws? Those same people, right?"

I shrugged, not sure how to answer, wondering what my mom with her law background would say.

"When the monarchies ruled the world, rich men plundered weaker nations. They took everything they had." He went to a rack on the wall and selected a piece of plywood. He carried it to the old transom where he started to trace a new piece. "Nowadays your officials, your politicians are elected, but I don't see much of a difference. I've never heard of a poor noble or for that matter a poor politician." He grabbed his jigsaw, and I took my spot holding the wood.

My arms felt like they were in a paint mixer by the time he'd finished. He looked up at me. "So when you ask, 'did I steal this?' I say 'no, I took it.' Because I don't consider it theft." He plugged in a hand sander and started smoothing out the edges of the plywood.

I looked at my watch. More time had passed than I thought. "I should probably get going. My mom's going to be waiting for me," I said above the noise.

"That's fine Tom," he yelled, without looking up.

I started to leave, but then the sander went off. I turned around. "By the way, I went into my grandparents' basement."

He'd taken out a piece of sandpaper and was working the edges by hand still not looking up. "And did you find anything?"

"I think so. There was a hole in the wall and a bigger space behind it." I paused for a minute, remembering the voices. "It looked like it'd been closed off."

He nodded but didn't say anything else.

"The thing I don't get is how you knew it was there."

Between strokes with the sand paper he answered, "Because I had my part in digging it." He offered nothing else, nodding his head goodbye. I left feeling confused, wondering what he meant.

Chapter 8

History Lessons

*I*t was hard to tell if the sun was up on Monday morning. The sky was gray and rain was falling. The teachers had a professional day, whatever that was, so I didn't have school. It would've been the perfect day to sleep in, only I was a paperboy. Sleeping in wasn't something I got to do anymore. I was in my grandparents' neighborhood up on the hill, hiding from the rain in the doorway of the town's library.

The building looked like a relic from the Middle Ages, made of huge stone blocks. It had heavy wooden doors with studded metal bolts going through them. It easily could've been the back door of a castle.

I didn't hang out here very much. I was a little scared of the head librarian. Usually, I left the paper near the entrance, careful to put it someplace it wouldn't get damaged, but for some reason, even though it was way too early for the library to be open, I tried the door. It was unlocked.

I pulled it open slowly and stood there with the paper in hand. Everything inside was dark, from the granite walls to the hardwood floors, to the giant bookshelves.

I wasn't sure if anyone was there. It was so quiet. Then I heard a female voice. "Well, you're up early." It came from behind a stack of books covering the front desk.

"I didn't think you'd be open," I responded.

"We're not. Is that the paper?"

"Yes," I said.

"Don't you usually leave it outside Tom? Why did you decide to come in today?" she asked. I'm not going to lie. It freaked me out that weird Miss Webster knew my name. Literally, I had never spoken to her. Of course, I'd heard the stories.

She owned an old Victorian house near my grandparents, but you never saw her there. She had these creepy wind chimes that rang even when there was no wind and these strange stone sculptures in her yard that could've passed for real. Some people said they moved at night, but that was probably just a story.

The real mystery was how she came to live in the house. Everyone assumed it was left to her, but no one could remember who the previous owner was or when exactly she started working at the library. It was like she'd always been there.

A pair of spectacled eyes looked over the books. The little bit of light from the desk lamp gave them a yellow glow. The outline of her coal-black hair tied up in a bun cast a shadow on the shelves behind her.

"You are Tom Donavan. Isn't that right?" she asked, stepping out from behind the desk. Her age was impossible to tell. She could've been in her late twenties or her early fifties. She wore a dark-blue dress buttoned at the collar that looked like it belonged to another century.

"Yes, it is," I answered.

"Can I help you with something Tom? Or did you just come in to get out of the rain?"

"Um," I started before turning to leave. "I'm sorry, I didn't mean to bother you."

"It's fine. I was only doing a little research for myself," she said. I looked at the book she'd left open on her desk. It could've held up a building. "If there's something you want to know, you're certainly in the right place."

"I guess I want to know about pirates…and, um, tunnels."

"Lose the 'um'," she said.

"Sorry," I looked at the floor, avoiding her stare.

"It's fine. It's a bad habit that's all." She waved for me to follow her. "So you want to know about pirate tunnels?"

"I guess. Someone told me about one that runs under the houses up here." I wasn't sure why, but I didn't want to tell her I already found it.

She looked back at me. I had a feeling she was waiting for me to say more. "If there were such a thing, it could be dangerous," she pointed out.

"Really?" I asked. I was thinking about the voices.

She nodded as we went back, turning down an aisle labeled American history. There was a fancy lamp with a pull chain hanging off the shelf. She turned it on, then reached for a book and opened it. "I assume when you say pirates, you mean the ones from the golden age?"

"Sure," I said.

She handed the book over, showing me a photograph. "This was a tunnel in Boston." The picture was of a brick wall with a large hole knocked in it. It looked like there was a cave behind the opening.

"The owner of an Italian restaurant in the North End found this in the back wall of his basement," she said while turning the page for me. There was another picture with musket balls, a rusted old sword, and a pair of leather boots. They were lined up on a dirt floor. "These artifacts were older than the Revolution, dating back to the early seventeen hundreds."

"Could anything like this be in West Harbor?" I asked.

"It's possible. We certainly had our fair share of pirates. Captain Kidd stopped at Block Island on his way to turn himself in, and Thomas Tew was from Newport. In fact, Rhode Island was a bit of a pirate haven. Merchants became wealthy trading with them, and the courts turned a blind eye to it. They were so much a part of the area that in the 1720s, England threatened to rescind Rhode Island's charter. I suppose if they were still active here during that time, they'd need some way of hiding their treasure and selling it."

"So it's possible."

"What's possible?" she asked, narrowing her gaze.

"Um," I started.

She closed the book I was holding. The sound echoed through the empty building. "Tom?"

"Sorry. I just meant that if there was a tunnel, then maybe it could've belonged to a pirate." I thought about Swift saying he had his part in digging the one under my grandparents' house. "How old would it be if there was one?"

"Well if it came from the golden age, which is the most recent time pirates were active in these waters, it'd have to be around three hundred years old," she answered.

I was quiet for a second, thinking. Then I asked, "So if someone claimed they'd dug a tunnel like that, you'd have to assume they were a little nuts."

She looked at me strangely. "Do you know some-one who is claiming to be that old?" There was an odd tone in her voice.

Looking at her, I thought maybe I'd said too much. "No I was just curious is all." I forced myself not to say 'um' first.

She gave me a strange look, as if she didn't believe me. I had a feeling she wanted to say more, but something held her back, some secret she wasn't ready to reveal.

"Careful of those bad habits Tom," she said, then she turned and walked back down the aisle.

I wasn't sure what she meant, but I followed her to the foyer and thanked her. She nodded, going back behind her desk.

Chapter 9

Taking Shape

I left the library and headed towards Swift's yard, riding along the waterfront. Water dripped like icicles down my spine. The rain made me feel alone, cutting me off from the real world. Streams in the road splashed my legs as I pedaled up the steep hill.

The cove looked alive, with swirling fog and mist surrounding the people standing out there. *'That's odd,'* I thought. *'Who would be out there today?'* I slowed down to look, but it was hard to see through the downpour. Something was wrong. I felt colder.

The longer I watched, the more I realized how many people were out there. Every time the fog moved more were revealed, as many as a hundred.

Quahoggers maybe? I didn't see any rakes or buckets for digging, things shell fishermen would have, and these people weren't moving either. They stood at the water's edge, staring up, remaining as still as posts.

It was bizarre. What were they doing? I stopped breathing, feeling my stomach sink. Have you ever seen something so strange that your brain can't make sense of it?

These people were as gray as the water and sky. Like all the color was washed out of them. I looked at their faces, at their eyes, and immediately regretted it. There was nothing there. Where their eyes should've been were dark sockets, pools of blackness. I started to shake.

They were all turned and focused on Swift's yard. It was like a nightmare, only I was awake.

I looked away, trying to focus on the road, trying to get the bike moving while my tires were wet and slipping. I shook my head and pushed hard on the pedals, feeling terrified. I wanted to get behind the next hedge. I was so afraid that those things would know I was there, that their eyes might turn towards me.

My legs ached as I struggled up the hill. My breath was coming quick now. I was blowing away the raindrops that dripped from my nose. I got behind the bushes and stopped, but I could still sense them out there. I knew I'd been too slow, that they'd seen me.

In that last moment, before I reached safety, they'd turned their heads. They'd turned all those dead, dark eyes towards me.

Safety? Who was I kidding? I pictured them leaving the water and climbing up the hill. Coming for me. I listened for their footsteps.

I was shaking when through the rain I heard something familiar. I pedaled again, even harder this time, reaching the end of the hedge, looking ahead to Swift's gate. He'd left it open. The sound got louder as I got closer. It was the dog. He was down by the fence by the water, and for once he wasn't barking at me. His deep voice boomed out, raging at the cove like a fog horn.

When I looked out again at the water it was empty. They'd all disappeared. I took off my hat and wiped the rain from my face, then I pulled it back down, snug on my head, and rode through the gate. I didn't stop until I was in the barn.

Swift stood by a wood-burning stove. It was hot and bright and a metal gas can was sitting on top of it. I'm sure there was a reason he was boiling a gas can. Either way, it was less scary than what was outside.

There was a contraption next to the stove, a series of PVC pipes strapped to a wooden plank. A rubber hose was running from the gas can to the pipes. Small wisps of steam were billowing up at the far end of the tubes. He was using the can like a large kettle.

"It's called a steam-box," Swift explained.

"What?" I asked shaking my head.

"I said, this is called a steam-box. We're going to use it to bend some wood. I loosened the keelson already, see."

I looked at the boat. The new transom and keelson were both installed. I leaned my bike against the wall and went closer, being careful of where I stepped. Scattered around the floor were plywood sheets with blocks screwed down to them.

"You alright? You look like you just saw a ghost," Swift asked.

Before I could answer the dog came in from the rain. He looked at me, snarled a little, then settled down by the stove to dry off. I wanted to thank him, scratch his ear or something. I have a feeling if I tried he'd probably take my hand off.

I looked back at Swift. He nodded then started to talk, ignoring the weirdness. "We'll use these jigs to shape the new pieces as they come out of the steamer."

"When did you do all this?" I asked.

Swift's eyes had deep circles under them. "Last night and today."

"Did you sleep at all?" I asked.

"No, not with that weather." His voice went low. I could barely hear him over the rain. "I don't sleep on stormy nights."

He showed me how to attach the blocks to the plywood. Then he gave me an old electric drill that weighed a ton. Its cord wasn't in the best shape, especially on a rainy day, but I didn't complain.

Swift glanced at the clock, "We should be ready for the first piece," he said, putting on a pair of gloves and opening up one of the pipes. I grabbed some heavy clamps that he pointed to on his workbench. He carefully curved the new rib with his hands then put the piece on the plywood jig.

I closed the clamps. "There we go," he said, groaning as he got up from the floor.

"Now what?" I asked.

"Now we wait. The next piece won't be ready for a little while."

"Oh," I said.

He looked at my face, "You look like you've got something on your mind, Tom. Like something's bothering you."

I didn't want to answer at first. If I talked about what I'd seen in the rain, it would bring it closer to being real.

Swift waited. Finally, I asked, "I was wondering. You said you had your part in digging the tunnel under my grandparents' house?" I felt silly. I wasn't sure if it was even a tunnel. "And you said it was a pirate tunnel?"

Swift nodded his head. "That's right."

"That means the tunnel would have to be really old?"

Swift nodded his head again.

"That would also mean that you're…"

"Really old," Swift finished my thought.

"But how's that possible?" I asked.

Swift held up his hand. "Hold on a second, let me get another piece started." He had a few strips of thinly cut wood lying near the boat. He picked one up and put it in the same tube we'd taken the first one out of.

I was waiting for an answer that made sense. I wasn't going to get it.

He turned and stared at me for a moment. Then with a long sigh, he answered, "It's because I'm cursed, Tom. I've been forced to live in and around this town for nearly three hundred years."

He was so matter-of-fact about it that it caught me by surprise. He had to be joking. I didn't say anything, but I'm pretty sure my mouth was open.

"Here at the water's edge," he continued, "I won't age, but if I stray too far from this place, I grow weak and frail. I come close to dying, but I never do. I'm forced always to stay here and hear their voices."

"Whose voices?" Those ghostly forms came back with far too much detail and then there was the whispering in the wall at my grandparents'. I wanted to sit down.

"They're waiting for me out in the water. I have to stay here on dry land," he whispered. He turned away, puttering around at his workbench.

This can't be true, I thought. Swift wasn't a pirate. He was an old man. "Um, how would that even happen?" I asked. "How would someone get cursed like that?"

He stopped what he was doing and thought about it for a moment. "You betray someone, someone who loves you very dearly." He turned back to me. "Her name was Sarah."

"Sarah," I repeated. I'd always liked that name. "Did you love her back?"

He looked at me as if he'd never been asked that question before, like he hadn't even considered it himself. "I don't know. I don't if I've ever truly loved anyone. I honestly don't know if I'm capable of it," he said, as if it had just occurred to him. "I'm not a good man. I never have been. From the start—I've been nothing but trouble." He went quiet. Then he looked down at his watch. "Time for the next piece."

Swift pulled his gloves back on and opened up the pipe. He pulled the piece out and started bending it. I stood there, staring at him.

"Tom, get the other set of clamps," he said. I came back to reality and went over and grabbed them, then helped him secure the new piece.

When more wood was loaded into the steamer he turned to me and asked, "I suppose you'll want to hear the

58

rest of the story now?" I nodded as he looked at his watch again.

"We have an hour to kill anyway," he said, pulling out two stools and offering one to me.

"Where should we begin?" He waited for me to answer.

"At the beginning I guess."

Swift rubbed the calluses on his hands and looked at the ceiling, trying to think, "I suppose it started when I was about your age. But if we go back that far, it'll be more than an hour," he said.

I shrugged my shoulders, not sure what to say. Part of me thought I should run now and never come back. The other part wanted answers.

"Fine then… When I was growing up, I knew one thing for sure. The only way a person like me could have anything was by taking it. Trouble was in my nature."

Chapter 10

Swift's Story

Cork, Ireland 1702

In a single afternoon I set my course, taking a path that led me to where I am today, here and cursed.

Where I came from, the wharves smelt like tar and were full of sails. On occasion one belonged to my father's ship. His life was at sea, coming home once or twice a year. A ship would've taken me on as well. Boys could join the navy or sign aboard a merchant vessel. But I had to stay home, so my mother could care for my sisters. I worked for a fishmonger, butchering the day's catch and stinking of entrails. I toiled through the morning, and in the afternoon I'd go looking for mischief.

I was at the market late in the day with a rotten apple in my hand. I was watching for someone to give me a bit more. Stalls full of produce brought in from the country lined the street. The merchants knew me there. Some were wary but most ignored me. They knew I wouldn't linger long.

I was getting down to the core of my apple when I saw a page off a naval ship. He wore the fine blue uniform of a British sailor with its white lapels and fancy brass buttons. He'd been in a hurry till his eyes fell on the baker's cart.

I knew what he was looking at. My own stomach had been rumbling for a taste of the pastries and cakes. They'd sat out most of the day, but they still looked delicious. The page had been stuck on a ship for months eating stale biscuits and hard tack.

I watched him reach inside his coat for his coin purse. He loosened the strap of his satchel and placed it on the ground. I started across the street.

"Here lad, a treat far sweeter than salt water," the baker said while wrapping a scone. The boy handed the money over, his eyes never leaving the food.

"Thank you, sir. You need not wrap it." The page took a bite while I hefted the apple core in my hand and tossed it in the air.

An old tinker was napping by his pots and pans. My apple core came down and crashed into his wares, *sending lids clattering and falling. He jumped and yelled. Everyone turned to see, including the page. I grabbed the satchel and went down an alley before he turned back.*

When I got home I went to the loft where I slept and tore into my prize. Right away I knew the importance of the papers I'd stolen, but it was a treasure I could never sell.

They were charts. The page had been sent to have them copied. Sending a distractible boy with something so valuable was a mistake. See, there were still places in the world civilized men hadn't seen. The globe was still being plotted. In my hand were maps of distant shores the British ship visited.

I was thrilled. My candle burnt through the night as I studied the foreign lands, dreaming of sailing away. I knew in the morning I'd have to get rid of them. They were too dangerous to keep.

I'd leave them somewhere to be found. But by the next morning, it was too late. A hundred British soldiers were sent to search for the charts, going over the whole town, door to door, tearing through people's homes.

I had to work for the fishmonger, but I couldn't leave the charts. What would happen to my mother if the Brits found them? I divided the papers, stuffing them down each of my pant legs. I walked like I had no kneecaps to the docks. When I passed a couple of soldiers they stared, but didn't stop me. I guess I looked too pitiful.

At the fishery, I slipped into a corner full of unused supplies and undid my trousers. I hid the charts in a spool of rope then dragged it behind the other supplies.

The manager walked in. "What's this then?" He pointed his fat, scared finger at my chest. He saw me closing my trousers and grabbed me roughly by the shirt, pulling me out onto the floor. "If you need to relieve yourself, use the damn privy." He pointed to the back room where a hole cut in the floor sat over a stinking latrine. "Get back to work." He walloped me across the head.

In the afternoons the manager went for a drink while I cleaned the floors and cutting tables. Over the next week, I'd sneak back to that spool and take the charts out for a quick look. I'd started copying them and hiding the papers under my bed. I became braver once the soldiers gave up their search. They went back to their fort and left reward posters around the city. I thought of collecting it when I finished.

At the end of the week, a Sunday, my mother popped her head into the loft. "Wake up," she said, "We need to get the house in order."

"Why?" I asked. The sun hadn't come up yet.

"Your father's ship is in port. He'll be home today. They're just waiting for the tide to turn." Her blue eyes sparkled in the candlelight. My mother didn't smile very much, but when she did, she lit up the room. The other women in town called her stuck-up and haughty what with

her raven-black hair and beauty, but to me she was amazing.

She was from the middle of Ireland. A country girl, the ladies in city called her. My father didn't see it that way.

"Your mother is from the heart of our island where hidden places are protected by the little magic this land has left. She's beyond the kings and queens of today. She's of the ancient people." He told us when he was home from the sea. My mother would laugh at it, but she'd never deny his stories either.

We were Christians, but she knew the Pagan ways as well, leaving little gifts for spirits and worshiping in nature when she could. We had a Bible, which was rare for a poor Catholic family. She taught us to read from it. Then she'd tell tales of Cúchulainn, Fin MacCool, his Fianna, and his son Oisín. Stories were what we lived on.

"Come along and be quick about it," she called as she climbed down the ladder. Months had passed since I'd seen my father.

My sisters and I scrubbed the floors and cleaned our home till midmorning, when we took a break to go outside the city walls and attend mass. My mother went to the market and bought a large bird. Then, while the girls prepared the afternoon meal, I ran down to the docks, hoping to watch him come down the gangplank.

My father had served on The Venture *for five years, becoming head carpenter. It was a large merchant* vessel, over a hundred feet from stern to bowsprit with three masts. They'd outfitted her with only a few guns for defense, none larger than a twelve pounder.

From a distance I could see something was wrong with the ship. Holes were blown through the sides, and the rail along the quarterdeck was splintered and smashed. They'd been attacked.

The first men to make their way down the gangplank were the ones who had to be carried. Five were hauled out in canvas stretchers. My father was one of them.

I ran to his side when the crewmen reached the dock. He was pale, and his eyes were closed, but his chest rose and fell, still breathing. "What happened," I asked, looking to the crewmen.

"He was injured saving my life and defending our ship." I turned to see a tall man dressed too well to be a common sailor. One of his arms was in a sling, and a bandage was wrapped around his head. This was Jonathan Beck, the first officer. "We were attacked by a French privateer, just north of Portugal," he said.

I didn't understand. "But we're not at war with France."

"Apparently things have changed, not that it would mattered to them. They had the wind and came in close enough to board us. They thought we'd surrender, but our captain isn't the sort. He'd sink us before letting the French cut into his profits.

"Your father and I tried to hold the quarterdeck while the French flooded over the side. I went down and most of our men retreated with the captain. But your father refused to give up ground. He stood over me and fought like a man possessed. He had a bludgeon in one hand and a sword in the other, holding out till our men finally rallied and drove the French back. They sounded a retreat, but as they pulled away, they fired a last broadside. Your father was helping me to my feet when his back was raked with debris. He protected me, but he was gravely injured. None of us thought he'd make it home."

I had tears running down my face as I listened. I grabbed my father's hand, and his eyes opened. "Shea-mus?" he asked, saying my real name. "Is that you boy? You've grown so much. Look-it how tall you are."

"It's me Da. We're going to take you home. Mom and the girls are waiting for you."

He squeezed my hand back weakly. "Don't cry boy, everything'll be just fine. You'll see. I'm not the type for dy'n, I guarantee."

The crewmen lifted my father as Beck led the way. I held my father's hand the whole time. When we were across the street from our home, I stopped, looking in horror. "Oh no, please no," I begged.

My mother and all my sisters were standing on the street. Guarding them was a contingent of British soldiers, dressed in their redcoats with their muskets at the ready. I could see the house being searched.

Beck stopped. All eyes turned on me including my father's. "Sheamus, what did you do?" he asked.

At the house, the manager from the fish market stood behind the soldiers leaning against the door, a smug smile on his ugly face. He'd found the charts and decided to collect the reward.

"I'm sorry Da, I'm so sorry," I cried. Then I confessed what I'd done.

My father listened and said nothing to me. Instead, he turned to Beck. "Sir I need to ask you a great favor."

Beck knew what it was. Without hesitation, he said, "It'll be done."

My father looked at me. Then he reached over and gave me what he could of a hug. I could see the effort it took. "Try to be a better man than this," he said.

Beck wrote a note. Then ordered me back to the ship. "Go now and give this to the officer on deck." I nodded but I didn't leave right away. Instead, I watched from the shadows as they carried my father home. It was the last time I ever saw him.

Chapter 11

Childhood's End

"'Be a better man than this,'" Swift said again, looking down at his watch and sighing. "The next piece should be done." He was silent for a long time.

"So you hid on your father's ship?" I asked.

He nodded. "And your real name is Sheamus?"

He shook his head. "That boy is gone." He put on his gloves and opened the tube, taking out the wood as he talked. "And it certainly wasn't and had never been my father's ship. At sea, a vessel belongs to the captain. I've still got the scars to prove it." He pulled up his shirt, showing angry-looking marks faded and pale with time.

"What did that?" I asked.

"A whip. We may not have been a navy vessel but our discipline was tight. Especially for a boy like me with a tendency towards trouble."

A whip? *That's insane*, I thought. Swift had been my age. I pictured my grandfather with his stern looks, the way he liked to tell me what to do. Good thing severe beatings were no longer allowed.

"But Beck was supposed to look after you?" I asked.

"He did—as well as he looked after every member of the crew. He couldn't show favoritism simply because my father saved his life. Still, it was Beck that gave me my name, taught me navigation, and prepared me to be an officer. And he was the one who brought my mother aboard one last time to say goodbye." Swift's thoughts went far away as he remembered the last day of his childhood.

Cork, Ireland 1702

I was hidden away in one of the ship's holds for a week, cowering in a darkened corner, just waiting to be discovered. I listened through the planks to the pounding of nails as the crew made repairs. Food was brought to me, but no one spoke, fearing they'd alert the captain.

I awoke one night from a fitful sleep to Beck's stern voice calling me from my hiding spot. "We'll be leaving in a day or two," he said. "We'll have to sign you aboard as part of the crew under a different name, but first there's someone here to see you."

I didn't recognize her under her hooded cloak, not till her soft hand touched my face. With tears in my eyes, I said, "I'm sorry mum."

"It's all right Sheamus. You've done a foolish thing, but all boys do. Only now you'll have to grow up faster than I would've wanted."

I asked her how my father was. In the week that passed, I hoped his wounds would heal enough for him to see me off. I'd been daydreaming down in the hold, imagining what it would be like if he made it back on board the ship.

"The night after you left, he stopped speaking. He lingered three days, but that was as long as his strength could hold. The funeral was yesterday morning."

I was shocked into silence. Almost in a whisper, I said, "I should've been told. Someone should have come to get me."

"Sheamus, you would have been seen. It wasn't safe."

"It's not fair!" I screamed. She covered my mouth. We listened quietly to see if the outburst had been heard. Beck, who'd been standing guard outside the door, looked back in. My mother gave him a nod, letting him know it was all right.

"You're going to find a lot of things in this world are unfair, especially when it comes to life and death."

Then, more softly she said, "I love you Sheamus. I don't know what will happen to you, but I hope someday you'll come back to us. If you don't though, there's something you must have."

She pulled a bundle from under her robes and handed it to me. "As the oldest in my family, I was given this. Now it goes to my son."

I pulled it open, not knowing what to expect. Inside was an ancient short sword, the kind carried by the warriors of the Fianna in the great days of heroes.

"Do you remember the legend of Oisín?" she asked.

"Yes," I said nodding my head.

"Well, there's more to it than most people know. A part of the story that's been in our family for hundreds of years."

Then she told me the tale. She told me the secret of Oisín's blade. The sword was the key to a legend, a pathway to a magical place. It was fantastic, but I knew my mother, and she never lied. There were instructions, words that had to be said in the ancient tongue. She whispered them to me and had me repeat them. I struggled with them, not only for their strangeness, but because I could sense their power. I felt the blade laid across my lap burning with enchantment. She kissed me on the cheek then left me there with my legacy.

"The next one should be done," Swift said. We went through the same process, taking the piece out and bending it on a jig. The smell of the steamed pine made me feel warm, safe from the rain falling outside. Swift took a kettle from the stove and poured boiling water over a tea bag. He offered me some, but I shook my head.

I wanted to hear the rest. It may have been a lie, but I still wanted to know. "Who is Oisín? What was this legend?"

He looked at me and smiled. "Oisín is a story for another time."

"What? Come on," I complained.

He looked at his watch. "It's getting late Tom."

I put my hands on my hips while he pointed to his watch. My eyes widened when I saw. We'd killed the morning and gotten into the afternoon. No wonder I was hungry. I'd told Swift earlier that I needed to get home before my mom. He was trying to help me out, but it was still annoying.

"It's too much to tell in a single afternoon," he said. "But I will say this; after that day I was forced to grow up fast. See, around that time, all of Europe was at war. I couldn't tell you why we were fighting, kings and succession, that sort of silliness."

I nodded my head as if I knew what he meant.

Swift snorted a little. "All I knew for sure was that the war involved everyone and you could make a lot of money with a letter of marque."

"A letter of what?" I asked.

"Marque, permission by our king to go hunting ships from other nations. We became privateers."

"Like a pirate?" I asked.

"I supposed, but it was all legal." Swift sat down on a stool sipping his tea. "I was good at fighting and I moved quickly through the ranks. The rules of promotion were looser on a privateer than in the Navy, especially in a time of war. I was given a commission at eighteen. The same day, our captain died in combat off the coast of Madrid, and Beck took command of the ship. I served under him until the war was over, when our ship was changed, turned into something... something not good."

He went quiet, staring off. "Changed into what?" I asked.

He looked into his tea. "The ship's owners refitted the Venture to be a slaver. Beck refused to captain her. I think he was disappointed I decided to stay on board, but at that time so many sailors and officers were out of work that I was happy to still have a job. I knew working a slaver was tough but..." Swift broke off, shaking his head.

He walked over to my little catboat and touched its side. "I watched the ship I'd grown up on, that my father had died for, turned into one of the most evil tools in human history. You can shrug it off and just say it was the era, but I tell you now Tom, there were enough people who knew it was wrong and still did nothing. There was too much money in it for people to care."

His hand dropped away from the catboat, falling to his side. "I'd killed men in battle, seen friends die on the deck. Still, nothing prepared me for work on a slaver."

I waited for him to say more, but Swift stayed quiet. His thoughts were somewhere else. Finally, he turned towards me. "That's how I ended up here. We took our slaves to Newport. I collected my pay and left the *Venture* behind forever. There were so many sailors and officers looking for work that it was probably a foolish thing to do, but I couldn't work that trade.

"I booked passage to the mainland, thinking I'd make my way to Boston or at best Providence, but when I reached West Harbor, I stayed."

"Why?" I asked.

"There was a merchant here, a local farmer, looking for a crew. You may have heard the name." Swift smiled.

"Summerlee?" I asked.

"Aye. And he had a daughter." Swift's smile widened, then he said, "But that's a story for another day as well."

Chapter 12

West Harbor Back When

The next morning I woke up feeling tired. The rain never let up. Thunder and bright bolts of lightning kept me awake. From our condo, I could see the entrance to the cove. I went out to the dining room around midnight and camped out on the floor. Yeah I know, weird right? We do own a couch, but I wanted to see the cove. So I set up in front of the patio door, looking for any sign of those things.

Eventually I must've fallen asleep, and that's when I saw them, in my dreams. They wore tattered and torn clothing. Their faces were blank and their dark, empty eyes were still staring towards Swift's home.

I dreamt I was walking through them. They were spaced like pieces on a chessboard, and even though they showed no emotion, they looked like they were waiting for something. I looked down and noticed that they weren't standing in the water, but were motionless on top of it. I saw that I was performing the same miracle, standing on the cove as if it were solid ground. Then, like Saint Peter in the Bible, I started to slip underneath. I felt something grab me, pulling me down. The last thing I remember before waking in a panic was looking up at those people and thinking, they look like pirates.

That was it for sleeping. After that, I couldn't keep my eyes from the door. I didn't see them out there, even when lightening made it bright as day, but I could feel them.

I made sure I was back in my bed by morning. I didn't want my mom to know I'd been lying under the table. That kind of behavior made her nervous.

She left for work and I was supposed to go to school, but on the way, I stopped at the library, hoping Miss Webster might be there early again. The door was open, but it was dark inside. I went in anyway.

I heard her say, with a chill in her voice, "The early bird catches the bookworm." The heavy door closed behind me with a thud.

"What are you looking for now Tom? More pirate tunnels?" she asked from behind a pile of ancient books.

"No, just a person, someone named Oisín, I think he was Irish."

"Well, that's an interesting one." She got up and walked back to the bookshelves, moving so briskly that I didn't have time to follow. She handed me a volume of Celtic legends. "Why don't you take this one with you?" she suggested in a voice that didn't sound like a suggestion.

I started towards the door with the book open, flipping through it with one hand. "Are you sure it's in here?"

She came up behind me, moving without a sound. The black cloth of her dress made her seem like another shadow. She took the book from my hand and opened it to a page with a picture of a sad looking old man with a gray beard. He was kneeling on the ground. It looked like the world was coming down on him. "That's who you're looking for." She went back behind her desk.

I thanked her and went to leave, but before I was out the door I heard her say something.

"Be careful Tom." Her voice was so soft.

"What's that?" I asked.

Her head peeked up from behind the stack. "Be careful with the book. It's old." I wasn't sure if that was what she meant the first time.

*   *   *

School was a struggle that day. I had a hard time keeping my eyes open or my head from bobbing. Some of my teachers were concerned, knowing I was usually a better student. At lunch, I finally got to read the book. Though if Swift's family had anything to do with the legend, I couldn't guess what it was. I brought it when I went to his place after school.

The gate was open, but Swift was nowhere to be seen. The dog was there though, sitting right in the middle of the yard staring at me. I rode in and watched his lip curl back showing his teeth. That's when I remembered that I didn't have any bones.

"Hey buddy," I said in the sweetest voice I could muster, realizing I had no idea what the dog's name was. I wouldn't be able to tell anyone who it was that ate me.

He started to growl as he got up.

I have to have something, I thought, taking off my backpack. I hadn't finished my lunch. I riffled through my bag. "Do you like peanut and butter, I mean peanut butter and jelly? I mean just- just give me a second," I begged.

He was right in front of me. The fur on his back was standing up, while he was still growling. The book fell out of the bag as I came up with half a sandwich. It hit the ground right in front of him.

"Oh no." All I could picture was what the dog did to newspapers. "Please don't, please don't," I begged, getting off my bike.

He opened his mouth as my hand reached down. Those teeth were going into something whether I liked it or not.

"Leave that book alone you beast," Swift called, coming out of the barn. The dog looked back. By then I was holding the sandwich out to him. I felt his teeth and slobber on my fingers as he took it. He snarled a little at Swift then he wandered off, disappearing behind the boats.

"What have you got here?" Swift asked as he came up to me. He bent down and picked the book up.

"Something I found in the library," I said.

He examined the cover before opening it and flipping through the pages. I waited to see what he thought.

His blue eyes twinkled a little. "Aye, Tom. This is grand. They're fine tales in here. I sparked a bit of interest in you, I see." He handed the book back.

"I wanted to know about Oisín," I said.

"Of course you did, and you couldn't wait for me to tell you. It's fine. But I guarantee that book doesn't have the whole story. The one person who knows the rest is right in front of you. But I think I might keep that secret a bit longer." Swift started walking away, back to the barn.

What else could there be? I wondered. According to the book, Oisín was a poet and adventurer. He met a woman named Niamh, the daughter of the sea god. She invited him to ride on the back of her horse to a mystical island called Tír-Na-Nóg. Of course, he went. She was beautiful and it's not like a sea goddess comes along every day.

Years later, Niamh, who was now Oisín's wife, saw that he was homesick for Ireland. She loaned him her horse and let him go. The one thing she said was that he couldn't get off the horse.

Oisín traveled all over Ireland looking for his old crew, these warriors and heroes he'd known, who could do all sorts of crazy stuff. But that time was over. He found some regular guys trying to clear the road of a boulder. Being heroic he figured he'd help, but when he leaned over, he slipped out of his saddle and touched the ground. All the years that had passed came back to him. He aged fast and died. Even his bones turned to dust. So, not a happy story.

"You're not going to tell me anymore?" I followed Swift into the barn.

"When you need to know. It's all tied up in that task you're going to do for me to pay for this boat." He touched its side. I noticed that the steam-box was already going and that the jigs had been cleared to bend more planks.

"'Need to know?' What are we in the CIA or something?" I asked.

Swift gave me that look. Eyebrow up, blue eyes staring. I'd gotten used to it, so it didn't work to shut me up. "You've got to tell me something. How did you end working for the Summerlees?" I was trying not to sound sarcastic, but there was a better chance of me believing in sea gods than in him convincing me he'd known my ancestors. The idea was just too weird. Yesterday maybe; after seeing those ghosts, I was more open to crazy ideas.

He laughed a little at my tone. "Still struggling with it, huh? That's fine, I'll tell you anyway."

West Harbor, 1715

I had no intention of landing in West Harbor, this town, my prison. I'd never heard of it, but I booked passage on the first ferry out of Newport, and its destination was Purgatory Cove.

There were other sailors going there. Two men from the town who'd heard their friend James Summerlee was planning a trading voyage. They said he was the most honest man they'd ever met.

Honest men are hard to come by, so I was interested. I stayed with those sailors when they landed. We walked together up the hill to the Summerlee house. West Harbor was a small village by anyone's reckoning. The town hall doubled as a church, and there were only a few buildings near the water. Most of the homes were spread out for farming.

James had four children. One daughter by his first wife, who'd died in childbirth, and three sons by his second. I met the boys at the house when their mother answered the door. She knew the sailors well and was happy to see them. She was friendly to me and told me that James was out in the pasture with his horses. He'd be back in a while. I asked her if I could walk out and introduce myself.

I went and looked over the cleared farmland. Most was for growing barley or left as grass for the horses, but near the house, there was a flower garden. It burst with color and fragrance. That's where I first saw Sarah. She was holding a book and sitting on a tall rock. Her skin was darker than most English girls, with an almost olive tan, and dark hair that made her blue eyes shine.

Her eyes met mine and I started walking towards her.

The sailors had told me a bit about her on the ferry. How she helped her father handling and taming the horses, and that she could ride as well as any man. They also said that any man who tried to marry her found she was too strong-willed to be tamed herself. "You must be Sarah," I said.

"If I must." She immediately turned back to her book.

I stood there, dumbly staring. I'd never had trouble coming up with words before, but at that moment my mouth felt frozen.

"You know some people consider staring impolite," she pointed out.

"I'm very sorry," I said. "I suppose I was curious to see what you're reading."

"It's John Dryden's last translation," she answered without looking up.

"Which part are you in? Ovid's writing or the Iliad?" I asked.

She took her eyes away from the page, mildly surprised. The habit of reading, learned from my mother, had never left me. "I'm halfway through the Iliad," Sarah said.

"Is this your first time reading Homer?" I asked.

She nodded. "My father recently added it to his collection. It's hard to get many volumes in the colonies. Most here are only concerned with the 'Good Book.'"

"As opposed to the rest, which are bad books?" I asked, smiling.

"Depends on who you talk to. I take it you've read Homer before?"

I nodded yes then asked, "Have you decided yet?"

"Decided what?" She was halfway between being annoyed and amused.

"Is the Iliad a love story or a war story?"

She rolled her eyes, then thought for a second. "A bit of both it seems."

"Funny how often the two go together?"

"Says a great deal about the nature of man," She pointed out, noting her page and closing the book.

"Or maybe it says more about the nature of women?" I suggested.

"So you would blame all the wars in the world on women?"

"No," I answered. "I blame the foolishness of man. And there is nothing that makes a man more foolish than a woman."

"I see," she said doubtfully.

"You don't agree?"

She got up. "Only in romantic stories are wars fought for love. Helen of Troy, if she was real, was probably ugly with a large dowry. That's the real reason the men in this story wanted her so badly. Men are always willing to kill for gold," she said.

"That's a harsh way of seeing things," I pointed out.

"And honest," she added, looking up to see her father coming into the garden.

"James Summerlee," he said putting his hand out. "How may I be of service?"

"Nathanial Swift," I answered, taking his hand. "And it's me who wishes to be of service to you, sir. I've come here seeking work on your trading voyage. I've served aboard the merchant vessel Venture, now docked in Newport, going on a decade. My last posting was as its first mate."

"First mate, you say? Well, I'll have to review your qualifications of course. That is, if you've passed your first employment test."

"And what test was that sir?" I asked, confused.

"You've been in conversation with my daughter and there's no better judge of character that I know. What say you, Sarah?"

She looked me up and down. "He may do. It'll be a few days before the Mayfair and Captain Burnaby arrive. I'll give you a more assured answer by then."

"Mister Swift, it's been a pleasure to meet you," she said, putting her hand out.

"Please call me Nathanial."

"Nathanial then," she said before leaving.

I turned to James, who was smiling. "I've raised a daughter who is more intelligent and has more will than any man I know," he said.

"It certainly seems so," I agreed.

He looked at me for a moment then said, "Come along Mr. Swift. Walk with me so I can know you better."

I stayed in West Harbor at the local inn for a week. James had the few men who were going to crew for him come to his house each night for dinner. It was a pleasant time in which I had several chances to speak with Sarah. We talked about books mostly. James was kind enough to let me borrow a few from his library. She'd also ask me pointed questions about my life. I had to fight the temptation to tell her my whole story.

Word came down that the Mayfair was making its way up the bay. The whole Summerlee family and I went down to the water's edge to watch. I saw that James had *invested much in the three-masted vessel. I could tell by the look of her that she'd be slow moving, but able to carry abundant cargo in her hold.*

A man named Burnaby captained her. He was retired from the British Navy. I'd only heard hints from Sarah about why he left. It sounded like he may have been a drunkard. She didn't think he was a good choice. I'd known enough of these men through my years at sea that I wasn't worried, but I should've considered it more carefully. He and James were acquaintances from years back, and as Summerlee was an overly kind sort, he gave the old man another chance at command. It would end up costing him dearly.

Chapter 13

Beginning the Journey

We worked late into the afternoon while Swift talked, telling me about meeting my ancestors. I suppose I asked for it. But if he wanted me to believe him, he should've made them more uppity, like my grandfather.

The lapstrake planks weren't as curved as the ribs, so they didn't have to be steamed as long. They were tougher to mount though. They made up the hull of the boat, sitting on top of each other, overlapping like the shingles on a roof. To get the new pieces in place, we had to loosen or remove the old ones. We were replacing four. We only had two attached when I looked outside to see the sun getting low. "Oh no! What time is?" I asked.

Swift glanced at his watch. "A bit after six."

I hurried to get up, brushing the sawdust off. "I got to go," I said, running to the door.

"Fine, but I'm going to keep working. I want this hull together so I can start painting her tomorrow." Swift got up and walked over to his calendar. "The time is coming."

He had a day circled, a Friday near the end of June that just happened to be the summer solstice. "What's so important about that day?" I asked.

"That's the day you pay for this boat," he said.

"Oh, right. How's that again?" It's not that I forgot, but so much weird stuff had happened that it'd gone to the back of my head. Seeing dead people will do that to you.

"You're going to sail out that evening and pick something up for me," Swift said. It didn't sound like a request.

"Why then?" I asked.

He scratched his beard. "There are days on the calendar that matter more than others. Days when things happen of an unusual nature, when for a moment if you have a keen eye you might see something truly special." Swift had a voice for storytelling.

I remembered the night his sword had done that trick. It'd only been a week ago. I looked at the boat; somehow it seemed magical too. How long could it take to put those last two pieces on? I didn't want to break the spell.

"Can I use your phone?" I asked.

Swift smiled and took me outside. There was a telephone pole next to the yard. A wire dangled down from it.

"Stay here," he said.

He came back from the tugboat with a metal box that looked like it'd come from a military surplus store. Inside was an old rotary phone.

Swift twisted some loose wires into the back of it. "I hardly ever use a phone, so I don't rightly see the point in paying for one." He handed it over to me. I stared at the numbers for a moment when I started to dial.

My mom picked up. I told her I was at a friend's place, working on a project. Not a lie, right?

Then she asked. "I didn't know you had anything due. What class is this for?"

"Um, history," I said, getting closer to a lie. "It's for extra credit," I added, finally crossing the line into full-on fabrication. "Can I stay a little longer and keep working?"

"Another hour but that's it," she said. "You have that interview tomorrow. Remember?"

How could I forget, I thought, but I didn't say that. I thanked her and promised I'd be home soon.

When I came back into the barn, Swift was already working on the other pieces. "So where am I sailing to?" I asked, coming over to help him.

"To an island that's going to be just outside the bay," he answered.

I didn't think about *how* he said this until later. 'Going to be?' Before I could ask any more questions, he started to tell me the next part of his story.

New York, 1715

We sailed the Mayfair *to the southern tip of Manhattan. Captain Burnaby said he'd take care of contacting the agents we'd be shipping for, while I and the crew off-loaded the cargo from New England. We were still short-handed, so I hoped to pick up a few more men for the longer voyage to the colony of Suriname in South America.*

I was at a warehouse by the wharf when someone approached me. "Nathanial Swift, I see you're doing well."

I turned to see John Sprowls, a mountain of a man. We'd been shipmates in my privateering days aboard the Venture.

"John!" I called out. He put a finger to his lips and winked. When he closed his massive hand around mine, he leaned in and said, "I'm going by a different name today. Call me Mathew."

"Well, it's good to see you alive either way," I said, noticing the way he was looking around, worried someone had heard me. The last time I saw him he'd been injured in combat. For his sake, we'd set him ashore in Jamaica with a fair sum from the prizes we'd taken.

"It's good to be alive, and back working." He smiled. "You've sailed in a fine craft. I wonder, is there room in the fo'c'sle for another able bodied sailor?"

I thought for a moment about what I knew of Sprowls. He was sharp, a hard worker, and even harder in a fight. I knew little else about him but I'd always liked the man. "Yes. Are you looking for work?"

"Much obliged. My shipmate and I have been on land a day too long," he said.

"Shipmate? It's two men I'm getting then?" I asked.

A man stepped from the shadows. "Paul Taggart," he said, putting out his hand. He was lean and looked like he'd seen a fair share of combat. I took his hand, not feeling overly sure about him. I passed a questioning glance at Sprowls.

"He's every bit the sailor I am. Trust me. You won't regret signing him aboard," Sprowls assured me. I nodded in agreement. Not knowing how poor a judge of character I was.

With Sprowls and Taggart our crew numbered eighteen. I returned to the Mayfair and found more bodies aboard. Twelve men stood in a line on the deck, their dark skin shining in the afternoon sun. Burnaby was looking them over, examining the chains that bound them together.

He turned at my approach as if daring me to say something. Back in West Harbor, James Summerlee had *made it very clear he wanted nothing to do with slaves. The horses we were carrying were going to a plantation, so Burnaby had suggested that it'd be profitable, but Summerlee, as a Quaker, was one of the earliest critics of the slave trade. I had my own reasons for hating it. I'd seen it up close.*

"Mister Swift, you're just in time to secure this cargo," the captain pointed to the men.

"Where would you like them? The Mayfair *has no slave deck," I pointed out.*

Burnaby dismissed my tone. "There's room with the livestock."

I took the twelve below. They were all strong men who'd been in the colonies working the fields. They were no longer in awe of the white man with his big ships and firearms. They'd seen our tricks.

We marched them down the companionway with their feet chained in a single line. They struggled on the ladder, having to sit and scoot on each rung.

The hold was big, nicer than any slave deck, but after only a few days there was a powerful smell of horseflesh and dung. One of the crew bent to secure their chains to the deck through bolts meant to hold a horse's lead.

"What are you doing?" I asked. Chained in a line below deck I couldn't imagine where he thought the slaves would go.

"Captain's orders sir. He doesn't want them to do anything foolish like throw themselves overboard."

I looked in their eyes and knew they'd do no such thing. They'd slit our throats first, I thought. "Fine," I said, taking my leave.

The next day, with the turn of the tide, we set sail. Burnaby came on deck but we said little to each other. I didn't trust the man and I doubt he liked me much better. At dusk, the watches changed and Sprowls was free to find me. "Mister Swift, might I have a word with you?"

We made our way to the bow alone. "So what are you wanted for?" I asked, not willing to mince words.

"Piracy, of course," Sprowls answered.

"Taggart too?"

"Aye, he was my shipmate, but we're both happy to have honest work now."

"Honesty is short around here," I said. Sprowls gave me a questioning look, so I told him about our captain, how he lied directly to the ship's owner. "I'd sooner trust an old pirate like you."

"So he's that concerned with profit?" Sprowls asked.

"It would seem so. Why?"

Sprowls watched the ocean. He was holding back an ace. Finally, he turned and said in a low voice, "There's a treasure waiting for me on a beach south of here. All I need is a ship to reach it."

"You're a lucky man. I've rarely found anything but sand on the beach," I said.

"It's a ship. We came on her in the lower Antilles. A Spanish vessel just returned from the Orient with a cargo of linens and silks, casks full of exotic spices. It'd been bound for Panama with enough wealth to make any man, or crew, rich. It was part of a convoy that lost its way in a storm. I was in charge of sailing her back to Tortuga with a small crew, while my captain, a man by the name of Finn, followed us."

"And where's Finn now?" I asked.

"Dead. The Spanish executed him." He spat on the deck. "Bloody Spaniards. Bloody weather too. With more bad luck than any ship should have, we were caught in another storm and separated. We were pushed to an island off the coast of South America. It's probably too small to even have a name. Our bottom caught hold of a nasty coral reef. It cracked the hull and broke the rudder chains. We were sinking. We had to beach the ship."

"How did you get off the island?" I asked.

He shook his head, "We waited three weeks, hoping our mates would return, but with few provisions, we had to act. We set out into the jungle and came on a tribe of Indians. We liberated one of their pirogues, those long war canoes they're so fond of. We rowed back to the civilized world and heard that the Spanish had captured Finn."

"So only you and Taggart know where the prize is?" I asked.

"Four other men were on the canoe, but they're imprisoned. Even if they weren't, none of them, including Taggart, are any good at navigating."

I thought for a moment, letting his tale sink in. Silks and spices, things like that could be worth more than gold. "We'll have to be careful with this," I said.

"You think Burnaby would change course for it?" he asked.

"Oh certainly. The trick will be getting the blow-hard to share." I scratched my chin.

"Oh he'll share it one way or another," Sprowls threatened.

"Calm yourself, man. I'm sure I can convince him." I had no doubt that Sprowls would be willing to kill the captain. In fact, he might even be willing to murder me, but he and Taggart weren't capable of sailing the ship alone if the other men didn't follow him.

"I'll trust you with it," he said. "You've always been a fair dealer."

I made my way to the captain's cabin. Though the space was small compared to most rooms on land, it was large for a merchant ship. Hung on the walls were relics from his naval career, swords and pistols, ribbons and awards. He was already deep into his meal. "I was wondering if you planned to join me. I thought you held a grudge for the cargo I brought on board," he said, barely looking up.

"I hold no grudge sir, but I can't say the same for James Summerlee."

"When he sees the profit I think he'll change his tone."

"Not from what I know of the man," I answered.

The captain finally looked up. He didn't betray any nervousness, but still, I sensed it. I motioned to the chair across from him. "May I?"

He nodded his head, never taking his eyes from me. "Do you have some suggestion Mister Swift?"

"No sir." I paused, holding the air for a moment. "Though the thought does occur to me that the only way Summerlee may know about your cargo, is by its profit. Or by loose lips."

"And how would you keep lips from being loose?" He pointed with his fork.

"As it stands, the men aboard this ship are working for a fixed wage. Perhaps with a small percentage of the profit, they'd feel less inclined to speak."

"Profit sharing on a shipping vessel? That could get expensive. I don't own those slaves. I'm only moving them. The fee, although substantial, wouldn't be much divided among a whole crew."

"What if I told you there was more to be had?" I asked.

He stared at me. "In that case, I might be open to the idea."

"We are bound for South America. I've been given word of a ship. One forced to beach in the Lesser Antilles, not far from our course. It's fresh from the Indian Ocean with a cargo worth a fortune. The crew of Spaniards abandoned her."

Burnaby's eyes lit with greed, but his face stayed passive as he brought his fork and knife back down to his meal. "Mister Swift, how is it that you've come to this knowledge?"

This was the sticky part. It could cost Sprowls his life if Burnaby named him as a pirate. "A member of our crew passed it to me. He knows the exact location and would be willing to tell us for a fifty percent share," I answered.

"Fifty percent, for one crewman, are you mad?"

I leaned over the table, "He's the only one that knows."

Burnaby was unmoving. He cut another piece and ate. "And you still haven't explained how that is."

"Does it matter? The ship is abandoned, fair salvage for the first vessel to find it. We wouldn't be going more than three or four days out of our way."

Burnaby cleared his throat and took up a wineglass. In a slow, precise manner he filled it. "I will allow for a thirty-five percent share and only for what we find."

He set the wine bottle down and offered me the glass, "Unless, of course, he's willing to come here and negotiate with me face to face. I'll also add that as a loyal servant of the king, I would not hesitate to make a full inquiry into how this ship came to be abandoned."

I took the glass. "Thirty-five percent and the information can stay anonymous?" I asked. It was a better deal than what Sprowls would've gotten when he was a pirate.

"Thirty-five percent for your mysterious crewman, forty-five for me, and the rest the crew can divide," Burnaby said from behind his glass.

"Ten percent? Only ten percent for the whole crew?" I demanded. I knew that this was where my share would come from. Burnaby watched me with a glint of joy in his eyes. He just learned for certain that I wasn't the one who knew the treasure's location.

"If this ship is as valuable as you say then ten percent could be quite nice."

I was half tempted to call the whole thing off, but it was already too late. Knowing this secret, Burnaby would do whatever he had to, to get to the treasure. He'd move through the crew and ruin the lives of eighteen sailors. "It's a fair deal I suppose. The men will take what they can in the end."

"We all do," Burnaby agreed.

Chapter 14

Nothing Good

Not long after coming home from school I heard a car horn in the parking lot. I was in front of the bathroom mirror, feeling trapped in my new suit. Everything felt tight and uncomfortable.

Outside the horn beeped again, this time longer and more impatient.

My grandfather was standing next to his classic silvery-gray Jaguar with a lit cigar. He looked at me disapprovingly when I came out. "You don't want to wear the jacket in the car."

"I don't?"

"No, it'll wrinkle. Put it over the back seat." He dropped his cigar to the ground and crushed it with his foot. He left it there. My mom and I lived just outside West Harbor. This wasn't his town.

A half hour later we reached the east side of Providence. It took almost as long for my grandfather to find a parking spot for his fancy car. We passed the main campus of Brown University. I looked through the gates at the shady yard and the old brick buildings, feeling out of place.

The interview was in an outlying building down the street from the campus. At the entrance, my grandfather bent over to straighten my tie and make sure my monkey suit was sitting on me just right. "Remember Tom, this is about your future. Try to do a good job." I nodded my head but didn't say anything.

We walked into an office where a young woman waited. "You must be Tom? I'm Miss Carson," she said, putting her hand out. She looked like a college student only better dressed, more teachery.

Boy, she's pretty, I remember thinking as I took her hand. "So should we get started?" she suggested.

"You're the interviewer?" my grandfather asked.

"We don't like to call it an interview. We're more interested in getting to know our prospective students. Keep it informal, you know," she answered sweetly before leading me into an office.

We talked for almost an hour. It certainly didn't feel like an interview. There were no 'what are your goals' type questions. It was more like 'what are your interests, what type of books do you read,' and by the end, I felt like I'd been talking to a friend. I guess that's the reason I felt slightly betrayed when we came out, and she started talking to my grandfather.

"How did he do?" he asked.

"Fine," she assured him while opening a file. Inside I could see a paper with my name, and more information than I felt was needed to describe me. "Your grandson is a very bright young man. I think he'll fit in just fine at our academy. However, there's a little concern about his academics."

"Really." My grandfather gave me a sideways glance.

"I get mostly A's," I said defensively.

"That's true Tom, but you have to understand that many of our students have been in private schools all along."

"You can blame his father for that. The man was impossible," my grandfather interrupted.

I felt like kicking him. Then I wouldn't have to go to this stupid school, plus I'd have the joy of kicking him. It was tempting.

Miss Carson smiled politely. "I'm sure he'll do fine, but we do move faster at the academy. We're concerned Tom might fall behind. We'd like to enroll him in a summer program at the Academy. You could call it summer camp, but with an academic focus. It'll give him a head start."

"What?" I asked, feeling slightly ill. "You mean like summer school?"

"I'll, of course, have to discuss it with his mother," my grandfather said, "but I don't see any reason she'd disagree."

Let the kicking and punching begin! Of course, I'm not a savage that beats up old men, no matter how tempting.

"The program starts the last week of June." She handed him a brochure. "Room and board are included in that price."

They spoke for a few minutes more. My grandfather had to tell her all about his time at the academy. I think Miss Carson said goodbye to me, or 'hope to see you soon,' something like that, but all I heard was a cell door slamming shut.

Chapter 15

Southern Sailing

'I'm going to summer school?' was all I could think the next day. The boarding school thing was bad enough; leave it to my grandfather to make it worse. I needed to escape, and soon. I got on my bike and rode to Swift's yard. I rode straight through the gate and into the barn, forgetting about the dog.

Swift was working in the boat, bent over, putting the floor planks in. He'd already installed the box for the centerboard.

"We gotta get this boat done," I blurted at him, but he hadn't heard me come in.

He startled, jumping back, nearly falling out of the boat. I had to grab his arm to keep him from falling. That's when I heard a growl. It was low and throaty, going right through me.

I didn't have any bones and I'd been dumb enough to eat my whole lunch.

"Oh no." I looked over my shoulder. The dog was stalking forward with his teeth bared, coming slowly at first. Then he lunged. This time there was no fence to protect me.

I dove headfirst into the boat, diving onto the floor. The dog's front paws were on the side while he leaned in, barking at me.

"Stop it Liam!" Swift yelled.

The dog stopped, starring at him. He snarled again then grumbled and got down.

When I was brave enough to look up I asked, "His name is Liam?"

"Yeah. What about it?" Swift sat down on the side of the boat.

"It's nothing, I just figured it'd be something scarier, like Scar or Killer."

"He's doesn't have any scars, and he rarely kills anything. The name Liam means 'protector,'" Swift said.

"Oh—Wait, what do you mean by 'rarely'?"

Swift motioned for me to get out of the boat. "I'd like to get back to work?"

"Right, sorry. It's just I got some bad news yesterday." I told him about the summer school thing. Then I told him about the Beecher Academy.

Swift didn't seem to think it was a big deal. "It's fine. We've made a good start."

"Yeah but—"

"But what?" Swift asked.

"Nothing. I've just got my own reasons for wanting the boat, something I need to do." For a moment he almost seemed interested, but only for a moment. If he'd asked, I'm not sure I would've told him about the trip I was planning. Luckily he didn't ask. Instead, he explained what he was doing. Then we got to work. Somewhere in there, he started to tell me his story again.

West Indies, 1715

The prize ship had wrecked on an island at the southernmost point of the Caribbean Sea. We rode close to the wind with all the cloth the Mayfair *would take. She was well made with tight seams and no growth on her bottom, making her faster than expected.*

A few days in the tropics and my skin glowed and blistered, eventually turning dark like leather. The pitch on the Mayfair*'s deck cooked our heels, boiling over the planks beneath our feet. At night the crew cabin was a sweltering hot box, stinking of unwashed sailors.*

Most men would have preferred to sleep on deck, beneath the stars, but the captain wouldn't have it. "They won't be lying all over my ship. If they're on deck I want them on their feet and working," he said.

Burnaby wouldn't win any friends among the crew. He worked them hard, running the ship like a military vessel. Many of the men would have jumped ship, but we never made landfall and the prize was waiting.

The captain thought I was too lenient with them. Giving them extra rations of water and fruit, running drills in the evening when the heat wasn't as bad. He thought me an even bigger fool for the way I treated the slaves. I gave them what kindness I could.

I couldn't look at them without thinking of the others I'd carried across the ocean on the Venture. *We'd had over two hundred when we left Africa, far less when we arrived in the colonies.*

In the tropics, I brought the twelve on deck to stretch their legs and see the sky.

The largest of the slaves looked around and asked, "Where are we Englishman?" There was nothing but ocean on all sides.

"In the tropics," I answered.

The slaves were still chained in a line. They stood near the main mast. "It's warm," the big man said, moving to the edge of the boat.

"Hold it right there!" a crewman called trying to pull them back. Four sailors grabbed the last two slaves, but the others pulled forward, dragging the white men and the other slaves with them. The large man crossed the deck to the gunwale and looked down. I followed him to the rail.

"It's deep here too," he said, looking at the white foamy waves beneath our hull.

"Deep enough," I answered.

"We came up here for exercise, yes?"

"Yes," I said. Standing next to him was like being in the shadow of a massive tree.

"Swimming is very good exercise," he said.

"You can't swim with chains on." I tried to imagine stopping him from doing anything. I would need a ladder to take a swing at him.

"You could always take them off," he suggested.

When I didn't answer he shrugged. The other slaves pushed up to the rail with the crewman close behind. I motioned for the sailors to back off. The big slave watched this.

"Are in charge?" he asked.

"No, the captain is." I pointed back to the quarterdeck where Burnaby watched.

"The fat one? Yes, I remember now. When we came aboard he was giving all the orders." He looked around at the sailors. "They listen to you better though. You don't have to speak as loud."

I looked at the other slaves. "And these men listen to you?"

"We've been together for a long time. We are brothers now. In our homeland we may have been different tribes, we may have been enemies, but here in the white man's land we are all the same to you, yes?"

Again I didn't answer, but I could no longer hold his gaze. I looked away and watched the waves.

"They call me Sampson," the big man said.

"I'm Swift," I answered.

Each day as we sailed I'd bring the slaves on deck, and I'd talk to Sampson. He was younger than he looked, but sharply intelligent. He was constantly watching and observing the work of the sailors. He told me that he and the others had belonged to a farmer in New York. Sampson almost seemed regretful telling me of the man's death the year before. "We worked and he'd mostly leave us be. He was too old to be overly cruel. Still, he was one of you."

"When they put him in the ground his son got everything he owned, including us, and the boy chose to sell us. When we reach port we'll be separated. They won't take us all together on the auction block."

"Probably not," I said.

"It'll be difficult for some of them." Sampson nodded to the others. "It'll be hard for them to be alone again."

"And for you?" I asked.

"No, it won't be such a burden. I was a prince in my land; one day I would've been king but when we were beaten in battle I was sent to the coast and sold. They took my name, Aboiye, and called me Sampson for my strength. I was young, maybe fourteen. When you are raised to rule you understand what it means to be alone."

"I had a different name once as well," I said.

"Was it taken from you?" Sampson asked.

"No, I cast it aside."

"There is power in names," I nodded then looked at him. He couldn't be more different from my mother, yet there was something about him that reminded me of her. Some sort of magic. I thought of the sword she gave me. It'd been a while since it crossed my mind.

It was a long voyage to the hidden cove where Sprowls's treasure lay, but by early summer we'd reached the Lesser Antilles, a chain of islands that marked the edge of the Caribbean Sea. As we passed each small piece of land, it fell to me to find out from Sprowls if it were the island we sought. He also told us which ones to avoid. There were Spanish outposts and the remnants of the French Buccaneers there.

Each night I'd bring the charts from the captain's quarters to Sprowls's hammock, and we'd plot the next day's course. Finally, we arrived. The island had no name, but it was larger than expected, with sandy beaches and a lush forest. "This is it," Sprowls said.

The captain was in his quarters where he spent most of his time. I ordered a man to let him know. A good twenty minutes later Burnaby came on deck, polished in *his sharpest suit. He wanted to be dressed well the day he became rich.*

We sailed round the island till we found the cove. The water lightened as we approached, turning azure blue. The entrance to the cove was marked by a tall piece of coral that jutted up from the sea bottom. It looked like an upturned trumpet. Below and around it were the angry teeth of the coral reef. It was a long, pale shadow below the water, where the incoming tide washed up into choppy waves and broke again.

"We'll wait till the tide is full then turn in," the captain ordered.

An hour passed before I gave the command. The wheel was turned hard over, and I held my breath as we passed over the natural barrier. At the bow, we dropped lead shot tied to a line and took soundings, checking the depth. We cleared the coral by five and a half feet. At high tide, this was as deep as it was going to get. I tried to picture the prize we were going for, imagining the weight it would add. How much deeper would we ride, I wondered?

We sailed into the cove and I saw the prize pulled up on the sand, listing to the side.

"What's this then?" I heard the captain say. He stood next to me. His eyes were wide as he stared at another ship. A double-masted schooner sat at anchor between us and the prize. It was smaller than our ship but much better armed.

I counted twelve guns that were being run out and turned towards us. I could hear them yelling across the water. They were as surprised to see us as we were to see them. They raised their colors, declaring themselves a vessel of France.

I looked at the captain and could sense his thoughts. Our men had practiced with our guns. We had a few swivels and four mounted. I was afraid of what he'd do with them, putting us in a fight we couldn't win.

"They'd have us quick." I pointed to the shore where a second anchor line was set. It was a spring line. With a few turns of the capstan, the Frenchmen could tug that line, turning their ship and pointing their guns anywhere in the cove. We weren't nearly as maneuverable with only the wind.

As I said, we were outmatched, but the captain's eyes were fixed. Most of his life he'd been at war with France. This old fool is going to do it, I thought. He's going to put us in a fight we can't win. I knew if I said anything else he'd attack out of spite. I stared at those guns and could almost smell the slow match burning. I held my breath, waiting to see what the old man would do.

Chapter 16

Smashed to Pieces

"Careful Tom!" Swift yelled. We were trying to stand the boat on its stern to treat the inside. It was heavier now with the floorboards and benches in. The fresh wood wasn't dried out like the old planks. The good news is if it slipped and fell on me, I could tell everyone I was crushed by an actual boat, one I put together myself. Nice, right?

We still had rigging to work on, and while Swift already treated the outside once, using a varnish he called his 'secret recipe,' we had several more coats of the finish to apply. I was excited, knowing how close we were, but I also wanted to know what happened.

"Did the French ship fire on you?" I asked.

"No, not then…I mean eventually, they did," Swift said, handing me a sanding block.

"Eventually?" I asked.

"Yeah, it was later that night. But even then, they weren't actually shooting at us."

"Okay," I said, wondering if Swift was getting confused by his own story.

Swift stepped back and grabbed a small ladder. He put it inside the boat and stuck his head up into the cockpit. "Burnaby saw my point. The French would've blown us to pieces," Swift called from the inside, over the sound of sanding.

I looked up for a second and got sawdust in my eyes.

"It crushed Burnaby's pride, but he knew we didn't have a chance. He went over to the French ship flying a white flag. England and France weren't at war so they held their fire, but they didn't like us being there."

"Burnaby met with their captain, who told him that he'd laid claim to the prize and that he had no interest in sharing. We had to leave. When the old man got back to the *Mayfair* he went to his quarters." Swift leaned down and looked at me. "That's when he opened his wine, and when he stopped making good choices. Never trust a drunkard Tom." Swift went back up and kept working while telling me the tale.

West Indies, 1715

Burnaby came up the ladder and through the entryway. "The Frenchman gave us permission to go ashore for fresh water, but we'll have to be quick. I want to be on our way to Barbados by the next high tide." He straightened his fancy vest and pointed at me. "Mister Swift, I expect you to take personal charge of filling the casks."

"What business do we have in Barbados?" I asked.

"My business," he said pointedly, "Is selling those slaves and hopefully reclaiming something from this journey."

I nodded my head and went about the business of making the ship ready to sail on the tide, but I was thinking of Sampson and his men. Being sold to a sugar plantation in the tropics was the cruelest of lives for a slave, but there was little I could do to help them.

The water-casks were emptied into the sea, then the casks themselves were tossed over the side. Sprowls, who was a boatswain, came up to me. "What are we going to do?" he asked.

"We're going to get these barrels full, then we're going to sail away from here as our captain ordered." I tried walking away from him.

He grabbed my arm with a hungry look about him. "Do you know how much loot is aboard that ship?

We're fools to go without trying."

"Attacking them would be completely illegal. Would you have us all hung for piracy?" I asked harshly, pulling away.

He held his tongue. Then he nodded. "You're right Mister Swift. I guess I haven't been off the account long enough. However, I'd still advise against setting sail just yet."

"Why's that?"

"My knees are aching, and if you look to the east, you'll see the sky is turning dark. There's a blow coming and this cove, even with those guns pointed at us, may be the safest place."

Sprowls was right. I could see it too, a darkening on the horizon past the trees. Storms moved fast in these parts. They could pass by one island and crash into another. "We'll keep a weather eye and see what comes with the tide, but for now we've got work to do." I climbed down into the boat.

Sprowls followed me. He looked at the Spanish treasure ship as we set the oars. "Aye, I'll never come on a prize that fat again. At least I won't have to share it with that devil of a captain."

"It would've been one way of getting rid of him," one of the men said.

"One way," Sprowls agreed.

We towed our water-casks up the river, landing out of sight of the cove. Sprowls advised us all to work quickly and quietly as we carried them inland to a stream.

This was the easy part. Getting them back up the river proved harder. They dragged like anchors when they were full. It took every strong back to row them to the Mayfair *where rigging had been set up to pull them aboard. Hours passed. We were barely done at the turn of the tide. In that time the storm had moved closer. The wind was picking up, and I could feel heaviness in the air.*

I went to the captain "What is it!" he shouted through his cabin door.

"Sir, it looks like there's a blow coming," I called.

"I'll be on deck in a moment. I still want to make that tide Mister Swift, make certain all is in readiness."

"Aye sir," I said.

Back on deck, I gave my orders. I listened to the songs and shanties of the crew as they set their backs to work. They were as nervous as me, watching the eastern sky become darker. If we could make it out to open water, we might have a chance. However, if the storm caught us outside the cove, but still near this island and its reef, it'd be the end of us.

The captain dumped the rest of his wine into a tin cup and staggered up onto the deck. He stumbled to the rail to see that the boats were pulled up and secured. Men waited by the capstan ready to hoist the anchor.

"Is all ready?" he demanded.

"We've just finished stowing the casks sir, but as you can see the weather is turning against us." Even in the cove, we could feel the rough water.

"Better the storm than the French blackguard with his guns pointed at us."

"Surely they'd understand if we're unwilling to leave in this," I tried to reason with him.

"They'll understand that my first mate is too cowardly to put to sea in a bit of weather," Burnaby shot back. He finished his mug. *"We are sailing with the tide. Is that understood?"*

"Aye sir," I answered. The wind came with force across our stern. As the anchor broke loose from the bottom, we felt the gusts pushing forward on our yards and bare masts. When the sails were raised the Mayfair jumped toward the beach. I joined the captain on the quarterdeck.

He called, *"Ready about!"*

The man at the helm turned us gently around. The crew hurried about the rigging, letting out sheets. The mizzen sail, the furthest back, which was at first hauled to the weather, was let go. It luffed above our heads. Then the wind took it, swinging it over the deck to the opposite side.

The men on the forward deck brought the jibs in tight, while more men scurried up the main and foremast to turn the yards. The sails were pointed into the wind. With it pushing against them, all forward motion fell away *and we turned slowly around. For a moment it seemed like we were dead in the water. Then the sails filled as they were trimmed. We started on our new heading, slowly moving across the cove on a beam reach, with the wind now blowing at us from the side, pushing us at an angle to it.*

The ship listed to the side. For such a large vessel the tilt felt odd, but I wasn't going to give up speed or direction. I could see the mouth of the cove ahead and knew we'd be passing close to the headland. By the time we approached the reef, it'd be impossible to turn around. We'd have to push through or end up making a rough landing on the coast.

The captain was reckless, and it was beginning to show on the nerves of every man on deck. It felt like we were lumbering forward, but we were making the best of the wind, riding as close as possible. "Mr. Sprowls," I called, "Throw out the chip, I want to know how fast we're traveling."

"Aye sir," he called as he and another man pulled out a spool of thin line. It had a small wooden float at the end. They made ready to throw it and let it drag across the water's surface. The line tied to it had knots along its length; by timing how long it took the line to go taut we could figure our speed.

"Belay that order," the captain called.

Everyone looked back at him in surprise. He still had his tin cup in his hand. He brought it up to take a sip then realized it was empty. In frustration, he tossed it over the side.

"But sir, don't you want to know how fast we're approaching that headland?"

"Go chase my mug. That ought to tell you." He pointed back. "No? Well then explain to me, if we're not going fast enough for your liking Mister Swift, what would you suggest, that we turn back like yellow sniveling cowards? I said we're leaving this cove and that's exactly what we're going to do."

"Aye sir," I answered. The men looked toward me with fear in their eyes. I walked around them, trying to say a few words of encouragement.

The captain called me back to the quarterdeck. "Stand here with me. I'll not have you turning my crew against me."

"Sir I have no interest in turning—" I started to say when he cut me off.

"Quiet! No more out of you."

I held my tongue and anger in check, watching the mouth of the cove approach. The wind blew harder as we headed further out. The waves were breaking on the reef, crashing like thunder. "Will we have a sounding?" I asked the captain.

"Why not? If it'll allay your worries," he mocked.

I ordered the sounding and listened as the men called out the depth. They dropped the line off the bow into *the foamy, roiling sea. It was deep for the most part. Then as the waves truly lifted us, they called out, "Two fathoms and barely that." I held my breath, listening for the next measure.*

"It seems we found your reef Mister Swift," the captain taunted me.

They called, "Six fathoms." And I finally let the air out of my lungs. We'd cleared it, but we still weren't safe. The wind was blowing out of the east, and the island was to the west. We could only turn so far into the weather and still keep moving. It was a dangerous game skirting the edge of the reef. We couldn't make much speed getting away from it. All it would take was a little change in the wind to send us back. The waves were lifting us higher and dropping us lower in their troughs.

"Let her off two points and tighten up those sails," the captain called. "I want a little more speed out of her." I heard the order, but I couldn't believe it. He was turning away from the sea, further into the island. True we might be able to coax a few more knots out of her, but we wouldn't be getting any further from land.

He watched his orders fulfilled. "You've wasted enough of my time here," he said. I could barely hear him over the screaming wind.

"What?" I asked.

He grabbed my lapels and pulled me to him. His breath stunk with wine. "I said you've wasted enough of my time with your promises and games."

I pushed him away. "This is madness. You aren't capable of command."

The helmsman, along with the rest of the crew, were watching us. They waited to see what would happen next. "I ordered you to let her off two points! Two points to starboard!" the captain screamed at the helmsman. The poor soul began to turn the wheel, but as he did, a wave taller than the others lifted the Mayfair *up and took the steering from him. Our rudder lifted out of the water, and the ship began to turn on its own. The helmsman tried to bring us back on course, but then the waves lifted us again.*

Why are we rising so high, I wondered. "At the bow, give us another sounding!" I called. The line dropped, and even from across the ship I could see it fell short.

My stomach lurched as at that moment the Mayfair *hit something. A sound like a single clap of thunder throbbed through the whole ship.*

We'd never gotten far enough from the reef, and in heavy weather, it was impossible to tell where we were. The force of the incoming waves had pushed us in too close.

Our sails were still full, and the wind was still pushing us, but the ship had slowed, shuddering as it was dragged across the reef. Timbers were being pulled apart. The only thing keeping us above water was the reef itself. I prayed the waves would give us a moment before they lifted us again. I knew if they took us up one more time it would be the end. The Mayfair would come apart when it dropped back down.

"Man the pumps!" I heard the captain call.

But I shouted above him, "Abandon ship, get to the boats if you can!" In a moment we'd be off the reef and sinking fast to the bottom. "You," I said, grabbing the helmsman, pulling him towards the captain, who'd been knocked off his feet and was having trouble getting up again, "see that he gets in a boat. I'll wager he's too drunk to swim."

Then I left the deck and made my way down the companionway. The walls were shaking and trembling with each incoming swell, one more violent than the next. A big one was coming, and that would be our end.

The water was already at waist height in the middle decks. Passing my quarters, I grabbed my pack with my short sword bound in it. I tore the pack open, making my way to the hold where the door was closed and locked. With the ancient blade, I cleaved the lock away and forced the door open against the pressure of the incoming sea. The twelve slaves were still there, chained together with the eye bolt holding them to the floor. They were trying to stay above the rapidly rising water.

I stood over the bolt and raised my arms high. With a guttural yell, I brought the iron blade straight down. It sliced through the water and with a single stroke of its dulled edge, cut the bolt in half.

The slaves looked at the ancient artifact in my hand. We were all thinking the same thing, that this piece of iron shouldn't have been able to do that. We didn't have long to wonder about it though, not with the ship sinking. In a line, still held by their chains, they half-swam to the ladder.

I stayed below, and as each one climbed, I took my blade and with quick strokes cut each man loose from the next. By the time they were all out and free, the water was well above my head. I could hear behind me the horrible sound of livestock drowning, and as I struggled against the incoming water, I thought for sure I'd join them. Then I felt Sampson's hand take my shoulder and pull me out.

We made our way up the flooded companionway, then to the deck. The Mayfair *came up again. This would be it, I thought as I felt her drop. I leaped, plunging into the ocean, hoping that the beach wasn't as far away as it looked.*

Swift got down and settled onto the ladder. He looked at me then at his sanding block.

"You saved Sampson and the others?" I was still blinking sawdust out of my eyes.

He nodded. "Probably the only decent things I've ever done." He looked at me, then at his sanding block. "The crew survived. Most of the men didn't know how to swim, but the beach wasn't far and there was enough flotsam breaking away from the *Mayfair* to ride in on. The boats landed roughly, smashing on the beach. Burnaby nearly drowned.

"He, of course, tried blaming me for the wreck. 'If I'd done that, or if he'd been allowed to do this, none of it would've happened,' all lies and excuses covering his incompetence. He accused me of inciting mutiny and ordered me detained.

"I said to him, 'What are you going to do, lock me in the hold? It's laying on the bottom of the ocean!'

"He didn't care for that. We separated into two parties. Some of the men, a very few, chose to stay with their captain. Most chose to come with me, including the slaves.

"Burnaby tried telling them that they were his property. Oddly enough, they weren't willing to listen. From that day forward they were free men."

Swift grabbed a broom to sweep out the inside of the boat, "It was the last time I spoke to Burnaby. Still, the man found ways to cause me misery." He handed me the broom then stood back to look at the boat.

"We're doing just fine, but Tom, something just occurred to me."

"What's that?" I asked.

"Do you know how to sail?"

Chapter 17

Learing Lessons

Somehow it never dawned on me that this might be a problem. I guess I thought I'd figure it out when the time came. Either way, when Swift asked me if knew how to sail, I was forced to admit that I had no idea. Of course, I didn't exactly say that. "I've turned the rudder. My father let me try doing that," I told him, "and I know if I turn it one way, the boat goes the other."

Swift didn't look impressed.

"I'm not completely clueless."

"Don't worry, we'll figure something out," he said. I left for the night, while he cooked up a plan to turn me into a sailor.

The next day after school when I came into the yard, the first thing I made certain of was that I entered slowly. No sudden moves. The second thing I made sure of was that I had a few bones out and ready, while the box stayed securely hidden in my backpack.

The dog came over to me and growled a little, but it wasn't as menacing as usual. It was like he was letting me know that he accepted my presence, but still wanted it to be clear that we weren't friends.

"Hi Liam," I said.

He tilted his large head, surprised to hear his name. Then he snarled, not caring for the familiarity.

"Okay, we're not there yet. I get it." I placed the bones down in front of him. He chomped them to pieces while I snuck past, going to the barn.

Swift was nowhere to be seen, but the door on the other side of the barn was open. I heard him call, "There's some pieces on my workbench. Get busy sanding them. I'm doing something else out here."

"Okay," I answered. The blade and handle for the rudder were on the bench. Swift left me the only two parts of the boat I knew how to use. "Figures," I muttered to myself as I took off my backpack. I had a strange feeling I was being watched. I turned and looked at the door. Liam was standing there. He wasn't looking at me though. His eyes were on my backpack.

I ignored him and went to work. Twenty minutes later Swift called again. I dropped the sanding block and hurried into the sunlight. Swift was standing by a cast iron bathtub, the old fashion kind with the clawed feet and deep sides. It was grungy and dirty, brown with grime.

"What do you think?" he asked.

I looked at him. "We're not doing anything weird, are we?"

He pulled a wooden sailboat from the tub, came over, and handed it to me. *So weird it is*, I thought. "What am I supposed to do with this?" I asked.

"Sail it," he said.

I moved the tiny boom back and forth on the mast while Swift explained. "A catboat is one of the easiest to learn on because it's only got the one sail. They're meant for work. The men who used them didn't want a whole bunch of complicated rigging."

I looked at the little boat. "Okay, well thanks."

"It's not a bloody present." He took it out of my hand. "I'm going to teach you how to sail with it, the basics anyway."

"You're going to teach me how to sail with a toy?"

"Well, I can't very well take you out on the real one now can I?"

I shrugged my shoulders.

"Would you show some imagination?" He handed the boat back and pointed to the tub. "This is the bay," he said. I placed the boat in the water, glad to see it stay afloat.

"And call me Neptune, king of the deep," he brought out an old fan, covered in dust and filth. It had metal blades and only half its safety cage. I looked at the frayed electric cord he handed me and thought, well at least I won't live long enough to drown.

He plugged it into an extension cord. The blades jumped to life. Blue sparks flashed inside and filled the air with a tangy smell. Swift raised his voice to be heard over the noise.

"You know how a rudder works, but that's not the engine that drives a sailboat. The thing you really have to understand is the one thing that's not attached. That's the wind." He pointed the fan at the boat in the tub. The breeze it was creating would have been like a hurricane if I'd been an inch tall. The sail whipped over and filled with air. The boat shot across the water and hit the other side.

"That's sailing with the wind," Swift yelled. "It's the simplest thing to do. But we have other options." He picked up the boat. There was a string running free at the end of the boom. Swift tied it off, putting the boom in the middle. He placed the boat facing the fan and turned it on low. The sail was at a slight angle to the wind. The boat looked like it wanted to go backward, but then the sail filled and it started to move toward the edge.

"We haven't come up with a way of sailing all the way into the wind, but as you can see we can get closer than you'd expect." He motioned with his hand, dividing the area of the tub into a big circle and dropping the boat in the center. "If you know the direction of the wind, all these different angles belong to you. It's not as simple as just dropping a motor and cranking it up, but it's certainly more elegant."

Swift spent the next hour teaching me the basics of sailing. Explaining how the wind moved across the sail faster on one side than on the other, creating areas of low and high pressure. The low pulled while the high pushed from the back, similar to how an airplane wing works. The centerboard kept the boat moving straight. I tried different positions with the sail, imagining how it'd be on the water.

After a while, we broke down the fan and went inside to work on the actual boat. I went over to the workbench. "Hey, did you move my backpack?" I asked Swift.

"No, I never saw it," he said.

I looked around, not sure what could've happened. Keep in mind, with the creepy stuff going on I had trouble trusting anything. "I know I put it right here. At least I think I did."

Swift opened a can of finish and started coating the boat above the water line.

"So how did you get off the island?" I asked while still looking.

"In the French ship," Swift answered.

"They gave you a ride?" I asked.

"Not by choice…"

West Indies, 1715

Between the twelve slaves and the men who choose my company over Burnaby's, I had twenty-five able bodies. They were looking to me for answers. It probably would've been a more strained situation between the whites and the now free black men, but they were all more concerned with getting off the island and surviving.

The storm moved through quickly, taking only a few hours to blow out its fury. By midnight the stars and the moon had come out. Some of the men thought it'd be best to make a fire, but Sprowls advised against it. "We aren't alone here boys. It's probably best not to attract attention," he said. It was bright enough for me to see the fear on the men's faces. They needed to know we had a plan.

I pulled Sprowls away from the others. "Tell me again how you left here last time?"

"In a canoe me and my mates pilfered from the natives," he answered.

"You crossed the ocean in it?" I asked, not sure if that was a trip I was willing to take.

"I didn't have to. There's a Spanish colony not far to the west. I wouldn't suggest going there, though. Taggart and I speak a bit of Spanish, so we fared well enough, but some of my old shipmates are probably still rotting in prison cells."

My men wouldn't be treated any better by the Spanish, I was sure. We'd be arrested without any hope of appeal. There was only one thing I could think to do. A plan was forming in my head. I knew of one boat that would surely be leaving the island. I planned to be on it. I told Sprowls my idea, and he nodded in agreement. We'd have to take the French ship if we wanted to escape.

We gathered the men and started off by moonlight, following Sprowls through the forest to the Indian village where he'd liberated a pirogue before. They were long war canoes dug out from the tall trees that grew in the tropics.

"We'll be in and out as quick as you please," Sprowls assured us as we moved through the forest, looking for the slow-moving river which split the island in two. It curved through the trees like a massive artery, making its way to the cove where the French ship was sitting at anchor.

We found the waterway and Sprowls went as silent as a forest devil. He followed the river, cutting through the woods near the muddy banks, not making a sound. In the distance, I could see cooking fires and hear voices speaking in a strange tongue.

As we approached the small encampment, Sprowls motioned for the men to hang back. "Last time I managed to sneak off in the dark before these buggers even knew I was there. I'll wager they're a little more careful with their property now. I don't want to stir them up if we don't have to. Some of these tribes have a rather fearsome nature, man-eaters and such," Sprowls whispered in my ear. It was a different tune than what he'd said before.

Sprowls took three men and disappeared into the forest while the rest of us waited at the next bend in the river. We listened to every sound and felt our anxiety grow as an hour passed. Finally, we heard the sound of oars breaking the surface of the river. The noise of splashing and pulling was a lot louder than I would've expected. Sprowls wasn't trying to be quiet.

"Hurry men, Hurry! They'll be on us in no time!" he shouted as he turned at the river bend.

I could hear the sound of more canoes approaching behind him and angry voices calling out in that foreign tongue. As Sprowls pulled his canoe into the shallows, we heard a rain of small arrows drop into the water around him. The men ran out and leaped like flying fish over the high bulwarks into the canoe. Near panic, they grabbed the oars and started paddling for their lives.

A sound I didn't expect to hear echoed out: the explosion of gunfire. I looked back to see where it'd come from. Mounted on the bow of one of the pirogues was a swivel gun. "Where did they get that?" I asked as another gun fired.

In the light from the shot, I saw what was chasing us. There were six pirogues, all loaded with angry natives. A few were armed with more swivel guns, and some of the natives had muskets. Though most still favored their arrows, which fell from the sky like rain.

"I thought you said this was a small tribe," I shouted at Sprowls.

"It is—apparently, they're having some sort of meeting."

"And where did they get the guns from?" I yelled as another shot fired.

Sprowls shrugged his shoulders, digging his paddle deeper into the water. "I don't know, but thank God they're lousy shots."

Another rain of arrows came down. Men in our boat called out in agony as some of them struck home. "Well they're much better with those," I said.

We came out the mouth of the river and into the cove. We were pointed directly at the French ship and the prize ship behind it. I could hear the turn of the capstan and see them moving on the spring line. They'd been alerted by the sound of the guns.

The French sailors woke to the worst thing any European could imagine. The natives were restless, and worse, they were armed. They ran out their guns and fired.

Their first round of shot blasted through the air, but fell far away from any of the canoes. It was enough to get our pursuers' attention though. The natives returned fire with their swivel guns and their arrows, finding the French ship a much easier target. They loaded and fired their small weapons at the French ship, making a lot of noise but not causing any real damage. We crossed the cove and found that for a time our canoe was being ignored. We didn't have anything to fire at anyone, so they didn't bother with us.

"Bring us round by the beach and out of the middle of this," I called to the man at the back of the boat. He used his paddle like a tiller. "Now paddle boys, paddle for your life," I said. We needed to be quick to get to the French ship in one piece. I couldn't imagine this fight lasting long.

We stayed in the shallows, beneath tree cover, while the natives were out in the middle of the cove. It was a crystal clear night under a bright moon. The only cover was the smoke of burning powder rolling across the water like a fogbank.

The French guns were reloaded and run out again. This time the crew took more careful aim. The boom and flash filled the night air, and two of the canoes were blown apart, shattered into splinters. They flew into the air and dropped back into the cove, disappearing below the water.

The natives gave up, turned, and started back up the river, but that didn't stop the French crew. We were nearly under the guns, pulling alongside the ship when the third round of shot fired. The blast left my crew blind and deaf.

I was angry as I thought of the damage those guns would do to the retreating natives. They were leaving. There was no reason to fire on them.

Sprowls had found a spear in the bottom of the canoe. He jammed it into the entryway and pulled us in close to the French ship's water line. Choked with smoke from the spent gunpowder, the air was hard to breathe. As my hearing returned, the sound of the French celebrating echoed out the gun port. I took up my oar and made a slapping motion with my hand, showing my crew what I expected from them.

Sprowls stood with his feet firmly braced in the canoe, and his hands hooked together, hanging down like a step. I climbed up him and onto the entryway, going over the side and onto the deck. I was unnoticed as I crouched and waited for my men.

Sampson and his freemen were the first to follow me up. The plan was to hold there till more were aboard, but these twelve had no interest in waiting. They pounced on the French, swinging their oars like clubs, shouting war cries.

In a moment of fury, they released weeks of frustration from being in the cargo hold of the Mayfair. Sampson led his men with those paddle-clubs, and beneath a bright moon, I watched them decimate all resistance.

Only the first few Frenchmen we ran into had to be swatted down. Most of their crew was too stunned to fight. Still, the freemen pressed on with Sampson leading the charge. I shouted for him to hold his men back, but in truth, there was little I could do.

"What happened?" I asked Swift. My bag was still nowhere to be seen, and I had stopped looking while I listened to his story.

"We claimed the prize and the French ship, an act of piracy by anyone's reckoning. I knew it. The men knew it. Any of us that believed we could return to the normal life was blind and foolish. Sprowls pointed out that there was only one thing left to do, draw up articles and elect officers. He nominated me for the captain's post. The men agreed."

"Sprowls wasn't one for speeches, but he gave a fine one that night. 'You've sailed your whole life for other men,' he said. 'They've profited from your labor and your blood. Think on it? Would you sail again for a man like Burnaby who'd take what's yours and throw your life away, or will you be a man and a servant only to yourself? I can't promise you a long life, but I can promise you a merry one.' He went quiet, but only for a moment, long enough for the men to think. Then he added, 'Oh and any man who signs the articles will get a share of the profits, including the treasure from that Spanish prize.'"

Swift shook his head. "There was such excitement. Every man signed."

"But what about the French sailors, what happened to them?" I asked.

Swift gave me a look, letting me know not to ask again. Then he said, "Understand this about violence, Tom. It's in everyone, and the more we're a part of it, the more it's a part of us. Sampson and his men had been taken from their homes and beaten down to serve as slaves. Even when they were free, the violence that had been enacted on them was going to be paid back. I learned a great deal from that battle. You see I was their leader, but in a way, I wasn't. It was the same for pirates. I was elected their captain and Sprowls the quartermaster, but on a pirate ship it's the men who are in charge."

"What do you mean?" I asked.

"Well, the articles we signed say that the captain is the supreme and unquestionable authority in time of chase or battle, but the rest of the time, all matters are decided by the crew. In other words, our ship was a democracy in every sense of the word. Any man who signed the articles had a vote."

Swift had that far off look on his face. "Some of the Frenchmen died without needing to that night. But more innocent people would be hurt by my men in the pursuit of riches. There wasn't a thing I could do about it."

We didn't talk much after that. I helped sort out the rigging then I left for the day.

Chapter 18

Denied and Denied Again

The moon looked out of place in the blue evening sky as I started home. I was thinking about Swift. He'd gone so quiet after telling me what happened to the French sailors. I suppose when you think about pirates, you don't always consider their victims.

I looked back at his yard. There was a hill that dropped from his fence straight down to the water's edge. Liam was at the corner, standing watch. The sun was getting low, going behind the trees, and it cast strange shadows on the cove. There was a spot at the bottom of the hill. It was darker than anywhere else. My stomach sank. That's where I'd seen those people in the rain. I pedaled faster.

I didn't even think about my missing backpack until I pulled in the parking lot and saw my mom's car parked in front of the condo.

"Where have you been?" she asked as I came through the door. She was sitting at the kitchen table with papers in front of her.

"I've been doing some work down at the marinas, cleaning boats and stuff," I answered, not feeling bad for lying. She'd taken the news about summer school a little too well.

"You know this country has child labor laws."

"I'm just doing some odd jobs. It's more for fun than anything else," I said.

I went to the kitchen to get a drink. Then my mother called me back. "This came for you," she said, handing me a letter. Once again she turned her attention to her papers. Even though her eyes were down, I had a feeling she was watching me.

The letter was already open. I turned it around and saw the postmark from Florida and my father's name in the return address. It read:

> *Dear Tom,*
>
> *I'm sorry I haven't called. Money's been a little tight down here, and I was having an argument with the phone company. Anyway, I've got my boat up and running for*

the season and I've started getting some char-
ters. I think it's going to be a busy summer and
I could use a deckhand. Maybe you could
come down and help out. Anyway, we'll have
to hash it out with your mom. I'll try calling as
soon as I get the phone thing sorted out.

Love you,
Dad

I was smiling so hard it hurt. Then I glanced at my mom and saw the way she was looking at me.

"Did you read this?" I asked her.

"I did," she answered.

"And…"

She found the papers in front of her more interesting. "I don't know if it's going to work with summer school," she said.

"So I just won't go," I said.

"You have to." She sounded sympathetic, but that only made me angrier.

"Come on Mom," I said.

"I'm sorry Tom, but this is the way it's got to be." She kept her eyes down.

I walked away feeling numb, but the rage was building. I went to my bedroom, yelling, "It's bloody tyranny!"

Yes, I know, it's hard to believe but I actually said that.

I tucked the letter under my bed with the guide book and the money I'd made. My mom came down the hall. She didn't say anything though. I think she thought it was better to ignore my outburst. I'm sure she was confused by my choice of curse words as well.

The next day was Saturday, so of course, the morning was gray and ugly. Welcome to New England. It wouldn't get any better as the day went on either. It fit my mood. I finished my paper route then I went to Swift's yard. He was already painting, putting on another coat.

He looked up as I came in the door. "I found your backpack," he said, motioning towards the workbench. "It was out by the fence."

It was ripped and torn and looked like it'd been buried. I turned and saw Liam by the door. He was already starting towards me, coming over with his teeth bared. "You know what you jerk, I don't have any more bones! Want to make something of it?"

The dog stopped in his tracks. "Bring it on," I shouted. I had my fists clenched. Liam growled a little, turned, and walked away. I think he may have snorted, but that could've been my imagination.

Swift nodded his head. "I think he's starting to like you."

I grabbed another brush and went over to join him. "So you killed some people? Go ahead and tell me about that," I grumbled.

Swift took my hand and slowed me down. I was brushing too hard. "Don't make light of it Tom. The fighting, the hurting people. It wasn't a good thing."

"I know," I said calming down a little. "But I still want to hear more."

West Indies, 1715

Sprowls stood beside me on the beach. It was near dawn the morning after signing the articles. We crammed the last of the Spanish loot into the French schooner. Not an inch of space was left for the crew to sleep below. The men were passed out on the sand. The sun was rising in the east over the tiny island, and we were looking at our ship in the morning light.

We decided not to maroon any of the surviving Frenchmen. We offered them passage to the next safe port and gave their crew the chance to sign our articles. The French privateers hadn't been much more than pirates anyway.

Sprowls and I were the only two left awake. He placed his hand on my shoulder. "How's it feel to have your destiny ahead of you Captain Swift?" he asked.

"'Destiny,' is that what's on my horizon, not a short dance at the end of a long rope?" I asked.

"That's for the unlucky ones, those who'd go down without a fight or have no guile about them. That's not you Swift. You're slippery. You always have been. This life was made for you."

I should have been scared. I wasn't. I thought of the wealth we'd already claimed, of all the treasure ahead of us. I was excited. I'd had enough of civilized men who set people like Burnaby ahead of people like me. I was ready to go to war upon the whole world.

"There's only one thing left to do," Sprowls said. "We'll need to rename her."

"Why?" I asked.

"La Princesse Hardie, it's just too blasted French. I'll tolerate them among the crew, but I won't sail a ship named by them."

"And what have you got against the French?" I asked.

"I married one when I was younger."

It was no light manner changing the name of a ship. Every sailor knew it could bring bad luck. All trace of the old name had to be erased, sanded down and painted over. Then a plea had to be made to King Neptune erasing the old name from his ledger. We sailed out from the cove a nameless ship till we were far from land. That's when we dropped our gifts into the deep, some gold coin and a bottle of rum. The old name was written down, placed in a box, and lit on fire.

A day passed before voting for the new name. Rum ran freely as I looked over the faces of the men sailing with me, including the freed slaves. I thought of the treasure already in our hold and called out. "Aye it's a grand thing this freedom we have, 'tis the greatest fortune that any of us will take. What say you to the 'Freedom's Fortune?'"

Sprowls was standing at my shoulder. "That's a bold name," he whispered in my ear, "Perhaps too bold."

"We'll offer it to the winds and see what our luck brings," I said.

He nodded while shouting, "Well what say you, men?"

The men cheered in answer, each one calling out in agreement. One man yelled above the others, "Aye, freedom and fortune, we'll have each in their turn!"

We made sail for New Providence in the Bahamas. I had no intention of taking any prizes along the way. Our hull was full, our crew was small, and the freed slaves, as frightening as they'd been in the attack, weren't trained sailors.

New Providence was a lawless place with a shallow harbor and safe anchorage, the perfect base for pirates. It wasn't far from the Florida strait where the merchants of Spain sailed their rich fleets. Sprowls introduced me to Benjamin Hornigold, a former privateer who'd built himself a flotilla of pirate ships.

He seemed more like the governor than a pirate, dressed in fine clothes tailored to his broad shoulders. He came aboard and surveyed our ship. *"Damn my eyes you've got yourself a small crew. We'll have to see about signing aboard more. But you've got guns. That's the important part."*

"What we need are men trained in firing them," I said.

"You'll have them." He motioned towards our quartermaster. *"Sprowls tells me you took her with nothing but oars."*

"We had oars, surprise, angry natives, and that big fellow over there," I said, pointing back towards Sampson. Sampson had the oar he used strapped to his back with a sling. It hadn't left him since that night. I told Hornigold the whole tale.

He laughed and patted me on the back, *"Well done Mister Swift. It may be peace in the rest of the world, but here in these islands, it falls to men like you and I to let these papist nations know that England has a stake in this New World. These lands and their riches aren't here for them alone,"* Hornigold said.

Like all pirates, Hornigold's men were a mix from every nation, but he believed himself loyal to the crown. He considered it his duty to continue attacking the ships of Spain, Portugal, and France. *"There's wealth in this New World, and the Spanish seem to think that it's all theirs. I disagree,"* he told me. *"Sprowls says you're a good man and I'm impressed by what I've seen. I'd like you to join* us. There's more treasure to be had working together," he said before taking his leave. We put it to a vote that very night and the men agreed.

Hornigold began our alliance well enough, giving us men to help offload our cargo and seeing that we got a fair price for it. Though we would have made more in England or the colonies.

Thirty men came aboard to fill out our crew. They were escaped slaves, old buccaneers, naval deserters, and out of work privateers. In three weeks' time, we'd meet Hornigold in the Gulf of Honduras to see what wealth the mines of Central America could provide.

We gave chase to every craft that came up on the horizon, taking six ships. Some fought back, some surrendered, but with each new victory, we improved, becoming more vicious pirates. We were a wealthy and better-prepared crew by the time we reached Honduras. Still, I was awed to see the fleet Hornigold put together.

Rough-looking men filled the decks of more than two dozen ships. They bristled with guns.

The Spanish fort outside the harbor was already under attack. Their heavy cannons were blasting back into the fleet with one salvo after another. For every shot from the fort, ten more returned from the water in answer. Finally, there was a great explosion behind their walls.

"We've hit their powder," one of our men yelled. The whole fleet turned towards the harbor and the Spanish settlement of Triunfo de la Cruz there in Tela Bay. Docked just inside the bay were merchant ships waiting to be loaded. It was a small town, but it's worth wasn't determined by its size. There was gold and silver waiting in their warehouses, ready to be loaded and sent back to Spain. Hornigold had timed his raid perfectly, just at the height of their shipping season.

"We'll attack with the incoming tide," I heard him call through his trumpet. The command was passed from *ship to ship, all down the line. I heard men from other vessels laughing and singing, boisterous at the thought of plunder. My crew was equally as merry, fueling up on rum, content in the belief they'd get more when we landed.*

I hadn't taken a drink yet, thinking that I ought to keep a clear head. Instead, I was looking at the town, trying to gauge what sort of resistance to expect. "Look there," I said to Sprowls, pointing to a man-o-war guarding the bay. I put my glass to my eye and surveyed it. "They'll put up a fight," I said.

Sprowls held a bottle in his hand, but it was only a prop. He was as sober as me. "I'd rather leave that work for some other crew. Those fat merchants, they're for us." He ran the glass over the bay then stopped. "What's this? What's that fool doing?" he asked.

I took the glass back.

"Look there," he said, pointing. A man was walking into the shallows wearing a black robe and a cassock. He held a large crucifix in one hand and carried a chair with the other. I watched him place the chair in the water and sit. The tide was at his waist. He put the crucifix on his lap and took a piece of rope.

"What's he doing?" Sprowls asked.

"He's tying himself to the chair," I answered.

"He's in the shallows. When the tide comes in, he'll be a foot under water."

"His mouth is moving. It looks like he's praying." I took the glass down, noticing how the crew gathered around us.

"Praying to hold back the ocean. Good luck father," someone laughed.

"He's praying for a strong westerly wind, the only thing that'll save this town," I said. The priest held the cross over his head. His eyes closed and his mouth moved. I ordered my men away from the rail. I didn't want them distracted from the job before us. I ordered them to check their weapons, to tighten this sail and let that one out. I even ordered more rum brought up, anything to keep their minds away from the man in the water.

As the tide turned, the pirate armada started. We were an unstoppable force, creeping forward with a strong southerly breeze, promising death and destruction. From time to time I returned quietly to the rail, putting the glass to my eye to watch the tide rise over the fool in his chair. The water went from the priest's waist to his chest, then up to his neck. *"Give up man,"* I mumbled to myself. In fifteen minutes I was sure he'd be breathing salt water, but then I felt it, the air shifting.

Coming over the mountains, in the distance I could see storm clouds, moving fast. *"The wind's changing,"* I heard one of the crew call. The men turned, rushing to the rail to look at the praying priest. To see if he were still alive or if he'd drowned in his chair. He was holding his *head up stiffly with salt water splashing into his mouth as he continued to pray. He stopped and coughed as the wind turned fully, coming straight from the west.*

We wouldn't be sailing in with this tide, I thought as lightning ripped the sky.

"We can't stay here," I heard a man call.

"Quiet you, or I'll throw you over the side, let the sharks have your cowardly carcass." I pulled my sword free, ready to cut down anyone who made another frightened remark. "Get away from that rail and get back to your posts!" I ordered.

I looked at the mountains and the dark clouds coming over them as the men moved back to their positions. I walked over to Sprowls, saying quietly, "He's right, though. If we stay here, that storm is going to rain havoc on us."

"Give the order captain," he said. I watched the storm for a moment more, moving at an incredible speed. I wouldn't be as foolish as Burnaby. "Ready about," I said, "Get us out of here."

One full coat of finish was done. I washed the brushes while Swift talked. "I watched the town's folk drag the priest in like he was the day's catch. I don't know if any of the other captains saw him," Swift said. "But they certainly saw the storm. Everyone turned towards open water to keep from being smashed on the rocks."

"You think the priest actually stopped the attack with his prayer?" I asked.

"Who knows? But the storm lasted three days. Hornigold still wanted the town, but half his fleet left. We put it to a vote and chose to leave as well. The gold of Triunfo de la Cruz was left in our wake, while we went looking for easier prey."

Swift's smile was crooked. "What are you going to do when the Lord himself decides to stop you?" he got up and went over to his workbench where I'd kicked the remains of my backpack. "Oh speaking of disasters and acts of God, don't forget your bag." He picked it up and handed it to me.

I stared at the dangling shreds and shook my head.

"You should see what he does to my laundry," Swift said while tidying up.

Chapter 19

Trapped and Nearly Trapped

"You smell awful," my mom said when I came through the door. There was a cloud around me from Swift's special recipe. "What have you been doing?" she asked.

"Finishing my paper route," I said.

She looked down at her watch. I'd been gone three hours, a lot longer than it usually took me to do my route.

"Then I went down to the marina. There's an old guy I'm helping out," I explained.

She was about to ask me more but then she looked down and saw my bag. "Is that your backpack? What happened to it?"

"A dog got it. I think I might need a new one."

She got up and came over, picking up the two pieces. "Where did this happen?"

"Um," I didn't want to say.

"Down at the marina?" she asked.

"Yeah, but it was my fault. I shouldn't have left it where it was."

She looked back at her pile of work on the table. "Go take a shower. We'll have to go to the store and get you a new one. One that you're going to be a lot more careful with, right?"

"Right," I said.

We grabbed lunch while we were out. When we got back my mom settled into her work again. After only a few minutes of watching me pace around bored, she gave me permission to go out on my bike. She suggested I go to my grandparents, but the look on my face told her what I thought of that. There weren't any kids in our condo complex, so if I wanted to see friends I had to ride to their neighborhoods. Of course, that wasn't where I wanted to go either.

The barn door was closed when I got to Swift's yard to keep out the wind and drizzle. I pushed it open and saw Swift look up, surprised to see me back. He was bent over, sanding a large piece of wood.

"Where's Liam?" I asked. I'd left my new backpack at home, but I had a plastic bag with me. I reached in and brought out the bone I'd bought him. "I've got something for him." True, he'd destroyed my backpack and true, he'd probably tear out my spine if given a chance, but we still needed to get along. I didn't want to look over my shoulder every time I came here.

"Out by the fence. Keeping watch," Swift said.

I almost asked, 'For what,' but I thought better of it.

"What are you working on?"

"The centerboard. It wasn't in terrible shape. A bit dry, but I think it'll serve you fine. Here, give it a go." He handed me the sandpaper. I had to step over the mast lying on the ground with the rigging still attached.

"My mom wasn't too happy with me."

Swift went over to the stove and threw another log in. "Why's that?" he asked.

I watched him fill the kettle in the slop sink. "The bag," I reminded him.

Swift shrugged his shoulders. "She's a lawyer, I'm sure she can afford another."

I didn't like how dismissive he was, but it only made me sand harder. I suppose what I should've been wondering is how he knew what my mom did. I don't think I'd ever mentioned it.

"Anyway, we had to go get another," I said.

"Nice that you can afford to." Swift pointed out. He came closer. "Careful Tom. You're going too deep into the wood."

I was sanding really hard. "Your ancestor, James Summerlee, wasn't as lucky. There was no replacing the ship he lost, the money he'd put into it. It'd nearly left him and his family destitute. He was close to losing everything," Swift said.

"Well, a backpack is a lot cheaper than a ship." Swift gave me that familiar look. "What happened? How did he pay his debts?" I asked.

"I happened," Swift said. He made his tea then settled down on a stool and started his story again.

New York, 1716

After Honduras, the crew decided to set out alone. Taking a city like Triunfo de la Cruz is fine if you can do it, but there were so many smaller prizes to be had. Besides, Hornigold wouldn't attack the British. My men had no such standards. They were from every nation, but their home was the ship. We made war on the world.

We went after every sail that came into view. Sometimes we were sent running; other times we took the prize with little effort. Occasionally, we got into a real fight. Blood was let and people were hurt. That was our life; fear and intimidation backed up by the threat of harm.

Months passed as we filled our hold. It wasn't all gold though. Most of it was trade items. Blankets, cookware, nails, anvils, and ladies' dresses piled high in every corner of the ship. We barely had a coin to show for

Pete A. O'Donnell

it. Most merchant vessels didn't carry a great deal of money. Their business was trade, not banking.

Loaded down with more odds and ends than you can imagine, we made our way back to the east coast, to Manhattan, where the men thought we'd get our best return. We sailed through the Narrows and sighted the city. There was the fort and the stone church and the red roof buildings lining the water's edge. We sailed past Nutten Island and dropped anchor up the Hudson River.

It was dark and I was nervous as we passed under the fort's guns. We weren't waving our black flag, but still, there was a lot about the Freedom's Fortune that made her look like a pirate ship. We'd cut gun ports in the lower decks and mounted smaller guns on the rails. When they were all run out, we bristled like an angry porcupine. We'd pulled down the forecastle and roundhouse as well, making a flat deck for fighting.

Twenty of the crew rowed the long boat across the Hudson. Sprowls had a list of everything we'd taken. None of it would be divvied up till it was all sold. The men pulled at the oars, and I could sense their anticipation. Months of work thieving had created an awful thirst in them.

Sprowls and I left them at the boat. He knew the merchants of New York, so I followed his lead. I hoped to get this business over with quickly. Instead, we spent most of our evening going door to door, selling our wares like a couple of tinkers.

"We'll get a better price this way," Sprowls explained as we turned down an alley leading to the back door of yet another merchant. They didn't like men like us coming to their front door.

This was the one he hoped would buy the ladies' dresses. I'd be glad to see them go. The men had enjoyed them too much, dancing around the deck in them while our fiddler played ladies of Spain.

Sprowls was about to knock when I saw through the window a group of men waiting in the merchant's parlor. "Odd that so many would be shopping for ladies' clothing this time of night," I said.

"Who can speak to the taste of New Yorkers," Sprowls answered.

I stepped to the side of the window and tried to get a better look. "They're armed. There's two by the door with muskets and the third is speaking to the merchant."

Sprowls leaned in and looked. "That's the constable," he said.

"Are you sure?"

"I've spent enough time as a sailor in this town to be familiar," he assured me.

"You don't think he's after us do you?" I asked.

"No. How could they know who we are? Still, discretion being the better part of valor and what not." Sprowls stepped back, motioning with his thumb to leave.

That's when a musket shot exploded, slamming into the wood.

"You there, halt!" A lone man called from the end of the alley, trying to block our way out. It didn't occur to him that he'd wasted the one shot he had on a warning.

"He must be new to this," Sprowls said, rushing the man while I moved a rain barrel in front of the door.

Sprowls threw his shoulder into the deputy, knocking him through the air. "Let's go, Nat," he called.

The other lawmen were banging, trying to get into the alley. "Hold a moment," I said to Sprowls while leaning down to the fallen man. "Who are you after?" I asked.

"You, the dread pirate Nathanial Swift," he answered.

I was shocked. "And how do you know who I am?"

He pulled a poster from his pocket. There was a crudely drawn portrait of me with an angry, stupid look on my face. "A captain Burnaby gave testimony against you. There's a warrant out for your arrest."

I grabbed the poster. "Thank you, young sir," I said then I hit him on the jaw.

Just then the barrel was pushed away. The shouting constabulary came pouring into the alley. Sprowls and I took off running, dodging in and around the tightly packed shops and homes, heading for the water with the lawmen not far behind. As we came close to the dock where our launch was waiting, Sprowls shouted, "Ready the boat!"

I shouted over him, "Ready your guns!"

We heard the footsteps behind us slow down and someone say, "Hold up men they're armed."

"Fine command," Sprowls said to me.

"What do you expect from the dread pirate Nathanial Swift," I handed him the poster. "I'm famous you know."

"Wonderful," Sprowls said, "And rich too, with a cargo we won't be able to sell."

Chapter 20

Homecoming

Swift slid the centerboard into its housing, then lifted it up and dropped it back down. "Works fine. Come up here and see," he said.

We'd lowered the boat down onto some sawhorses that didn't look all that sturdy. I hesitated. "O-kay." The whole thing was shaking as I grabbed the side and pulled myself up. I lifted the centerboard and dropped it back in.

"Not everything on this old boat was junk." Swift took the board out of the housing and passed it to me then he climbed down. The boat bounced around like it was going to crash before it ever made it to the ocean.

"You came back here after New York?" I asked, passing the piece down.

"I had a cargo I needed to get rid of. Sure I could've sold it in Tortuga or one of the other lawless ports, but I never would've gotten what it was worth. We needed a merchant in the civilized world. With a warrant out for me, showing my face in Boston or New York would not have been wise."

He put the centerboard down on the workbench. I couldn't be sure but I think Swift's face turned a little red, and it wasn't from the stove. "I suppose I was tempted to return for other reasons."

West Harbor, 1716

We put the Freedom's Fortune *deep into Purgatory Cove sounding at the ebb tide with just a few feet of clearance below our keel. Most can't see it from the land, but there's a little turn to the shore where tall trees once grew. They were perfect for hiding a mast or two.*

I left a shore party at the water's edge and made my way through the woods, up the hill, and to the Summerlee home. It was hidden in the trees, more rambling than most colonial houses.

I stood at the door for a long time with my hand ready to knock. I'd only spent a few days in this happy place, but there was something about it that made me feel at home.

I let my hand fall and waited, expecting James or maybe his wife to greet me. All these long months thinking of Sarah and never once did I consider that she might be the one to open the door. Her eyes fell on me and widened. "My God," she said.

My mouth hung open, but I couldn't find a word to say. I'd been telling bawdy tales, giving orders, and bringing men under my command, but as before, when I first met her, my voice failed me.

"You're here, and still it appears that all you can do is stare," she said.

"Hello, Sarah." I finally managed to get out. Then for some reason like a preening fool, I bowed. I looked the part of a pirate captain, wearing silks and fine stockings. Long gone were the simple work clothes of a sailor. At that moment I missed them. "May I come in?"

She nodded and stepped back.

"How've you been?" I asked.

She wanted to berate me. I could see it in her eyes, but as she opened her mouth she softened. "Things have been hard here Mr. Swift."

Sarah leaned back into the house and called, "Father, we have a visitor returned from the sea."

There was no answer. "Come along," she said leading me through their foyer. I noticed how bare the house was. All of the fine things James owned, lamps, tables, good china, the silver they'd eaten with, were gone, sold to cover the family's debts.

The house was quiet. Each time I'd been here before I'd heard the boys laughing or arguing. Sarah took me to the back room where a bed was set up. James lay there. He was pale and his eyes were drowsy, though they opened wide when he saw me.

He stared for a moment then said, "I hope you're not here to raid us. I assure you our cabinets are quite bare."

"What's happened?" I stepped into the room.

"From the way Burnaby tells it, you sunk my ship," Summerlee answered with barely contained venom.

"I sunk your ship?" I was astounded. "That bloated, lying parasite. It was him, James. Burnaby set the Mayfair on a reef. The fool was drunk and ordered us away from safe harbor in a storm. For God sakes, I wasn't the captain!"

"Mind your blasphemy in my home," James tried to yell but the effort was too much. He had to steady himself before he added, "Burnaby said it was you that brought the Mayfair to that island with the promise of treasure."

"Yes, I suggested it, but he was in charge. It was his choice. I did nothing to twist his arm."

Summerlee stared at me for a long time before finally shaking his head. "He still hasn't been back here you know? He sent a letter. That fat fool didn't have the strength to face me."

James looked at Sarah, then back at me in my pirate clothing. "You look ridiculous. You know that right?"

"*Well, you have to keep up appearances.*" *I thought I could at least get a smile from him, but James was beyond that.*

He pulled his blanket aside and motioned to where his left leg had been. "*Of course. That's why Sarah's been hemming all my pants. So I can show off my new leg. That is, if I can afford one.*" *At his knee was a stump.* "*Perhaps you've got an old piece of hickory you can loan me.*"

I gasped in surprise. Being a sailor I'd of course seen this sort of injury, but it was still a shock.

"*I'm very tired Nathanial,*" *he said, pulling the blanket back over and turning his eyes to the window.* "*Sarah, would you entertain our guest?*"

Sarah took my arm. "*Come with me.*"

We went out to the kitchen. When we were out of her father's hearing she said, "*It is good to see you safe.*"

I smiled and nodded, but I had to know. "*How did this happen to him?*"

"*The debtors were coming for everything, so we needed to make some quick sales. He was working too hard, trying to get the last of our horses to market in Providence. He fell from his mount and lay in the road for hours with a broken leg. We sent out a search party and brought him back. I did what I could, setting it, but the fever took hold. The leg had to be removed. Luckily, I'm a steady hand with a stitch.*"

"*You did that?*" *I asked.*

"Who else?" She sat down. "The midwife gave me some herbs for the pain, but he's refused to take them. Like every man in this town, he's afraid of a woman who might know more than him."

"I find it easier to assume that every woman knows more than me." I sat across from her. "Where are the boys?"

"The oldest two are apprenticed to craftsmen; shipwrights in Boston. The youngest is in school in town. My mother-in-law took the position as schoolteacher. I've been doing what I can for my father and trying to keep the farm running."

"I'm sorry Sarah."

She took a deep breath then asked, "Tell me your part. What happened to the Mayfair?"

"Burnaby and I were not well suited," I said. "He showed himself to be a liar and a tyrant. We'd barely begun our journey when he agreed to ship slaves from New York."

"I warned my father about him." Sarah shook her head.

I told her the rest of the story.

"He claimed that you turned the crew against him," she smiled. "A pamphlet has gone from here to London, chronicling his escape. Apparently, Burnaby kept his few loyal men alive, hiding in the jungle and keeping their *spirits up, telling them of the justice he'd bring down on you. A few days after the crash, a Dutch vessel found him."*

"Since his return, he's done everything he can to blacken your name. Not that you haven't done enough yourself. They've got a call to take you dead or alive. You're the dread pirate Swift now, the most wanted man on the high seas."

"If I were smart I'd turn you in for the reward," she added.

I sat back in my chair and wondered if she were serious. "I don't think that'd be wise at all," I said.

She raised a single eyebrow.

"Oh, it's got nothing to do with my bloodthirsty crew only a shout away. It's more the financial opportunity you'd be giving up."

"Do tell," Sarah said.

I leaned in again. "My ship has found itself in need of an agent. Someone here in the colonies that we can trust to sell our wares."

"Your stolen wares," she pointed out.

"Stolen and valuable, and sitting out in the cove."

"And who did all these things belong too?" I didn't answer her.

She squeezed her fingers together. "You want to trade on my father's name? Make us criminals as well?" she asked.

"Look around you Sarah." I got up from the chair and motioned to the empty house. "You call what I'm

doing thievery, but we live in a world of thieves. Kings and monarchs say they have a divine right to rule, to tax you and take what's yours with little regard for who earned it. And why do they claim this right, because their ancestors stole or conquered enough land for them to rule, gave them power that they neither earned nor deserve?

"I'm called a criminal because I no longer listen to their rules. I'm low-born with nothing to call my own, but I tell you aboard my ship all men are equals, all princes of the sea. The Africans, the French, the English, and the Irish; we serve only each other and ourselves. We determine our destiny. Call us thieves if you must, but know that we are freer than any man has ever been and if we have to take from others to maintain that freedom, then so be it. I have as much right to make war on all the nations of the earth as any monarch who sits on a gilded throne. Remember that when they drag your father off to the pauper's prison."

When I finished, Sarah stared at me, saying nothing.

"I'm sorry." I started to turn towards the door.

"Nathanial wait," she called. "I do understand you. But give me some time to think."

She looked back at her father's room. "He'd hate it," she said.

"Starvation is worse. I would not ask this of you if I thought it'd harm you, Sarah. You must know I'd never do a thing to cause you harm."

"Is this a new tactic? You've been impassioned and now you hope to make me swoon by saying sweet things?" she asked.

"I would say a thousand more kind words, but as you know you leave me speechless."

"On the contrary, it seems you're quite good at making speeches." She tapped on the table and stared at me. "Am I as blind as my father?" she asked herself.

"I'm no Burnaby," I said.

"No, but what if you're worse?" She motioned for me to sit again, then we discussed the terms of our partnership.

Swift had a folding knife in his hand. He didn't look happy as he cut away the lines from the mast. They'd been twisted around the gaff and boom when they were taken down. My dad had wrapped them together. Apparently, he stunk at storing boat stuff too.

As Swift tore the frayed rope away he looked at the mast, running his hand up and down its whole length, checking for cracks. "These might just do. I'll sand them a bit tonight and then see if I can treat them." He looked up at the ceiling, listening to the sound of rain hitting the roof. "Probably going be a long night anyway."

It took me a moment to understand what he meant. I tried telling myself that Swift had a thing about the weather. He was crazy, right? But what I'd seen a week ago, when that last storm came through, was still too fresh.

I knew it was time to head home, but I didn't want to go outside. "How did James take the idea of working with you?" I asked while pulling the lines away from the gaff.

"Not well," Swift said, handing me his knife. "But what choice did he have? He was ill and Sarah was trying to save her family." Swift looked up. He heard something above the sound of the raindrops. We stared at the barn door and listened. I could hear it not far away. It was Liam, barking at something outside. He sounded more upset than usual.

"Is he alright?" I asked.

"Yes, of course," Swift said, but he didn't sound completely sure. He went over to the door and touched the handle, but he didn't open it. Not at first. He stood there and listened. Liam's bark sounded manic. Then it went quiet.

I was squeezing the knife so hard that my hand started to hurt.

There was a sound outside, a scratching noise, followed by a thump. Swift pulled at the barn door, sliding it open. The sky was grey and overcast and it was getting darker as the sun set somewhere behind the clouds. Liam was a shadow against the fading light. He looked up at both of us. Then he came in and shook the rain off, spraying Swift before turning and settling back on his haunches so he could look out.

Swift came back to the workbench, running his hand over his face to get the water off. "I swear he does that on purpose."

He looked back at Liam, but when his eyes drifted to the outside and the weather, he had to shake his head to break the spell it cast on him. He spoke quickly, but his eyes were unfocused. "After Sarah agreed, I put the crew to work."

His hand was going back over the mast. "It took us five nights to dig the tunnel. It was a quarter mile from the inlet, back along the creek in the woods. We cut down trees and moved stones to shore it up. Then we moved the cargo in.

Sarah would sell it piece by piece to avoid raising suspicion. I left two men with her to help. They were the ones who'd sailed with me that first day when I came to West Harbor. They'd enough of the pirate life."

"We returned to the shipping lanes, back to our bloody work. We were gone for months before bringing back more loot. Each time we returned we'd only stay long enough to unload it and to take our pay. I could see how it weighed on Sarah."

"I took what time I could with her when we were here, while James healed slowly. He'd speak to me and tell me how much he hated what we were doing, but he'd never say as much in Sarah's presence. I suppose he didn't want to add to the hard choice she'd already made."

"Of course the one question he'd always ask was, 'When will this be over?' I didn't have an answer. When the end arrived, it was just as much a surprise to me."

Chapter 21

Petty Pirate Scumbags

It was time to leave. I stopped next to Liam before going out into the rain and took the bone out of the shopping bag. I held it out to him. The look on his face was something to see.

I think he was surprised, maybe even touched. Or maybe I was reading too much into a dog's expression. It wasn't just a treat. It was an actual bone filled with some sort of chewy stuff. "Go ahead boy," I said.

He took it as I stepped past him. I pulled my hood up then saw that he was following me. He stood next to me in the rain as I got on my bike with the bone hanging from his mouth. He was alert and guarded, like my own private security detail. He followed me to the gate.

"Thanks, buddy," I said. I almost patted him on the head, but then I thought better of it.

I didn't look up, or out at the cove, as I rode home. In fact, I kept my head low, watching the wet pavement. It was better when I got to Main Street. Even on a rainy night, there were people going to the restaurants. The white lights decorating the trees were on, and I could see the evening crowds through the windows.

It was quieter near home. Fewer cars, fewer people. I pulled my bike into the condo complex and went in through the garage. When I came into the living room my mom looked up. She was sitting on the couch watching TV. "You're soaked," she said.

"Yeah, it's really coming down." I may have had a jacket on, but that didn't do anything for my blue jeans.

"What's going on with you?" she asked.

"What do you mean?" All I wanted to do was climb into a hot shower.

She turned the volume off. "Is it a girlfriend, something like that?"

"Oh God no," I said, feeling my face turn red.

"If you have any questions you know you can ask me? I want us to be able to talk."

"Mom, I really don't," I said. I looked at the slider, debating over throwing myself from the balcony. It was raining hard enough out there that it was spraying the glass door. The deck light was off, but the curtains were open.

My eyes stayed on the glass for a moment too long. I thought I saw something out there. I wanted to look away. I should've looked away, left the room, and not come back.

The evening news was reflecting off the glass, but that's not what I saw. There was something moving in the dark, just at the edge of the deck where the rain was falling hardest. Someone was standing in the shadows.

"Well, maybe you can talk to your grandfather?" my mom suggested. She didn't see how tight my spine had become as I inched forward.

I went to the window, keeping my eyes away from the glass, looking at the carpet. "Yeah maybe," I said, though I hadn't actually heard her. I grabbed the curtains and closed them, then I backed away slowly.

"We'll see him tomorrow at church," my mom said. Again I was only half listening. I was worried that the door was unlocked.

Can ghosts open doors?
Do they even need doors?
I really need to lock that door.

I breathed out and told myself, 'it was a trick of the light. There's nothing out there. Still, just to be safe….'

I went back to the slider and pulled the curtain aside just enough to reach the lock. That's when everything inside me sank, like I was falling through the floor. I looked at the other side of the glass. There was a hand there, reaching out. It came from a tattered sleeve with bones showing through the rotting flesh of long fingers. I could see right through it in the flickering light of the TV. I closed the lock fast, jumping back.

"Tom, what's wrong with you?" My mom got up.

Throwing yourself across the dining room in a panic is a quick way to get a parent's attention.

She came over to me, grabbing my shoulders to look at my face. I was pale with shock. "What is it, Tom? Are you doing drugs or something?"

I looked back at the door. "I wish," I said. That wasn't a good answer by the way.

It stopped raining sometime before dawn, but everything felt wet when I went outside. There were puddles on the sidewalks. The streets glistened and reflected the blue sky.

I needed to deliver the Sunday paper. It was the biggest bundle of the week; the most customers, the most pages, and mostly just advertisements. When I reached the bottom of the hill where I always picked them up, I saw something was wrong.

There's an old factory building at the corner of Water Street, just past the train trestle. That's where a truck dropped the bundles for me. The pavement was wet of course, and clinging to it was an entire stack of Sunday papers. They'd been shredded, torn to pieces.

Like I mentioned the Sunday paper is big, so when an entire stack is ripped to confetti, it covers a lot of area. Scraps of newspaper were plastered all around.

My first thought was of Liam. We were becoming friendlier; maybe he couldn't deal with it, so he came down here to teach me a lesson. A dog would have to have serious issues to do this much damage. I came closer and saw how the papers were dragged towards the water. On the few dry pieces, I noticed something that looked like footprints. They didn't belong to a dog.

There were hundreds of wet steps, like an army coming up from the shore. It was low tide now, but when I looked at Water Street, I remembered how it flooded. So apparently I wasn't just dealing with vengeful ghosts, they were a bunch of petty scumbags too, making my life harder just because.

I didn't want to think about what this could actually mean but an awful realization dawned on me. They'd torn these pages apart, what would happen if they got a hold of me?

I called my boss when I got home. That was fun. As you can guess he wasn't happy. He asked me if I cleaned it up. I hadn't; that's when he offered to fire me. I thought about it for a moment. Another week's pay would've been nice, but honestly, I was leaving soon anyway. "I'm sorry sir, but I need to go to church."

There was yelling, lots of yelling, and some words that weren't polite to say to a kid. I hung up the phone. "Everything all right?" my mom asked.

"Not really," I said.

She was still worried about me. Last night I told her that there was a ghost on our deck. My mom doesn't believe in ghosts. Officially I don't either. She'd turned the deck light on and threw open the curtains. Nothing was out there of course. These ghosts weren't trying to mess with my mom, just me, because of Swift. As I said, they were 'petty.' I didn't sleep well after that, which stinks because I used to like sleeping on rainy nights.

I sat through church hardly listening to the sermon, trying to keep my eyes from closing. Every time my head started to fall, the image jumped into my brain of those men in the water. They were out there, watching and waiting. I think I may have fallen asleep once or twice during the service because when I came up with a start, my grandfather was scowling at me.

We left the church and went to the diner on Main Street. My grandmother used my shoulder as a crutch as we walked down the steepest part of the hill. "Thank you, Tom," she said at the bottom, "You're becoming such a strong young man."

I smiled and nodded, holding the door open. She struggled a little going in, then after looking around the diner, confused, she waited for someone to guide her. Something was wrong with her. She had moments like this, but today it seemed worse. I took her arm while my mom and grandfather sat at our usual booth. "They're over there," I said pointing.

She stared at me strangely, before mumbling, "of course."

Mom and my grandfather were already arguing about taxes or politicians or any combination of the two. "I don't care how much you make, the tax system is unfair—" my mother was saying, until my grandmother interrupted in a wavering voice.

"I can't believe it's Sunday already," she pointed out.

Mom paused, having her thoughts interrupted. "I know, the week goes by so quick."

Grandma went quiet, staring off again. My mom and grandfather returned to their conversation. I half listened, glad the subject wasn't the Beecher Academy. My grandmother let her silverware drop to her plate noisily and they stopped talking again, both staring at her. "Oh my goodness," she said, as if the action had surprised her as well. There were tears in her eyes. She wiped them away then reached across the table and touched my mother's face. My mom pulled back a little from the sudden gesture. Then she relaxed, allowing her mom's hand to brush her cheek.

"You've grown so fast…I'm sorry dear," Grandma dropped her hand back to the table. "I'm so tired today. The whispering was loud last night."

My mom leaned forward. Her hand was gripping the table.

Everyone was quiet, then finally I asked, "What whispering?" I was hoping she wouldn't answer.

"I heard them in the walls," she said. "I couldn't sleep. They were too loud."

We stayed quiet, waiting for her to say more. She remained silent though, her eyes returning to some distant point.

"It's fine." My grandfather patted her hand and tried getting the conversation going again, bringing up the academy, but the strangeness wouldn't leave.

They saw us off in the parking lot of the church where my mom's car was. "Do you mind if I go see a friend?" I asked her.

She was looking in her rearview mirror, back at her parents who were making their way home. "Maybe you should spend some time with your grandmother. She's hardly gotten to see you lately."

I was quiet at first. "That's not the reason she's acting so weird. There's something wrong with her. Half the time she doesn't know who I am… then there's that other thing," I said reluctantly.

Like I said, my mom doesn't believe in ghosts. She believes in drugs though, and she asked me again last night if I were on them. "This friend, is he the one filling your head with this stuff?" she asked.

"No, of course not." *Lying, lying—I'm a liar!* I thought, before adding. "I'm telling you Mom, I thought I saw something, and maybe Grandma heard something—" I was almost going to tell her about the tunnel, but then I'd have to fill her in on the rest, including the boat. I wasn't willing to do that.

"She hasn't been feeling well, that's all," my mom said a little too quickly.

"You mean she's sick—like in her head, going crazy or something," I answered.

"My mother is not going crazy!" she yelled.

I turned away, looking out the window at Main Street as it passed by. "You and Granddad just want to ignore it anyway. All he's worried about is having a grandson at that stupid school, and all you care about is your job."

"That's not true," she said.

"Please, that's the reason you said I have to go, so I can get a good job just like yours. That's the reason you're sending me away." I was still looking out the window, surprised by how fast I'd become angry.

"Tom, that's not fair."

"And that's the reason—" I stopped before I said something terrible, before the words came out. We looked at each other and I knew, she knew, what I was about to say. "Never mind," I turned away again.

*And that's the reason Dad left.*I thought, but I wasn't cruel enough to say it aloud.

I didn't look back, not till we were in the parking lot. I got out of the car and went over to my bike. "Where do you think you're going?" she asked.

"I'm going to see my friend," I said, getting on my bike. "If that's alright with you?"

She wanted to say no, I could tell, but she only nodded her head as I rode off.

Chapter 22

No Escape

Swift wandered across the yard, coming back from the tugboat. I pulled the gate closed behind me, not something I usually worried about doing. I liked to leave it open in case I ever had to escape the canine catastrophe. Speaking of Liam, he was out by the fence, contently chewing on the bone I gave him yesterday. He looked back at me and waved his tail just a little. Then he stopped, stared at the tail, and growled at it. He grumbled, picked up his bone, and went off to hide.

"It's good to see you too," I said, going over to the barn.

Swift looked rough. His hair was as crazy as ever. The dark circles under his eyes made his droopy face look deflated. He was doing a lot of scratching, the tired kind that people who just got out of bed do.

"You alright?" I asked.

"I just woke up, grabbed a few hours after the rain." He pulled the door open. It was dark inside so I couldn't see anything, then Swift flipped on the light switch. The boat sat on the floor on its flat bottom. The coamings and rub rails were in place. The new decking was shiny under the varnish and the rudder hung from the stern. Inside, the floorboards and seats were finished, and outside, all the hardware, including the cleaned up traveler and rail, the first things I'd taken off, were back in place. It was a thing of beauty.

"What's left?" I asked.

"I saved the rigging. It's all been treated, but I thought you'd want to help set it up. It'll give you a chance to learn a bit too. We'll need to get it on a trailer then I want to rig up some navigational lights. They're going to be eyesores, but you'll need them."

"Need them? For what?" I asked.

"Your favor. Remember Tom, you still owe me."

"I didn't forget," I said.

He nodded. "You'll be going out at daylight, but returning after sunset."

"So in the dark?" I asked. I was doing some figuring in my head, wondering what it'd be like on the water, at night, when there were ghosts who seemed intent on messing with me. The little boat suddenly seemed a lot smaller.

"You'll be fine," Swift said, turning and heading into the yard.

I followed him to a beat-up old trailer. We had to hook up an air compressor to fill the tires before we could move it into the barn. We backed it up to the boat and started to work it under the hull.

It helped that Swift was freakishly strong. He lifted the bow and put his shoulder into the keel while I pushed the trailer back. He laid the front of the boat down and blocked the wheels to keep them from moving. Then he attached a metal cable to the front. I turned the crank on a winch while he pushed, guiding the boat up into place. We towed the whole thing outside when we were done.

Swift was trying to teach me the name of every line and I was listening, but I wanted to know something else. He still hadn't gotten to the part of his story where he was cursed. Considering that the ghosts had turned their attention on me, I wanted to know more.

"So what went wrong?" Swift looked at me. "With your ship? It sounds like you had everything figured out, the whole piracy thing. Was it the curse? Is that why you quit?"

"No, the curse was something else. That happened here." He motioned back towards the town. "Our piracy days ended, because—well, you see, every party has to come to an end. And you can only rob and steal for so long before someone'll try to stop you."

West Indies, 1718

We made the Caribbean near the end of winter and found the pickings thin. We took what we could well into the spring, but prizes were few and far between. It seemed that every sail we chased outclassed us, or was part of a convoy, traveling with armed vessels ready to fight and force us to run. The men never liked retreating. It didn't pay.

Rampant piracy was strangling trade, and Mother England had enough of it. They wanted law brought to the islands. The king was offering a pardon for pirates who swore an oath and gave up their wicked ways.

On the Freedom's Fortune *there were few familiar faces still aboard. The freed slaves were with us, and a couple of the men from the original crew, but most of the sailors from the* Mayfair *took their pay and left. Log cutters and former privateers filled the deck, men hungry for treasure.*

We were low on provisions when we sailed to Nassau in July with little to show for our months at sea. We came round the windward side of the harbor clearing Hog Island to find the town a dark patch of destruction.

Nassau was a roughly built and roughly lived in town before, but with each passing year, it seemed to fall further from grace. The few buildings leaned dangerously into the sand-swept streets, while most of the locals slept in tents and ramshackle huts strung together with spare rope or banana leaves.

The walls of the fort, broken since the last war, were overgrown with vines, while the shore was the heart of decay. In the shallows and on the beach were the carcasses of thirty or forty captured ships, run up on the ground and pillaged. Rigging, masts, and any metal fittings were stripped. The rest were burnt, left to rot or be swept away by the tide. Tattered and torn shrouds hung from spares blowing in the wind like mourning veils.

The shallow harbor was hard to navigate. It was narrow, boxed-in by Hog Island. We dropped anchor and loaded one of our boats. I sent Sprowls and a party of men to the shore for the supplies we needed, warning him to be careful. Pirates feeding on each other wasn't unheard of in these desperate times. I saw the Ranger, *captained by Charles Vane at anchor. He was flying the death's head flag from his ship. The remains of the fort had the same flag. It proudly declared that this island and all the things on it belonged to pirates.*

I'd never met Vane, but I'd heard plenty about him. His reputation was as fierce as Blackbeard's, known for his cruelty and viciousness. There were stories of him torturing and terrorizing captured crews, burning ships and leaving survivors abandoned. When he was cornered by the HMS Phoenix *he took the king's pardon. Then he disregarded it a few days later, going back on the hunt.*

Sprowls rowed ashore at midmorning. It was my hope to get what we needed and leave quickly. I watched as the shore party was greeted. It seemed friendly enough. They were guided up the beach and taken into the largest of the camps that littered the sand. An hour passed, then the morning gave way to afternoon, the sun began to sink lower in the sky, setting in the west. It wasn't till the first stars twinkled above that I saw activity on the beach. A party of men were returning to our launch. There were more of them than had left. I wasn't sure what was coming, but I sensed ill tidings.

I glanced at my crew. They'd been finishing off the rum in the belief that more would be brought on soon. Sampson stood apart from the others, in the way he often did with a lit pipe in his hand. Many of the men freed with him had taken to the pirate's life, becoming almost indistinguishable from the rest of the crew, but Sampson had somehow stayed different. It wasn't the color of his skin; many of our men were freed slaves. It was his demeanor, he was aloof, standing back and taking everything in, constantly watching. His eyes were on the shore when I waved him over.

"Something troubling you captain?" he asked.

"Many things, but right now mainly that." I motioned to the boat.

He nodded his head. "There's more coming than we sent," he pointed out.

"Perhaps we should get ready for trouble," I said.

"Oh, I don't know if they have enough for trouble," he answered.

I looked back at the crew. "With all our men drunk and jolly..."

"It's true." His eyes were still on the approaching boat. "There is something else. My eyes are very good, but..." He motioned for my telescope then placed it to his eye, saying, "That's better, now I can tell for sure. I don't believe our quartermaster is aboard that boat."

"Sprowls is missing?"

"He's not returning, that's for sure. He's a big man, nearly as big as me and bigger than anyone coming this way."

I looked back at our crew. They wouldn't be much good in a fight, especially if they were caught by surprise. "Sampson, would you do me a favor and quietly gather your men?"

Sampson nodded his head then stepped back, only to return a minute later with a small group behind him. Though they'd joined the ranks, wore the clothes of pirates, and taken to the sea as their home, the men freed with Sampson were still loyal to him. In short order they were all gathered. I wasn't sure what was going to happen when the launch approached, but I wanted to be ready. I outlined my plan. Then stood and waited.

When the launch was halfway across the harbor, I called for all lights to be extinguished. The men groaned and were slow to do it. It was hard to play cards and dice in the dark. Eventually, they followed the order, and our whole deck turned black. The moon was a narrow sliver in the sky. "See now boys the launch is returning," I said, pointing over the side.

"Ahoy the Freedom's Fortune," *someone called. I recognized the voice of Taggart, the man who'd signed aboard with Sprowls.*

"Ahoy the boat," I answered back.

"Would you lower the ladder?" Taggart asked.

"Aye, but where's our quartermaster? Where's Sprowls?"

"He's enjoying the hospitality of Captain Vane," Taggart said.

"I see, and have you returned with the supplies we need? The men are running short on rum."

I could hear a bit of whispering below before I added. "With the extra guests you've brought, I think we'll find ourselves in need."

There was more whispering below. Then Taggart called up, "I've come with an invitation from Captain Vane. He wishes your company on the shore. These men are an honor guard for you."

"Certainly, I assumed as much." I looked around in the dark at my crew. Even in their drunken stupor, they

could tell something wasn't right. For a moment I was tempted to be done with all these charades and order them to open fire on the launch, but that would leave us here in this harbor till morning with any number of enemies on the shore. We needed time, and there was only one way to get it. I stepped back from the rail and motioned for my men to follow me.

They gathered round and I said quietly, "Listen up me hardies, there are strange games afoot. I don't know what they've planned for me, but I've got plans of my own in place. Hold the ship till morning. Let no one aboard unless you hear from me, Mister Sprowls, or Sampson."

The crew looked around, realizing for the first time that Sampson's towering form wasn't with them. I took my leave, dropping down the rope ladder and into the launch. As I sat, I uncovered a small lantern that I'd brought with me. "Who've we got here anyway?" I asked.

Taggart reached his hand up and brought the light down. "Don't worry captain. Vane only wishes to make your acquaintance."

"I'm sure," I said looking at the men, noting that not a single one was from the Freedom's Fortune, each was a stranger, and each was armed. I suppose that wasn't all that unusual. They were pirates after all.

They shoved off and I held my lantern at my waist saying, "It's a dark night, too dark not to see what's coming." In truth, I wanted to keep them blinded.

Taggart nodded his head as we rode to the beach in silence. At the camp, I could see bonfires and hear music playing; fiddles and drums, fifes, and men singing. I was escorted up the sand and into the pirate camp. I could smell the meat roasting above the open fires. Whole pigs were hanging on wooden shafts. Some of the pirates looked up at my arrival, but most were too interested in their rum.

I was brought to a large tent where fine chairs were set in the sand. Three men were leaning over a wooden table, each holding a cup with dice. They slammed the cups down then each carefully lifted and looked under to see what they had. Sprowls was there. His eyes met mine, but he didn't say anything. He only smirked a little while waiting to hear the bids from the others.

The man to his right called, "Two threes."

Sprowls answered back, "Three threes."

The third man had seen Sprowls smile. He looked up at me and nodded his head in welcome. "You must be Captain Swift?"

"And I take it you're Captain Vane."

"I am, pardon me for a moment." He turned back to the dice, peaking under his cup one last time. "Four threes," he said.

"I'll challenge that," Sprowls told him.

Vane turned to my large quartermaster. "Are you calling me a liar Mister Sprowls?"

Sprowls's eyes met mine again before answering, "I'm not calling you anything, but I am saying that there isn't four threes on this table. You've been challenged, what say you?"

Vane lifted his cup. Not a single four on the dice. He handed a few coins over to Sprowls. "It was a gamble, but nothing ventured, nothing gained, wouldn't you say, Captain Swift?"

"I'll agree to that," I answered, knowing for certain that the boat he'd sent to the Freedom's Fortune *had been meant to board us. I walked over to the table. Vane stood up and shook my hand, squeezing tight to test my grip. "Otherwise I'd have nothing to do with this life of ours," I added.*

"It's true," Vane said, nodding his head, looking me over. "You're a fair bit more handsome than that wanted poster they put out."

"I think they were trying to capture a certain viciousness that I must confess is not in my nature."

Vane laughed as he sat back down, motioning for the third man at the table, a member of his crew, to leave and give me his seat. "Aye, they want the evil pirate Nathanial Swift, thief and murderer."

"And free man," I added.

"I'll drink to that." Vane took a swig from a bottle that sat at his foot then offered it to me. I sat down, taking a drink of the rum. "You've heard of the king's pardon?" he asked.

I'd been hearing about it for weeks, but I had to wonder what the king would ask from us in return. I'd heard many were given the duty of hunting other pirates. "I have. In fact, I heard you took it."

He laughed. "It's true, but it didn't last. Got me out of a tight spot though. Cost me a fine ship and a cargo." He took the bottle back, taking a swig. "There's more than one old pirate on this island that I think plans on being more faithful than I. I ought to cut their throats now. It'll probably come to it before long anyway." He waited a moment looking at me. "At least I don't have to worry about you. There's no chance of you getting excused."

"The idea of not being chased by the crown anymore doesn't sound all that awful," I said.

"You misunderstand me." Vane sounded amused. "You are in the same boat as me. You won't be offered the pardon. The king's men only have a rope and a short dance planned for you. You've managed to find yourself on a short list of captains whose crimes are too heinous to be forgiven. Don't worry, you've found yourself in the best of company." He brought the bottle back up again.

I was confused. In my time on the account, I'd only used what force was necessary to take a prize. "It's Burnaby again," Sprowls said. "As big a fool as he is, he still has friends in the navy."

"In fact, your old captain is sailing with Woodes Rogers," Vane added.

"Poor Mister Rogers." The name meant nothing to me.

"Poor Governor Rogers," Vane corrected. "According to the king, this town and island will belong to him. He's to be our new governor. He's bringing order to this lawless place. What he doesn't know is that this island already has law. It's mine." I looked around at the drunken pirates celebrating. In a few hours, they'd be fighting each other or passing out.

"Since my near capture by the Phoenix I've worked hard to make certain we'll be able to defend this island. I've taken ships that can fight. You've seen the Ranger. She's a bit large for hunting, too deep a draft for some of the shallows, but I'm certain she'll get the job done. Now that beauty of yours, the Freedom's Fortune, you've sailed several seasons aboard her, haven't you?"

I nodded my head. I knew where this was going.

He leaned in, "I dare say she's got more guns than even my own vessel."

Vane fell silent, waiting for me to respond. I tapped the table and idly lifted one of the cups before saying, "She's armed well, it's true, but she's also quick. That's her real value. We were able to pass over that sandbar without running aground. We'll have to be more cautious leaving if we can get our supplies."

"Caution is always advised in these waters," Sprowls said, making Vane snort.

Vane sat back and brought the bottle to his lips once more. "Leaving may not be in the cards for you."

"Oh, and why is that?"

I noticed that the men who rowed me ashore were coming closer, closing a circle around us. Vane leaned over the table again. "Because I'm not about to let a ship that fine leave when this island is in need of defense."

"I see. So you want me to stay and fight for you. Is that it?" I asked as my eyes searched the armed men. Taggart wasn't among them. He was off near the cooking fires. I looked to Sprowls. His face was unreadable.

"I want the Freedom's Fortune. I can find someone else to captain her if need be. Either way, I promise you that ship won't be leaving till I say so. You've anchored in my harbor and are now subject to my rules."

"And if I try to run?"

"I'll blast you to splinters and burn you to the waterline. Of course, that won't be happening. You and your quartermaster are here, and your ship is out there," He pointed out.

"I'm sorry Captain Vane, as much as I've enjoyed your hospitality I must tell you I have no intention of staying here tonight." I stood up and rested my hand on my sword. "Come on Mister Sprowls."

Vane was quick to his feet, bouncing back out of his chair. He pulled a charged pistol from his bandolier.

His men closed in even tighter around me, brandishing their weapons. Pistols and swords were pointed at Sprowls and I.

I held my hands up. "There's no need for blood-shed tonight," I said. Then there was a sound, a heavy 'thwack.' One of Vane's men fell over, smashing into the gambling table.

Everyone turned to see Sampson standing behind him. He towered over Vane's men, holding his Indian oar. The rest of Sampson's men had taken up position behind each of Vane's. They held cutlasses, darkened with soot so they wouldn't glimmer in the starlight.

"Well there might be a need for a little bloodshed," I said, looking at the back of the fallen pirate's skull. "His I mean…hopefully, that was enough."

Vane looked around. His men, dozens of them, were only a few yards away dancing drunkenly around the fire. He had a loaded weapon pointed at my chest and twelve of his best, hand-picked pirates ready to fight. But then there were these other men who'd come from the shadows like ghosts with murder in their eyes. Whatever happened next he wouldn't escape. Sampson would close the distance and smash his head in with that oar before he could defend himself.

Vane had only one play. I saw it in his eyes before he ever started to move. He made as if he were going to drop his weapon, but instead, he turned quickly towards Sampson. Sampson and I reacted at the same time. He swung down his oar while I dove and tackled Vane. At the moment, *before the oar struck, and before I could take his legs out from under him, I heard the hammer strike on the priming-pan. There was a sizzling spark.*

That should've been it for Sampson. My friend's chest should've been punched through. But there was no explosion. The pistol misfired.

I scurried to my knees with Vane beneath me in the sand. Before he could lift his arms, I pummeled him, slashing viciously down with my fists like a madman. They crashed into his mouth and nose till Sprowls grabbed my arms and pulled me away. "It's enough now Nathanial," he said firmly.

I caught my breath. "We're going to return to our ship," I said, looking down at Vane. A few of the men who'd come with Sprowls's landing party, including Taggart, came forward, wanting to see what happened.

Vane spat out blood and nodded slowly. "Go to your ship and get comfortable there. You're not leaving this harbor without my permission. You'll stay and defend the freedom you've enjoyed, or I'll see you dead."

"We've got teeth of our own," I threatened.

"Go now, captain. We'll make sure this man behaves himself," Sampson said, his eyes never wavering while his oar rested above Vane's head.

I turned to one of Vane's pirates. He had a knife held to his throat. He'd lowered his musket. Its barrel had been chopped, but it was still the longest weapon there. I took it and leaned into Vane. "I'm a crack shot on a moving deck, and I'm far deadlier on land. After my phan-toms disappear, if I see you move, I'll put this ball directly through your skull. Do you understand me?"

Vane nodded his head. "You'll not get out of this harbor without a fight."

Sprowls and the others from Freedom's Fortune *followed my lead, taking the charged weapons and dis-arming Vane's guards. We headed toward the shore and our boats. I kept the musket pointed back, watching to make certain that Sampson and his men cleared away safely. He wouldn't move till he saw me in the boat, then in quick succession each of his men vanished into the scrub brush, making their way back to the broken and burnt ships down the beach, where they'd landed the* Freedom's Fortune*'s second boat.*

As our men began to pull at the oars, Sprowls said to me, "It's a good thing you're a talented gambler, I've seen you shoot."

"You don't think I could hit Vane?" I asked, still holding the musket.

"If I had faith in that then I'd tell you to do it now. Save us the trouble we'll have in the morning."

"You think he'll attack us?"

"No, he may talk about defending this island, but it's clear he's preparing to pull anchor himself. He's mov-ing everything into a few heavily armed vessels. He knows the king's men are on their way."

"Then what does he care if we stay?"

"If it's as he said, and Burnaby is truly a part of the king's convoy, then it's probably Vane's hope that they'll try harder to capture you."

I nodded, watching the beach disappear behind us. There'd been no alarm raised. No men sent after us. Vane had made his play and lost. The fight was over. He wouldn't waste ammo or men coming after us, but we had few stores, including freshwater, and we had no real way of getting any. I was certain that anyone I sent ashore would not return. My men would either be captured or tempted to join Vane. Looking back at those bonfires, those merry pirates, I wondered why they wouldn't want to go. That was the life that most of them had signed on for, short and happy.

I held my musket and looked over at Taggart. He was rowing and keeping his head down. I wasn't angry at his disloyalty. I knew that many men aboard the Freedom's Fortune would have done the same thing. For a moment though I thought of Vane's words, cutting the throats of the pirates who were going to turn on him anyway. I held the musket and thought about how easy it'd be to lift it to my shoulder and shoot Taggart.

If I could take the king's pardon, even a cold-blooded murder such as that would be forgiven. Quietly I handed the musket to Sprowls. He said nothing as he laid it across his legs, but I think he could sense my thoughts.

Chapter 23

A Sail on the Horizon

*N*assau, New Providence 1718
At daybreak I had men in boats charting a course out of the harbor. It'd be high tide by midmorning, and I wanted to be underway.

It wasn't going to happen. As the tide came in I saw boats at the entrance of the harbor. Vane's men were towing a six-gun merchant ship there. They pointed the guns at us. The *Freedom's Fortune,* given the right position, would blast the ship to splinters, but in this narrow waterway those six guns could devastate us.

The little merchant fired a single shot. It dropped into the water near one of our boats. Sprowls stepped up behind me. "Should I call them back?"

I looked at the merchant ship. All the guns were on the top deck, and I could see their tiny crew. Not many volunteered to stand in our way.

"Let them finish," I said.

"Even under fire?" Sprowls asked.

"They aren't under fire. That was a warning shot. We'll be leaving eventually, and I want my course carefully plotted."

Sprowls nodded his head. A few hours passed and our boats returned with crude drawings of each sandbar and shallow. In the heat of the day the men were regretting the rum they'd drank the night before. They grumbled, wanting to send a watering party ashore.

"Surely Vane wouldn't deny us fresh water," someone said.

We were not in battle, nor were we giving chase. Officially our decision had to be made by a vote.

"You can ask Mister Taggart there," I said. "Vane's intention was to take us last night. He wants the Freedom's Fortune. *He wants us trapped here till the British navy arrives. Any of you that go ashore won't be coming back. They'll be forced to stand with Vane, die with him if they must. We'll be gone from this harbor and out from under his guns by the morning if you'll give me your trust." My eyes never left Taggart. I could see that he was thinking being ashore wouldn't be so bad.*

Other men spoke up. Most of it amounted to whining and bellyaching. They were thirsty and tired, and despite my warning, they believed their brothers ashore didn't wish them any harm.

In the end, they took their vote.

Twelve men went ashore with half our water-casks floating behind them. They left at two, and by five it was clear they weren't returning. I didn't say anything. I just drank a cup of stale water and waited, watching the shore. A half hour passed and I noticed some bustling going on, men moving about with urgency.

Even across the harbor, I could hear them calling on the wind. They were shouting from ship to ship that a sail was approaching. I turned my telescope to the harbor entrance. White sails were crossing the Point of Hog Island. There were three masts, and the ship's sides were painted gold and black. It flew the flag of Great Britain.

"Dear God," I muttered. This was a Royal battleship, a man-o-war. It was a small one, but still, it was more than enough. It had twenty guns at least, but that wasn't what made it so deadly. It was the men aboard, well-trained sailors accurate with those guns and over a hundred marines capable of raiding and taking any pirate ship.

The pirates on the island may have outnumbered them, but a ship like this didn't sail alone. More would be here soon. My time was up. We were at anchor, as were all of Vane's vessels. There'd be no escape under those guns.

I turned my telescope back to Vane's blockade vessel, the little merchantman who'd been standing guard at the entrance. Already the ship was being rowed back to shore. I thought of cutting our anchor chains and making a run for it. But without momentum, we'd be passing the British at a lazy pace. They'd capture us or blast us to hell with a single broadside before we reached open water. In fact, if we were the first to go, then I'd only be giving Vane what he wanted, a distraction.

The British ship was called the Rose. She sailed to the entrance of the harbor not far from where the merchantman had been. They dropped anchor, blocking our way and Vane's. The message was clear, they were our prison guards. Only moments after their anchor splashed in the water Vane answered their message.

Three shots rang out. I turned in time to see the puffs of smoke from Vane's flagship. The cannonballs flew. Two missed, but the third tore into the Rose's rigging.

"Do you think he intends to fight them?" Sprowls asked.

"No, but I think he wants them to think he will...Look," I said, pointing at the Rose. They'd raised the flag of truce.

"They're playing for time," Sprowls said.

We watched a boat lowered from the Rose *and sent across to the* Ranger. *All the while the sun was setting lower. In my glass, I could see the uniformed lieutenant standing at the bow of his boat. He had that arrogant way about him as he shouted through a speaking trumpet. "We demand to know why you've fired upon the Crown's vessels."*

Vane needed no trumpet. His angry voice was loud enough. "I'll use my utmost endeavor to burn you all, and all the vessels in the harbor this night!"

"What bluster," I said.

Then I felt Sprowls tap me on the shoulder. "It won't save him." He pointed to the harbor entrance where more ships were arriving. Vane looked up, seeing them as well.

He stepped back from the rail. I half expected him to come back with a pistol to shoot the lieutenant. He held a letter instead. "Give this to your governor. I'll await his answer."

"Is this your surrender?" the lieutenant asked.

"It's my demands," Vane shot back. "Now be a good boy and deliver."

Before the sun set three vessels joined the Rose; *the sloop of war,* HMS Shark *with its ten guns, followed by the twenty-gun transport* Willing-Mind, *loaded with hundreds of soldiers, and the privateer* Buck, *with ten more guns.*

There were reports that two larger ships, the Milford *and the* Delicia *waited outside the harbor with Governor Rogers aboard. Burnaby was with him. He'd been appointed to some lower office in these islands. I thought of that old man, then I looked at the town of Naussau, its wreckage and waste. This is the place he deserves. I promised myself that whatever happened in the next few hours, I wouldn't be captured. I'd see my freedom or my grave.*

My men watched the British ships without any rum to calm their nerves.

"What will we do captain?" Sprowls asked.

"The tide comes up tonight and the eastern passage is unguarded," I said.

"There's a reason for that. It's barely passable in daylight. In the dark it's madness."

The wind had turned us on our anchor so that our stern faced the British ships. Meaning the curious and all too sober crew were crowded behind us near the wheel.

"Would you rather stay here?" I asked.

"We run up on a sandbar, and we won't have a choice. The king's men will claim us at their leisure." Sprowls could only point out problems. He hardly ever gave solutions.

"I've had enough of this arguing!" I shouted then I lowered my voice to a growl. "We escape tonight or not at all." I looked around at each man. "There won't be any blasted vote either. This is combat. My word is law and I say we go tonight."

I grabbed the man closest to me by the shirt, not even sure who it was. I threw him across the deck, kicking him. "Now find a post and stay away from the rail!

Watching those bloody ships isn't going to make them leave." The men skulked away, leaving Sprowls and I alone. In the dark, with only starlight, I could barely see his eyes. I wouldn't look away though, not till he turned and left my deck.

An hour passed and I ordered Sprowls to get a party of men into our remaining boat. "When they're ready I want the capstan turned as quietly as possible. Get our anchor up, but set no sail. The men in the boat will tow us out."

Sprowls nodded then went to work. He wasn't wrong. The eastern passage was nearly impossible, but we had to try something. In the morning Vane was going to be forced to surrender. Raiding parties would storm the beaches with first light, and the pirates would see just how pitiful their defenses were. My eyes fell on Vane's flagship. All its lanterns were dark, but I could see its outline against the stars. Men were busy on her deck. I couldn't tell what they were doing, but I could only assume they were preparing for a fight.

I looked on as our men climbed into the boat. They were some of our strongest. Sprowls led the detail himself. He dropped down the rope ladder, leaving me to order the hoisting of the anchor. When I saw that the boat was in position, I ordered the men to set their backs to the giant wheel and slowly turn it. I listened as each of its teeth caught the stop with an incredibly loud clap. The ship began to move beneath my feet. From the bow, I could barely see the boat, but I could feel its tug. Not a single oar could be heard splashing as Sprowls brought us out into the middle of the channel. We had to go far south, close to the beaches of New Providence to avoid Potters Cay.

We reached the passage and just when I should've been looking ahead, something called my attention back to the British ships. Out of nowhere, it seemed like the sun had risen. The whole harbor was alight, reflecting the glow of a burning ship floating across the water. It was Vane's own Ranger, his flagship, and it was on fire.

Two small boats were coming away from it after cutting their lines. I knew in a moment what Vane had done. His words to the Lieutenant came back. "I'll use my utmost endeavor to burn you, and all the vessels in the harbor this night," he'd said. Turns out he was telling the truth.

He'd sacrificed his own ship to destroy the British. The fire was spreading across the Ranger, moving with incredible speed. The decks and sails were soaked with tar. That's what his men had been busy doing an hour before. Now he was sending this burning vessel straight at the anchored British ship.

On the Rose, men hurried to cut their anchor line. Then the heat reached the Ranger's guns. Vane had double stuffed them with two cannon balls and extra powder. When they cooked hot enough, the cannons exploded, sending their deadly load in every direction.

Loud eruptions echoed through the night, blasting at the British ship. Amazingly, nothing hit them. Their lines dropped into the water, and they started moving with topsails set and a strong easterly wind. The crew of the Rose *didn't show a sign of panic. They came about, setting their sails, moving slowly away from the* Ranger.

I shook my head. It was a waste to stand still watching this and not take advantage. The men in the boat had stopped rowing, turning to see the show as well. This wasn't good. We were so close to shore that the wind could easily beach us. I ran to the bow and shouted down. "Put your back to the oars and turn us around. Make way for the western passage!"

I ran back to the helm, pushing the man at the wheel aside. I started to turn us about and ordered each man to his post, calling for the sheets to be raised.

I looked back at the British ships. They were in a slow-motion race with the flaming Ranger. *It was closing in on them. It wouldn't take much. A single touch from that ship and the flames could spread like a disease. Slowly the British started to gain distance. Their sails filled with the wind as they made their way out of the harbor's entrance.*

With our sails set our tow lines slackened, falling into the water. We had enough speed to overtake the longboat. I ordered the men brought aboard as quickly as possible. It was a tricky thing with us moving the whole time, but we were able to get them on deck.

With pulleys and gears, we lifted the boat out of the water. Moments passed as we moved recklessly through the harbor. By the light of the Ranger, I examined the chart the men made that morning. I held the helm, giving orders and watching our position. The water was full of strange shadows in the flickering light of the fireboat.

We came up to the Ranger; its masts and spars were gone, along with most of its top deck. I watched it only for a moment as its bowsprit dropped away, splashing into the water, sizzling with steam. The air near the ship filled with smoke and the smell of burnt tar. The warm up-drafts danced over our sails as I listened to the hissing and crackling of flame in the Ranger's lower decks, then we were past it and into the mouth of the harbor. We passed through without touching a single bit of ground, staying on a course that gave us the best wind. In the distance off our port and starboard were the British ships. We sailed through them. When I looked back, they were attempting to give chase. But we were moving too fast. We sailed away from New Providence and off into the night with no destination in mind, only the idea of staying free.

Chapter 24

Madeline

I had no idea what time it was when Swift and I finished setting up the mast and rigging. It probably would've gone faster if Swift hadn't been reciting his life story. I'm not saying I wasn't interested, but I still didn't know why those things in the water were after him. The closer we came to finishing the boat, the more I worried.

"Tell me what this is." He pointed to a line that ran from the back to the boom.

I'd attached it only a few minutes before, but I couldn't think of its name. My head was still full of fire ships and evil pirates.

He breathed out heavily, tired and a little cranky. "Pay attention, Tom." He grabbed another line, "This is the halyard. It's used to raise and lower the sail." He pointed out the pulleys above the mast and showed me where the line connected to the gaff, a pole that spreads the top of the sail out.

He touched the boom, "And this is?"

"The boom!" I called loudly. Swift sneered.

It was attached to the mast. It was the long pole that held the bottom of the sail. It moved back and forth across the boat and would crack you in the head if you weren't careful. Swift grabbed that first line again. "This is the mainsheet. Careful with it. It controls the boom."

Swift ran through each piece and part of the boat then he had me recite everything back, all the rigging and what it did. "Now let's see you raise the sail. Let it out for some air."

"You want me to do that here?" I asked.

"Would you rather wait till you're on the water?" Swift nodded towards the cove while Liam wandered up next to him. The dog was watching me intently. Even he knew this was a bad idea.

"Okay," I said, hoisting the sail with the halyard. The mainsheet was still in my hand when the wind grabbed the sail and flung the boom over. It nearly pulled me out of the boat as the trailer started to tip.

Swift jumped on the tire, putting his weight against the side. "Get that sail back in!" he yelled.

I stumbled on the loose lines that were coiled like angry snakes in the bottom of the boat. One rope wrapped around my ankle and pulled my leg out from under me like a Bugs Bunny snare. That was the halyard, which was attached to the heavy gaff, which was attached to the sail, which was falling, and was also attached to me.

It pulled at my leg and naturally I pulled back. The sail started to rise again. Then the boat started tipping once more. I may have been a dope on a rope, repeating himself, but I think I was starting to understand how this stuff worked.

"Loosen that line," Swift yelled.

I wanted to tell him that this was all his fault. But I was too busy trying to do exactly what he said. I dug my fingers into the rope, but every time I moved my leg the sail would bounce. Every time the wind blew, even a little, the rope would get tighter. This is what we call learning.

I finally got my leg out. Then I let the line go. Bad idea. The sail and gaff came crashing down. Unfortunately, none of it hit me. I say that because I'd rather be knocked out than have to listen to Swift yell.

"Look at this mess! Straighten those lines. Do it neat or don't do it at all." He shouted at me like I was lowliest of sailors. I picked up the sail and gaff and folded them back and forth, laying them on top of the boom. I kept one hand on the bundle while Swift handed me some cloth strips to tie them down. I did my best, but of course Swift wasn't impressed. He started calling out scenarios, telling me how to handle the boat with only the mainsheet and rudder. 'Set it to this point…No, no I told you the wind is coming from the northeast…Mind that line.' There was a lot of this. I'll spare you the details.

"Now let's talk about navigation," Swift said. He'd finally let me climb back onto solid ground.

He must've seen something in my face that made him decide to give me mercy. "Or we could take a break," he said, walking towards the tugboat and motioning for me to follow. We went up a rickety ladder to the boat's deck where he had a lawn chair set up. It was at the very edge of the yard where you could see all of Purgatory Cove.

Swift went below, coming back with two icy-cold brown bottles. He offered me one.

"It's just root beer," he said after I stared at it a bit too long.

I took a swig while Swift said, "You're doing good. You learn quickly when you pay attention. The question is how you'll do tomorrow."

"Tomorrow?" I asked.

"You've got the maiden voyage."

"Tomorrow," I said again, looking out at the water. I should've been excited; instead, I was trying to find dark spots. The sun was high, blotting out the strange shadows. That didn't mean they weren't there though.

"What are they?" I asked.

Swift took a long swig, avoiding my stare.

"You said something was waiting for you. You know I've seen them, the…" I couldn't get myself to say ghosts. Swift turned and stared at me, waiting for me to finish. "Are they your victims?"

"No, not my victims," he said. "They're my crew."

"What happened to them?" I asked.

"They came for me. They came to take me."

I waited for him to say more, but he found his bottle more interesting. He was staring at it.

Finally, he looked up at me and sat back in his chair. "It was after Nassau. We hadn't had the best of luck. The men were looking for someone to blame. We were low on provisions and we had the stormy season coming in fast. There's little loyalty in this world Tom, only the takers and those being taken, and it's better to be the latter."

West Indies, 1718

The trade winds pressed gently on our swaying masts as we waited without a single sail sighted in days. In the distance were tiny islands, places to run to if need be.

Freshwater was low. We'd refilled at a muddy spring on a small spit of land, but half our casks were left behind weeks before. I leaned against the rail, looking up at the shrouds, letting my eyes lose their focus. That's when Sprowls came to me. "Captain, a word if you don't mind?"

I could feel the eyes from the deck. The men were sober, having drunk through their rum in port. It was my hope to catch a prize, even a small fishing boat to replenish our stores, but the sea gave us nothing. At nightfall I was going to set sail for the nearest settlement. Apparently, the men weren't going to give me that time.

I answered Sprowls loudly, "Say what you will as free as you please."

Sprowls and I hadn't spoken much lately. "The men are worried about this bad luck we're having."

"Bad luck?" I asked.

"It's been over a month since we've taken a prize. Even before Vane, we were running more than we were fighting." Sprowls tried leading me back to the stern, but I wouldn't follow. If this was going to happen, I wanted it to be public.

"We take what we can and live another day," I answered.

"The men think there'd be more to take with a different man in command." He set himself between the crew and me.

I looked into Sprowls's eyes then I pushed past him, moving to the center of the deck. "Is it true!? You want another leader!?" I shouted at them.

"Aye we do!" one man called. I was certain it was Taggart. I should've killed him before, I thought as I heard others echo him.

"It's time to change our luck and our fortune," someone yelled.

"And our captain," another added.

The crew began to move toward me. I was losing my rank today and if I wasn't careful my life too. These weren't my men anymore, not a single loyal soul among them.

My hand rested on the hilt of my sword. If I were going down, I'd bring as many with me as I could. I looked through the crowd and found Taggart. He wouldn't be in the first press, too cowardly. I'd find him when the action started. It didn't matter how many I had to cut down.

I looked at the lines, wondering if I could use them to get up and through to him. I put my hand on the shroud, pulling myself up while my cutlass came free of its scabbard. I stood on the rail ready to fight.

That's when a number of men pushed through the crowd ahead of the others. Sampson and his men gathered in a circle around me with their swords drawn. "No harm comes to our captain," he said simply. His carved oar was ready to split heads.

Sprowls stood before Sampson without a glint of fear. "No one's going to harm Swift if he steps down without a fight. I'll promise you that. There's no need for blood this day."

I believed Sprowls, but looking at the rest of the crew, I didn't think their intentions were nearly as kind.

These were all killers. Deadly men who wanted blood, and I hadn't provided any lately.

I looked towards the ocean for an answer. All the attention of the crew was on me. Otherwise, someone else might've noticed it first. Out there, almost too far to see, a sail was lazily crossing the horizon.

I sheathed my sword and jumped down, putting myself between Sampson and Sprowls. "Hold your elections for today and I promise you a prize by sunset."

"And how's that trick done?" Sprowls asked.

"Luck of the Irish, or perhaps I'll open my blasted eyes." Squinting into the sun, a smile cracked my face as I pointed. "Make sail me hardies, four points off the starboard and nearly out of view."

The men looked about in confusion, not sure what to do. They milled about the deck for a moment before Sprowls yelled, "You heard your captain, get to work you mangy dogs!"

The ship was sailing from Barbados, straight across our bow with the wind behind her. We set our sails pointing to intercept a few miles to the west. Their watchman wasn't very sharp. They took their time before starting to run. We'd closed half the distance before they began to tack.

She was almost half again our size, but that didn't matter because she was poorly handled and we were better armed. I could see they were shorthanded. Their turn had been slow and sloppy, with sails billowing lazily before her crew could tighten them.

Our crew grumbled as we gave chase. Such a large ship in the islands was probably a slaver. As disloyal as these men were, they'd fought since the beginning with freed slaves. They had no interest in getting into the trade, nor did they have any interest in freeing more Africans.

Sprowls stood near me and listened to the same grumbling. I could tell he was wondering, trying to decide what to do. I think he wanted to give me a chance to live out the day, but if it came to it, he wasn't above being my executioner.

I called out to the crew, "She's leaving Barbados, not heading towards it. Slaves never leave that island. I'll wager anyone's cut that she's offloaded her cargo in exchange for sugarcane and molasses, maybe even some rum or coin. It'll be a fine payday."

The sun was setting low in the sky as we came upon her with the water turning rougher and the wind beginning to gust. Often at the end of the day, as the air began to cool, you'd feel the breeze pick up. This was more violent. A squall was coming.

As the prize lifted and fell with the waves, I saw her name, the Madeline. It was a pretty name for a ship that worked an ugly trade.

I could see the first storm clouds darkening the horizon. They were black and haunting, swallowing the *sky and ocean in shadow. The* Madeline *was aiming for them, running straight into the storm.*

Before we were in firing range, the men started to chant. Their swearing and cursing gave way to a single word repeated over and over again, "Death. Death. Death." They beat the rail with swords, axes, and cudgels, anything that would make noise. The rhythm became faster as we closed the distance. Through my glass, I watched the panicked sailors on the Madeline. *The waves began to roughen as we cut through the water, closing and closing, white caps disappearing beneath our hull.*

I gave the order, and two shots were fired across the Madeline*'s bow. With the wind and spray blowing in my face I watched them drop in the water closer to the prize than I liked. It was enough. The* Madeline *was convinced. They heaved to, dropping their sails as we circled round and came up beside her.*

Hooks were thrown across, and the men rushed the deck, eager for anyone to fight back. I led the party with my sword out, angry and ready to strike down anyone who dared look at me wrong, but the Madeline*'s crew had no fight in them.*

I had the captain brought before me. "You have my surrender, sir. I ask only that you do no harm to my crew," he said.

Rain began to fall, making the deck slippery. "You have my word. But I'll expect a full tally of your cargo."

"Um, yes sir, there is only a slight problem with that."

"I don't much care for problems," I answered, putting my sword to his chest. "If you've sold your slaves we'll take whatever you traded for them." My men were busy breaking open hatches, tearing through what they found.

"It's the owner sir. He holds the manifest and all the ship's papers in his cabin. He didn't wish to give up, so he locked himself below with a keg of gunpowder. He's threatening to put fire to it if anyone tries to break in."

I lowered my blade. "He must put great value on the ship's contents if he's willing to kill himself for it."

The captain leaned in close and whispered. "It's all he has, all the wealth he's made trading flesh. He sold his plantation, all his holdings, and is returning home to England to retire and enjoy his wealth. There's a king's ransom."

"You're rather free with your tongue," I whispered as well.

"You have the ship. If that fool wants to blow himself up it's no benefit to anyone. The coin is in his quarters. He's been perched on it since we left; three heavy chests full."

I wiped the rain from my face, wondering how to solve this little snag. A keg of powder probably wouldn't sink us, but it would do more damage than I'd like with this squall coming.

I looked at the men, these pirates I'd robbed and pillaged with. Most I hardly recognized. I knew their names but little more than that. They'd been ready to toss me overboard a few hours before. Would they ever admit they were wrong? Or would they drink through this prize like every other, only to keep moving? They were sharks, stupid animals that could only consume. I owed them nothing.

I called Sprowls over. He'd gotten a report from the men breaking into the hold that made him smile. "You were right Nathanial, this is a fine prize. You should see the wealth they travel with, an entire household of goods worthy of a nobleman."

"We have a problem," I said. Then I told him of the ship's owner, embellishing a little. "The man is held up in his quarters with three kegs of powder, more than enough to sink the ship."

Sprowls blustered and raged. Saying he'd bust in and kill the owner first.

I held my hand up. "Calm yourself. There's no time for action with this storm on us. The captain here is willing to help us for a cut of the take. He'll lie to the owner."

Sprowls looked at the captain appraisingly. I'd warned the man not to say anything. I'm sure he was wondering why I'd lie to my quartermaster and why I didn't tell him about the gold, but he kept his eyes on the deck, knowing I'd kill him if he spoke.

I continued, "He'll tell the owner we left. Meanwhile, we'll make sail for New England. I'll take a small prize crew to maintain order. We'll wait till the owner comes out then it'll be simple, without bloodshed or explosions."

"But who's going to sail it when there's a madman below?" Sprowls asked. "I'm sure you'll have no volunteers." He had no idea how valuable the ship was.

"I'll do it myself. I'll take Sampson and his men with me, they're a loyal bunch."

Sprowls looked at me. Was that a hint of suspicion? "I would have done the best for you that I could," he said, almost like an apology.

I have no doubt you would have done for me, I thought, but I said, "It's all right. You were in a tough spot."

The storm was picking up. We had no time to stand and talk. The deck was rising and falling below us, and the rain was turning fiercer. "We'll sail back to New England. Follow as best you can, but if you lose us, we'll meet in Block Island Sound."

Sprowls nodded his head, "Fine then." He turned and called to our crew to close the hatches.

Before the hooks were let loose, I asked Sprowls to retrieve one thing from my quarters. He was quick about it. As the last grappling hook fell from the Madeline, Sprowls threw across a small, heavy bundle. A plan was *forming in my head, a thought that carried with it a quality of legend.*

We left the Freedom's Fortune *as the true brunt of the storm fell on us. I ordered the helmsman to put the* Madeline *on a course that took us north and away from my fellow pirates. I'd every intention of meeting them again, but I swore it wouldn't be with the gold.*

Chapter 25

Putting In and Going Under

Swift and I climbed down from the tugboat and went to the front of the trailer. "I'd like to put her in the water before the sun drops much lower," He said. He tied a rope through the hitch with an end hanging over each side for handholds.

Pulling the little boat was easy until we reached the hill going down to the boat launch. We had to put the trailer down and dig our feet in a couple of times to stop it from running away.

The cove was glassy still, except for the little waves made by a motorboat coming out of the water. The operator cut his engine and allowed his craft to drift up onto his trailer. There were a couple of men on the ramp waiting for him.

Swift watched, strangling his hands with the rope as he twisted it across his knuckles. The men weren't moving in any sort of hurry. "Bloody fools, I'd see their heads caved in," he muttered.

"It looks like they're almost done," I said.

He looked at the sun falling behind the trees and breathed out heavily. Quietly he said, "Magic time." He squatted down and picked up a stone from the parking lot and tossed it out into the water.

"What was that?" I asked.

"Nothing Tom, it's just this time of day, it's special."

I waited for him to say more. He settled down onto the trailer and added, "There's ancient magic in transitions. Every day must fade into night and every night into day. Those times are doorways."

He picked up another rock and threw it. "Can you feel it, that power in the air?"

I looked at the pink and purple sky. "I suppose," I said.

He shook his head then went quiet. We had to wait till the ramp was free so I asked, "What happened with the *Madeline?*"

West Indies, 1718
We were in the storm the entire night, with the sea swelling and the deck swamped. It was past dawn before

the ship's owner left his keg of gunpowder. When the sun rose in the east, it was in a dark and angry sky. The Madeline*'s captain went below and knocked at the door.*

"Who's there?" the owner demanded.

"Sir, it's the captain, we've got things to discuss. This blow has taken us far off course." I stood silently at his shoulder in the companionway.

"The pirates, did they take everything?" the owner asked.

I motioned with my sword for the captain to answer. "No sir, they took quite a bit, but they had to clear off because of the storm."

There was silence on the other side of the door.

"They knew to have this ship was to sink it and the cowards were too afraid," the captain added. Above the wind and ocean noise, I could hear someone moving in the cabin. I motioned for the captain to stand aside.

The door opened slowly then the owner stuck his head out. He held a lantern ahead of him in the darkened hallway, shining it up to find my smiling face and my less than friendly blade. I was soaked to the bone and exhausted, but my hand was steady. The owner tried shutting the door, but I rammed through, knocking him back. The lantern fell from his hand and smashed on the ground, shattering and spreading flame as its oil leaked across the deck.

"I'll send us all to the deep!" he shouted, rushing to the other side of the room and picking up his flint.

I closed the door to the cabin. Then I stomped out the spreading flames. The deck was rising and falling, tossing the ship's owner about, nearly knocking him off his feet with each rise. The treasure chests were between us, with the keg of gunpowder on top and a short piece of fuse ready to be lit.

"Then do it you bloody coward," I said.

"What?"

"Do it. Light it off. We'll die here together, the two of us, and we'll see that nobody gets your treasure. It'd be far better on the bottom than in the hands of a man like you."

"You're mad. I earned this money through my own labors."

I slashed at the air near him. "Liar, I know who you are sir. Some low-born noble, a younger brother who earned his way on the back of black flesh. You're laughable. I'll put this blade straight through you."

"Don't come any closer!" he cried as step by step I moved in.

"You're going to die here today. Do you understand that?" He went to strike the flint, but I lunged at him. I drove the blade deep into his shoulder. He looked shocked. Not just because of the sudden onset of pain, but because he could no longer move his hand to work the flint. A nerve was severed.

"*Or maybe you won't die. But you'll watch me take everything you have.*" *My smile was grim as I saw his face drop. I had his wounds treated and locked him below in the same hold where he'd held so many slaves over a lifetime in that awful trade.*

The storm held on, tossing us about. Without the stars there was no way to navigate, no way to tell where we were; we could've been swept halfway across the Atlantic for all I knew. The men waited for me to do something, pick a direction and try running from the weather, but I told them to hold us where we were till the clouds blackened in front of the setting sun. I gave them the task of filling a large basin with seawater. I told Sampson and his men to hold back all the ship's regular crew.

"*Send them below,*" *I ordered as I took out my leather bundle and unrolled it to reveal the ancient iron sword.*

Sampson looked at the blade. I'd taken it out only once when he asked to see it, after the Mayfair *crashed. He'd questioned me then about the legend, in the way that only Sampson could, pointedly and with a little smile, never letting on whether he believed me or not. I'd told him the whole story. Little did I know that he'd been waiting all this time to see if it were true. I was curious as well, but also afraid.*

I watched till the light of the sun faded in the west, till I believed it'd be touching the earth on the horizon. Then I set the short sword in the sea water. At first, it sank, but then I recited the words passed down from my mother.

'There's safety,' she'd said, 'even in the heart of a storm; there's a magic place. But never go there lightly and never stay too long.'

Sampson stood over my shoulder, his eyes growing large as he watched the blade spin. It'd been explained to me by my mother what would happen, but I had trouble believing it until I saw it with my own eyes.

Just as the sun slipped away below the horizon, turning the gray and heavy clouds to darkness, the sword stopped and held rigid in the water. I took a compass from my pocket and matched the path of the blade with the heading. "This is where we're going," I said to Sampson. "Bring the Madeline*'s men above and set sail."*

"Are you sure Swift?" Sampson asked.

I was afraid, but I was also angry. I thought of the gold and my crew nearly betraying me. "Yes," I said. "I'm sure."

The pick-up pulled away with the motorboat. We turned the trailer and slowly backed it down the ramp. The cement was slippery and I was trying not to fall as we guided it down. The boat touched the water with a splash, then Swift ordered, "Climb down there and guide her out."

I stepped onto the front of the trailer and pushed the boat off. There was a tag line tied to the bow. I held it like a leash while the boat floated off.

"You best keep it, boy," Swift said when I tried handing it to him. He walked off and motioned for me to follow.

There was a small wall beside the ramp that ran twenty or thirty yards down the shoreline. I followed Swift with the boat in tow. "You'll have to get your feet wet if you don't want to scuff up all that fine work we've done," he said, pointing to the boat.

I took off my shoes and sat down. My toes were dangling, barely touching the water. With the sun setting, the surface was dark. I sat there afraid. I couldn't tell how deep it was, but that wasn't what was making me hesitate. It was the darkness. I couldn't tell what was underneath, but I felt like something was there, something in the water.

"It shouldn't be much more than waist deep," Swift said.

I tried to shake it off. Then I took a deep breath and dropped from the wall. I nearly jumped back out yelling, "Jeez!"

Swift came running over. "Are you all right?!" He went to his knees and held his hand out.

"This water's freezing." I looked up and saw how shaken he was. "Sorry," I said.

"Let's just get this done." He got up, going down the wall.

I followed him through the water, stumbling over the large loose rocks on the bottom. I stubbed my toes a bunch of times, but no matter how much it hurt, I didn't say anything.

"Grab the mushroom anchor," Swift said when I got to the end of the wall. I pushed myself up on the side of the boat and grabbed it from the bottom.

He pointed out into the cove. "Toss it that way."

I held the hunk of metal and swung it back and forth a few times before letting it fly. It plopped out into the cove.

"If you feel around the wall, along the bottom, you should find an eye hook you can tie the boat off to."

I did what he said, searching under the water, but there didn't seem to be anything there. "I don't feel it... just more wall," I said.

"Keep looking, it's there," he answered. The sun was behind the trees. Soon it'd be completely dark.

"I'm sorry, I just can't find it," I explained as I felt every other slimy thing.

"It's got to be there. We don't have time for these games," he growled at me.

"I'm not playing games. I just can't find it" I was suddenly aware of just how alone we were and how quiet it was. Swift was almost always cranky, but right now he looked different. He was angry and scared.

"Bloody hell!" He took off his shoes and sat down on the edge of the wall. He sucked air into his chest then he dropped into the water. "Give me that line." He grabbed it away then started feeling around.

"Here it is," he said, bringing the line down and running it through the bolt.

His hands were on the wall ready to pull himself up. Suddenly he was jerked down, ducking below the water as if something had grabbed him. Bubbles came up as while tried to scream. I watched his hands struggle, grabbing for anything.

This had to be a joke, I thought. It was only three feet of water.

His arms flailed around, reaching out, trying to find anything to pull himself up with. The back of his head surfaced and I could see blood streaming from an open cut where he'd scraped his head on the wall. I grabbed his arms and tried pulling. It didn't work. Instead, he dragged me down.

Swift was already freakishly strong and when he was scared he was even more powerful. He pulled, and I went under. I had just enough time to close my mouth from the salt water.

I was plunged into the dark, shoved down against the rocky bottom. Swift was holding me with my face pushed against the wall. He was trying to shove off of me, but something kept him there. Like the water itself didn't want to let him go.

Unfortunately, he wasn't letting me go either. The only thing I could do was put myself directly under him. His hands were like claws digging into my back. I managed to get my feet down. Then I kicked off as hard as I could, as if my life depended on it, which it most certainly did.

I pushed Swift's head out of the water. He reached out, grabbing the wall. Then he pulled himself out, thrashing and kicking with his legs as he tore free. I came up, trying to avoid getting smashed in the face.

"Are you out of your mind?!" I yelled while hacking up sea water. Swift scurried away from the wall. He nearly collapsed in the parking lot as he tried to catch his breath.

He lost his voice in a fit of coughing. When it cleared he yelled, "See boy, see what happens?! They want me."

He got to his feet and stumbled away. I was left there in the dark, still in the water, wondering what I'd gotten myself into.

Chapter 26

Mostly Illusions

I fumbled with my keys at home. I don't think I had a concussion, but my head had been bleeding from where Swift slammed me into the wall. I'd gotten it to stop—mostly anyway—and I was wet too, like head-to-toe soaked. Let's face it, trying to keep an insane old man from attempting to drown you could leave a person a bit disheveled.

I walked into the living room to see the glow from the television and a small lamp in the corner. My mom was on the couch. The TV went off, and I knew I was in trouble.

"I'm sorry," I answered lamely. Then I said it again. "I mean I'm sorry for earlier. I shouldn't have said—well, any of that."

"It was really hurtful, Tom. Then you stay out this whole time. What was I supposed to think?" She turned with that stern mom-face. Then her eyes widened. "What happened to you?"

"Um," I started. You would think I would've come up with a cover story on the way home. But I hadn't. "I fell in the water…um, off my bike." *Please don't ask me how, please don't ask me how.*

"How?" Of course.

"Being stupid," I said, always a safe answer, and maybe, sort of the truth.

"You're bleeding."

I touched my forehead. "I am?"

She got up and grabbed my hand, leading me to the bathroom. "I swear Tom. I don't know what's come over you."

"I don't know, but I am sorry." I followed her.

"Is this what they call acting out?" she asked.

"I don't think so." I wasn't sure what she meant.

"You're so worried about that school, but I'm trying to do what's best for you. I bet you'll end up liking the place after a while."

Not likely, 'cause I ain't going, I thought.

I didn't say that of course. I'd decided earlier that I was done arguing. There was no point. I had my boat and a plan. I only had to survive Swift's weirdness a few days longer.

I sat down on the toilet while she examined the cut. "It's not just the school," I said. "It's grandma. It's like no one else sees what's going on with her... And it's Dad. I miss him. I miss talking to him." I wanted to ask her to let me go see him again, but I didn't bother, sure I knew the answer already.

Mom was quiet for a moment. Finally, she said, "I'm worried about grandma too." She was looking at my scratched up arms.

"She doesn't know who I am half the time," I said.

"This isn't something you should be worrying about. It'll be alright." She held some balled-up toilet paper to my head. "I called your grandfather earlier to see if he'd bring her to a doctor."

"What did he say?"

"He didn't want to hear it." She stepped back. "I don't think you need stitches. I'll just wrap it up for you."

"Why don't you let me take a shower first," I said. I was cold and the salt water made my skin feel sticky.

She nodded and turned the shower on before leaving. I took my shirt off slowly, feeling sore. I didn't know what I was going to do. I didn't think being around Swift was safe. He was obviously insane. Either that or haunted by murderous ghosts. I liked the idea of him being nuts better. Either way, none of it was safe. I was sure of that. I sat down on the bottom of the shower and let it wash over me, wondering what to do.

I was up early the next morning, and it wasn't for my paper route. Remember, I got fired yesterday. Without me, my boss had to deliver the papers himself. I saw his old pick-up truck circling the roads I used to cover. He didn't look happy. One more for my fan club, but at least he wasn't a ghost.

I went to the door of the library and pulled it open. Again, it was well before operating hours. I couldn't help but wonder if maybe Miss Webster left it that way on purpose, like she knew I was coming and she wanted to help me.

The library was dark and cold. Only her little desk lamp lit the foyer. "You again? Tom, we're not open yet." The annoyance was clear in her voice. So much for my theory.

"Sorry," I said, turning around. My hand was still on the heavy door.

"What is it this time? Are you in some sort of trouble?" she asked.

I stopped. "No, I don't think so. Well—maybe." I thought about the hand I saw on our patio. "Do you know anything about ghosts?"

"Ghosts? Why yes," she said. Then she went quiet, coming out from behind her desk. Her feet didn't make a sound on the hardwood floors as she seemed to appear in front of me. It was dark in the library and her black dress blended into the shadows. "A fair amount," she added as she pushed the heavy door closed behind me. "You could say they're a hobby of mine." I don't know what it was about the way she said that, but it made me shiver a little.

"I was wondering. How do you stop them from messing with you?"

"Messing with you?" she asked. "Tom, have you actually seen a ghost?"

Like a hundred—all lined up and floating on the water, I thought, but I didn't say that.

"Tom, answer me?"

"Yes, I think so," I finally said. "They tore up my newspapers yesterday and got me fired."

She raised an eyebrow. "I guess that explains why we didn't get a paper."

"Sorry," I said.

"What makes you think it was a ghost and not something else?"

"I saw one the night before. It was on my deck, trying to get in my house—I mean condo."

I'd never seen Miss Webster look surprised before. "Well, that's interesting." She motioned to a nearby table. There was a lamp on it that she flipped on. "Have a seat."

I did as she asked. She took the chair next to me. It was a little odd being so close to her. She smelt like flowers, not perfume, actual flowers and herbs, fresh from the garden. "Ghosts don't usually bother people unless they've gotten themselves into something strange. Started looking into things they shouldn't. Tell me Tom, what have you gotten into?"

"Nothing," I said defensively. I didn't want to tell her about Swift. I knew if I did, she'd tell me to stay away from him. That would be it for the boat and for my plan to see my dad. In other words, she'd tell me to be smart.

"Really?" she asked, sitting back and crossing her arms. "Okay then." She wasn't going to call me a liar, but I could see that she didn't believe me. "Well then, I'll just tell you this, when ghosts want something they don't quit. They've got all of eternity to wait. And usually what they want is the reason they're stuck here in the first place."

"So what do I do?"

"Give them what they want," she said.

I thought about it. They wanted Swift. What was I supposed to do, hit him on the head and drag him to the water? *I'd have to get Liam another bone to distract him— wait, no, I couldn't do that.* It scared me that I could come up with a plan that quick. "That's not really an option," I said.

"Well, then you have two choices. One is religion. Whatever your faith is, you can use it as protection. Of course, you have to be strong in that faith. It's all about belief."

I already went to church every Sunday, what else was I supposed to do?

"The other option is to go in the opposite direction," she said.

"What do you mean?"

"Don't believe. Close your mind to all these ideas. Ignore them, pretend they're not there. These otherworldly things feed on your beliefs. If you ignore them, try to hide them from your thoughts, they have no power."

"You're saying they're not real?"

"No, that's not what I'm saying at all. They're as real, and dangerous, as you make them. You'd be surprised by how many things in this world are like that." She leaned in a little and whispered while motioning around the room. "Most of it's an illusion anyway." Again, she gave me shivers.

I focused on the floor until the feeling left. Then I asked, "So all I have to do is pretend they aren't real? That's kind of tough when they're staring right at you."

She got up abruptly. "So close your eyes, control your mind, and get out of my library. Come back during regular hours or when you can tell me the truth about what you've gotten yourself into. Then maybe I can help you."

"What?" I asked, surprised by how abrupt she was.

"That's all I got for you, Tom. When you're ready to tell me the whole story maybe I can give you more. If you survive." She pointed towards the door.

I got up, sensing that if she had to ask me again, it wasn't going to be pleasant.

"Okay…thanks," I said, still having no idea what to do.

Chapter 27

Questions and Answers

I went to the pharmacy after school. Did you know that most local pharmacies have a small religious section? It's a good place to go when you need to get a cross or a Star of David in a hurry. We went to church every Sunday, but I wouldn't say my family was super religious. We were moderate about our faith like we are about most things.

I got both by the way, the star and the cross. I'm not Jewish, but I figured every little bit would help, and the star came with a chain. I left it on and put the cross right next to it. I'm fairly certain the cross wasn't supposed to be a necklace. It was big, more like the kind you'd hang on a wall. *More cross, less ghost*, I thought.

I went to Swift's yard and found him sitting in a lawn chair at the front of his tugboat. He was staring down at something in his hand. Liam was lying under the boat. I passed him a rawhide I'd bought at the pharmacy. It's amazing all the different stuff you can find there.

I may've been trying to protect myself with religion, but the only thing I'd seen that could keep those ghosts away for sure was this cranky old dog. I had every intention of keeping him on my side.

Swift didn't look up when I dropped my bike in the dirt, or when I climbed the squeaky ladder, or when I jumped down loudly onto the deck.

He couldn't still be angry with me over yesterday, I thought. If anything, I should be the one holding a grudge. "Hey," I called.

He finally looked up. "There's something I forgot to do. It shouldn't take long. Here." He threw the thing in his hand to me.

After I caught it out of the air I looked down. I was surprised. Then I was worried. It was the gold coin. The one Swift showed me before. The one he'd gotten weird about. I thought he was going to kill me last time if I didn't give it back.

"What do you want me to do with this?" I asked.

"We're going to find some place in the boat for it. It's an old tradition for luck." He stood up, leaning against the gunwale. "Put it in your pocket." He was staring at me like he didn't want to look down at the coin.

"Okay," I said, getting it out of sight. "But I think it's time you told me a few things."

He waited for me to continue.

"You need to tell me where I'm going. Where it is I'm supposed to be sailing to." I hated how whiney my voice sounded. "It's time you told me what my part in this is….and what exactly happened yesterday."

"Come with me." He went into the tugboat and closed the door behind us. He pointed to an old wooden chair, motioning for me to sit. The cabin was dark and tight, smelling the way only an old hermit's hole could. He lit a propane lantern sitting on a beat up old table. It was next to a cot, one of those army ones with a metal frame. Swift sat on it and reached down to a loose floorboard. He pulled it away and brought out a leather bundle. "Do you know what's in here?" he asked.

"It's your sword," I said.

"It is that. But it's also the way to Tír-Na-Nóg." He hadn't looked up yet.

"Okay."

"Don't tell me you already forgot Oisín's story."

"No, I didn't forget, but it's just a myth, not a real place," I said.

"That could be a point of debate." Swift un-wrapped his bundle, bringing the two-and-a-half-foot long weapon out and handing it to me.

"It's made of iron. If you feel the edge you can see how dull it is."

I touched it. It felt more like a rock than a blade. A butter knife would've been sharper.

"Not that impressive?" he asked.

I didn't know how to respond. It was the oldest thing I'd ever held.

"This sword was given to Oisín by his wife Niamh, daughter of the sea god, along with the horse that carried him back to Ireland. It was his guide to Tír-Na-Nóg."

"But it's not a real place," I stated again.

Swift threw his up hands. "Think what you want, but since ancient times men have believed in this island. Some call it Tír-Na-Nóg, some call it Hy-brazil, others call it Avalon." He sat back and asked, "You've heard the name Avalon before haven't you?"

"Maybe," I said, trying to remember.

"It was the island where King Arthur rested after being mortally wounded. Where he's supposed to wait un-til the world needs him again."

"Okay, but that's just a story too," I answered.

"They're all just stories," he said, "but if you don't mind I'll go ahead and finish. Then you can choose to be-lieve whatever you like."

I motioned for him to continue.

"In Ireland, they believe the island shows itself once every seven years, off the shores of Aran. If you know where to look for it though, you can find it more often. It rests in the heart of powerful sea storms, but finding it there is dangerous. It's safer and more predictable when it appears twice a year, at dawn on the winter solstice, and at sunset on the summer solstice. It moves in the Atlantic, following powerful ley lines that cross the ocean."

"Ley lines?" I interrupted.

"Yes, not that I'm about to explain those to you," he said impatiently.

"I'm sorry. Please."

He furrowed his brow, thinking of how to explain. "Have you ever wondered why the ancients would lay roads in certain ways, why animals follow the same trails through the wilderness, or even why fish migrate in certain courses in the ocean? Some believe there are lines of energy that cross the earth; they can't be seen, but they can be felt."

I gave him a look that let him know what I thought of that.

"It sounds silly I know, but then again you're talking to a three-hundred-year-old pirate about a magical island."

I stayed quiet.

"There are markings in the stars that tell where the island is going to appear. The sword works like a compass. It tells you the exact direction to look in."

I held the sword, wondering if it was my imagination that made it feel warm. "So this island is going to show up on the summer solstice?"

He nodded his head.

"Why do you want me to go there?" I asked.

"Because that's the safe place where Sampson and I hid my treasure," he answered.

West Indies, 1718

Setting sail in a tropical storm was suicide, but I knew we had distance to make up. I ordered the men into the rigging while waves tossed them side to side. The Madeline*'s canvas dropped, and the fierce winds began to pull.*

I took the helm, calling orders above the storm, knowing that the weather could tear our masts away at any moment, or that a wave could twist us and toss the whole ship down into the dark. We'd all die soon if nothing changed, but I didn't relent. I held us on the course the sword promised.

Again and again we rode up the face of one swell, then down another. Finally, the ocean formed liked a wall, climbing as high as a mountain. Men were looking over the side as the ocean dropped away. I held on till we reached the peak. *That's when I saw it; there was light, and beneath was the island.*

Time seemed to slow. The sky above was suddenly clear and calm. The sun had returned, held in eternal twilight, carving an unnatural hole across the horizon. It shined like a spotlight behind the island while stars twinkled above against a background of purple and pink.

The bow of the Madeline *dropped, chasing down the front of the wave. We crashed into a calm piece of water, bobbing like a cork pushed through a bottle. The wind gave way, and we stalled. I looked back at the storm behind us and smiled. It churned and raged, held back by some invisible barrier.*

Sampson and his freemen spoke in their native tongues, while the Madeline*'s crew cursed and prayed, usually in the same breath. I ignored them, staring at something I didn't think I'd ever actually see; a magical place.*

The island was rugged in spots like those off the coast of Ireland and tropical in other places, swelling with green. Only in the distance, beyond the trees, could I see anything that looked like civilization.

Tall towers made of marble appeared in the distance. They looked ancient and alien at first, the watchtowers of some prehistoric civilization. As I gazed longer though, they appeared only to be mountains that had weathered oddly. I strained through my glass, but it was as if the more I focused on them, the less clear they became.

I looked at the shore at a rounded beach of soft sand. A fine spot for landing a small boat, but my eyes fell on something better. There was a long pier jutting out into the water, made of marble polished so hard that it gleamed like a ray of light. That's where I'd take my gold.

Sampson came up next to me. "This is your safe place?" he asked.

"It is."

"Why are we here? What do you plan to do?" His face was impassive.

I slammed my hand on the rail, letting my rage show for the first time. "The men of the Freedom's Fortune *care nothing for what I've given them. They only care about what else they can take." I looked back at the deck of the gently swaying* Madeline. *"I'll give them this ship, but the gold on it is mine, and I mean to keep it."*

Sampson nodded his head. He was quiet for a long time, thinking. Finally, he said, "This is foolishness. You've found a place of legend. A place so special, and all you can think of is your gold." He shook his head. "I suppose every legend needs a fool in it, someone whose mistakes others can learn from. I owe you, Swift. So I'll go with you even though I think you're making a terrible mistake." He turned and walked away.

A boat was unlashed and lowered for Sampson and I. The trunks of gold were loaded, but I left behind a small sack, a fortune for any man. With this and the goods in the hold, I hoped to dissuade doubt from my old crew.

We cast off and pulled at the oars, afraid it would take us too long to make it to the dock and that we'd be landing in the dark. We had nothing to fear though. Time didn't move the same here. It didn't appear to move at all. In fact, the sun stayed still in the sky.

We came to the pier, pulled alongside, and tied our line around a stone block. The marble was clean. There was no seagrass or slime growing on it where it touched the sandy soil. Tiny waves lapped gently at our boat as Sampson and I lifted each trunk from the bottom and placed them on the pier. Sampson climbed on the dock and moved the trunks back from the edge. "Shall we bring them inland?" I asked.

"They'll be safe here. Nothing on this island will trouble with them." He was looking away. There was a sound in the distance distracting him. Sampson turned to me and asked, "Can you hear that?"

"Aye, the singing," I answered, knowing exactly what he meant. I'd been hearing it too.

"It's wonderful isn't it?" he asked.

"Pay no attention to it. Songs at sea are never safe things to listen too," I said.

Sampson's eyes were back on the island. He wouldn't look away. "How could it be anything bad when it's sung in my mother's own voice?" he said.

249

"*Your mother?*" *I asked.*

"*I haven't heard her voice since I was a child, but yes, most certainly that's her, singing the loveliest of songs.*" *Sampson started walking, almost in a daze. He broke into a run, bounding on his long legs.*

"*Sampson wait!*" *I called.*

He turned, waving with a bright smile on his face, the likes of which I'd never seen. Then he darted off towards the beach. He was gone into the wilderness, and I was left alone rowing back to the Madeline. *I knew that if I went after him, I'd never return. I'd stay here forever.*

When I rowed away, I noticed the sun dropping from the sky again. The water became rougher. I rowed hard, making the best time I could while swells climbed and dropped around me. By the time I made the Madeline *it was full dark, and the wind was blowing hard. Her stern lights appeared over the crest of one wave. They were the only guide for me. She was turning with the wind. It was a tricky thing coming up next to her. I held the ladder and pulled myself up. Once on deck, I turned to look at the island, but it was gone. The storm moved in around us. We rode it out for the night and in the morning we set sail for Block Island Sound to rendezvous with the* Freedom's Fortune.

I was still holding the sword when Swift stopped and stood up.

"What happened?" I asked.

"Nothing good," Swift said simply as he turned and came back to me. He held his hand out for the sword. "We're burning daylight. We can sit here all day, or you can take that boat out for a bit."

Chapter 28

Taking to the Wind

*I*n the middle of the cove with my arms tired from rowing, I turned to hear a motor firing up. Its loud rumble echoed across the water, but Swift's voice was still louder.

"Far enough! Raise the sail," he called from the shore.

I pulled the oars in and stowed them. Then I rubbed my swollen hands while glancing at the base of the mast, seeing the tiniest corner of the gold coin. Hopefully, it'll bring me luck.

I was in it now. Out far enough that if those ghosts wanted me, there wouldn't be a thing I could do. I touched the cross around my neck, so big it was silly, and I said a little prayer. It went like this: 'God, don't let me drown—or be pulled apart by cursed ghost-pirates.' Whoever thought that'd be at the top of their holy requests?

I stood up and untied the gaskets holding the sail. I pulled on the halyard, tugging hard, hand over hand, sending the sail and the gaff up into the blue sky and into the wind. It billowed out a little. I was excited watching it, waiting for something to happen, but it did exactly nothing, just flopped around limply.

I yelled across the water. "What now?"

Swift shouted back, "Let the sail out. Find the wind," Heads were starting to turn on the cove, looking for the loud old man.

I let the mainsheet out a bit, then a bit more, and just as I was ready to give up and shout that this was stupid, a breeze touched the sail. It started to move, dancing a little, like a puppy rolling over in its sleep. It filled slowly, till suddenly it snapped out. The mainsheet line hopped out of my hand.

"Tighten up a bit," Swift shouted.

I pulled it back in, cinching it off. That's when something strange happened. There was a jerk, seemingly from nowhere, grabbing hold of the boat and pushing. Like magic I was moving, actually moving. I couldn't believe it. "Hey, it's moving!" I called.

"That's what it's supposed to do," Swift said. He was following along the shore.

"What do I do now?"

"Try not hitting anything," he answered.

"Okay," I nodded. That sounded like good advice to me.

My hand went to the rudder. In my excitement, I turned it too hard and fell away from the wind. Swift was shouting something from the shore, but I ignored him, wanting to solve the problem myself.

I steered the rudder back and let the mainsheet out again, finding my lost breeze. I pulled the line in, tightening the sail till it was full. I took the rudder and slowly guided the little boat out into the main channel.

From the docks, I probably looked like I was moving in slow motion but from the boat, it felt wild, like I was moving way too fast. The boat was a living thing and I was only half in control.

I turned into the channel and adjusted the sail, letting it out. I tried to do it one-handed, not wanting to let go of the rudder while the boat leaned on its side.

The docks, that little park where I first met Swift, and the bell tower at town hall all came and went. Then I passed a red buoy on a beam reach, with the wind hitting my sail on the side.

I entered the bay and turned further into the wind, passing the point. To the east I could see green hills on a broad island, and the top of the Newport Bridge peeking above it. Boats were moving in and around the smaller islands. The wind picked up in the open, and the water moved faster against my hull as the boat tilted further.

Swift gave me a list of tasks. He'd told me to play a little before I got too far from land. I could hear his lecture in my head. *Get used to the wind coming from*

different directions. It's not as simple as turning a wheel. Momentum is the key, especially with a single-sailed boat.

Momentum wasn't an issue on the bay. The wind never let up. *There are little turns, small course adjustments you make when steering a boat; then there are big turns called tacking,* Swift had said.

Might as well try it, I thought as I pulled the rudder hard-over, coming across the wind and feeling the boat stall out. I held the tiller, spinning the boat around ninety degrees. The wind hit the sail again and it quickly tossed the boom over my head.

I pulled the sail in and trimmed it till it felt right, then the boat started to move forward. It was sluggish at first, but slowly it sped up. Unfortunately, this new direction was on a crash course with a bunch of rocks. I tried tacking again, but it was too soon—no momentum.

The boat stopped halfway into its turn. This time it had no interest in catching the wind or turning any further. Swift had said *Boats like yours can find themselves in irons if they turn without enough speed.*

He'd told me what to do to fix it. I pushed the boom across in the direction I wanted to go and felt the wind start to push me backward. I turned the rudder, experimenting. Eventually, the boat started to make headway again. After that, I sailed further out into the bay.

Hours may have passed, but I was having too much fun to tell. It was only when the sun started to set that I turned back towards home. I tacked across the bay until I was at the mouth of the cove. I came in close to land before dropping my sail and picking the oars up again.

Swift was sitting on the stone wall. "If your smile were any bigger it'd shatter your face," he said. I tried not smiling for a minute. The salt air and falling temperature had me cold and bone-tired, but it didn't matter.

I grabbed the old milk carton that kept the line floating near the wall. Then I threw out the mushroom anchor and secured the sail and gaff to the boom.

Swift tossed a tarp across to me. I hung it over the boom, making a cover, like a tent for the cockpit in case it rained. *A person would be dry and warm underneath there*, I thought.

Swift reached down, helping me out of the water. "Let's head out. I don't like being down here at this time of day." I had to jog to keep up with his long strides as he hurried up the hill.

"I wish we didn't have to go so quick." I glanced back at the boat.

He stopped and pointed at a spot in the water not far from the wall. "Look closely, Tom. Look and tell me what you see. Then tell me if you want to stay here."

The water was calm and glassy. My eyes, of course, were drawn to the boat. But that wasn't what Swift wanted me to see. There was something else there, something below the water, a dark mass. "Maybe it's a school of fish." I suggested while thinking to myself, *Don't believe it*.

The Spot didn't move or undulate the way fish did. It clung to the wall. I was thinking about yesterday as I stared.

The darkness wasn't one thing, but many. There were lines, rows across the surface. It dawned on me what I was seeing, and the smile fell from my face. I felt my breath catch. I remembered that morning in the rain, the people I'd seen. I knew what the dark mass was.

It was their shadows. If men stood above the water, then these would be the shadows they'd cast. I breathed in quickly, turning away. Had that been there yesterday, I wondered. Was it there just now, when I waded over from the boat?

I understood why Swift was upset. An icy chill grabbed hold of me. They nearly had him yesterday.

Swift placed his hand on my shoulder, "Now you know why I never went back for my treasure. It's because of them, because of my curse." Then he began to tell me what happened when he met his crew again.

Rhode Island, 1718

It was a hard voyage back to Block Island Sound. Sampson's men didn't trust me anymore. I'd conjured an island; made magic and disappeared their leader and brother. They started hating me the moment I returned without him.

I was anxious, worried all the time that Sampson's men would plot against me. They hardly ever spoke

English so I wouldn't know till a knife was at my throat. Only fear held them back. I didn't wear my cutlass anymore; instead, I carried my short sword. If they had no respect for their captain, they at least dreaded his magic.

The crew of the Madeline *served grudgingly, knowing that I'd taken the treasure from the ship. Fear, again, was the only reason they followed my command. The island had terrified these sailors too, but they were even more afraid that I was the only thing keeping Sampson's pirates from slaughtering them.*

I was left alone most of the time, given a wide berth by everyone. It gave me time to think, to wonder if I'd made the right decision. I'd been rash, just like when I was a boy. Now I was left waiting to be caught. I didn't want to share the treasure, but too many people knew what I'd done.

There were fourteen sailors and ten pirates. Sampson's men had never developed a knack for sailing, so I had to keep the Madeline*'s men aboard to run the ship.*

I could get rid of the captain and the ship's former owner though. We sailed along the coast of North Carolina and came to one of its many islands. The ship's owner was brought on deck and lowered into a boat. I asked the captain to accompany me ashore then I left him there, out of sight of the Madeline.

When I returned to the ship I said nothing about either man, letting the crew assume the worst. "My sword will take anyone who speaks of the island where I hid my treasure. It'll damn them." I pointed the weapon around at each man's chest. "Keep your tongues in your mouths or I promise your soul will find pain beyond death!" It was an empty threat. Oisín's sword was not meant for murder. It was forged for heroes. My criminal hands sullied it.

In under a week, we came upon the Freedom's Fortune *in Block Island Sound. I'd hoped never to see that ship again. If they'd wrecked or been captured by the crown, it would've been fine by me.*

They signaled for us to come about. I watched as a boat-full of men was lowered into the water. Sprowls was among them. He was cheery as he came up the side. "Ahoy there, captain," he called.

"Ahoy." I tried to sound happy as well.

We dropped a ladder so they could climb aboard. Sprowls was the last man up, "Glad to see you survived the storm," he said, offering his hand. I reached out to take it. As I did two men from my former crew grabbed my arms. They pinned them behind me, and Sprowls closed his fist and drove it into my gut.

"Where is it?" he demanded. "What have you done with it?"

"What are you referring too?" I asked, struggling to breathe.

"The gold you lying snake." He hit me again. I was bent over coughing, spitting up an unhealthy amount of blood. Sprowls's fists were like hammers.

"I don't understand," I said.

Sprowls pulled back my head with my hair, forcing me to look at him. "We were only a few days ahead of you Nathanial. We had to resupply in the Chesapeake. A few miles north of where you left the Madeline's captain and owner." He stepped back. "A smarter man would've killed them both. They were on that island for less than a day when their campfire was spotted by a fishing boat. The story reached us just before we sailed, three trunks of gold taken from the ship, left on some tropical island."

Sprowls dropped my head and struck me again in the gut. "Tell me where it is."

"That's all they had to say?" I asked, coughing.

Sprowls eyed me suspiciously as he clenched his fist. "No, there was more. The captain was mad, going on about some magical island. Nonsense I'm sure."

"Why don't you ask the men on this deck?" I nodded to the Madeline's crew.

Sprowls looked around. The freed slaves had been standing by, making no move to protect me. Sampson was gone, and so was their loyalty. One of them pointed to my sword. It was still tucked in my belt, though I had no way of reaching it with my arms pinned.

Sprowls followed the man's finger to the weapon. He took it out of my belt and held it up. "What about it?" he said, pointing.

The man's face was twisted in fear as he stepped back into the crowd. "What are you afraid of? Not this little pig sticker?" Sprowls looked at the sword, examining the carvings on the blade and handle.

I looked at Sampson's pirates. "It's alright men. Tell your new captain what you saw. Tell him about the magic place. I give you my leave."

The man who'd pointed out the sword stepped forward, looking at me nervously. I nodded my head, letting him know it was alright. "The story is true," he said. "Captain Swift conjured a place in the storm. He used that to do it."

Sprowls nodded his head. Then in a single sudden motion, he threw my sword to the ground and pulled out his cutlass. Quicker than a man his size should've been able to move, he crossed the deck and slammed the man who'd spoken in the face with the pommel of his blade. "I've heard enough of this blithering story!" he yelled.

He grabbed a sailor from the Madeline*'s crew and held him by the throat. "You, you'll tell me where my gold is, or I swear I'll run you through, and I'll kill the rest of you," he yelled at the sailors. They ducked and cowered, but none spoke. There was no answer they could give.*

"It's ashore and gone for a while, but guaranteed safe," I said.

"Enough lies!" Sprowls threw the man.

"It's the truth. I left it on an island that was there and now is gone, left for God knows where, a place that only I can find. Ask them," I said, motioning towards the Madeline's crew. Sprowls looked over his shoulder. They, and the African pirates, were nodding their heads.

"Then you're going to find it," Sprowls said, turning back to me.

I laughed a little, but it turned into another coughing fit. "Now that you believe me, do you think I'd give it to you and your disloyal crew? You don't know me very well. You were ready to set me aside before I found this ship. Feel free to take everything aboard it, but that gold is mine. I'll not share it with any of you."

"I'll just have your life then," Sprowls said, placing his blade to my chest.

"No one gets the gold that way," I answered.

He was frustrated, ready to kill me, but the treasure held him. He thought for a moment, and an evil light went off behind his eyes, "You may not care to save your own skin, but Summerlee and his clan, especially that doxy daughter of his. You always kept us far away from them. You didn't want our stink rubbing off." He leaned in till I could smell his sour breath. "Well let's see how much they stink when we get really close."

"Leave them out of this!" I demanded.

"You leave them out of it! The dice are in your hand Swift. How will you cast them?"

I was quiet for a moment, looking at the mainland. She was only a few miles up that shore. I imagined Sprowls's hands on Sarah, the horrible things I knew he was capable of. I had my answer. I was caught and bested. "The island won't return for a year, not to here anyway," I said. "And I'll need that to find it." I motioned to the sword.

"A year?" Sprowls demanded.

"Magic is a tricky thing."

His hand went around my throat. He squeezed hard while his face twisted with rage. For a moment, as the world went dark, I thought this would be my end, but then he let go. They dropped me to the deck.

"Bring him back to the ship and chain him below," Sprowls ordered as I struggled, nearly unconscious.

I was bound in shackles and rowed across to the Freedom's Fortune, stowed in the ship's belly like so much meat. I passed out in the cool darkness, smelling the stench of the bilge water below me. A single night or maybe two passed before I heard the anchor run out, dropping in shallow water. We were in Purgatory Cove.

Time passed as I lay listening to the ship sounds. I was denied all comfort, given no food or water. In the morning there was activity. Boats were assembled, and most of the crew left. There were few footsteps above my head, only a small watch.

I heard the crew row a short distance to the Madeline *where they went to work, pulling hatches and setting up rigging to unload the hold. The possessions of the Englishman were hoisted up, swayed over the side, and lowered into boats.*

They worked at this for the better part of the day before returning. There was loud thumping and groaning above as the crew brought aboard water casks and other supplies. Time passed, and all went silent.

There was a smack outside my hatch, then blinding light scorched my eyes as a torch was shoved into the darkness. "Here he is then, still strung up like a Christmas goose, let's have him on deck." Rough hands grabbed me and pulled me out. I was lifted and thrown face first onto the deck, where I was spat on and kicked.

They removed my shackles, and a heavy hand smacked me across the head.

"On your feet!" someone yelled. My eyes were beginning to clear, but I didn't care for what I saw. The crew had me surrounded, torches in their hands. Most wanted to see me dancing at the end of a yardarm, hung for the worst crime any pirate could imagine; holding back treasure from his brethren.

Sprowls stepped forward from the mob. He took the tatters of my shirt in his hand and pulled me close to his face, "Be here Swift when we return, or the Summerlee clan and this whole town will regret your leaving." I nodded my head in understanding, then he threw me away. "Over the side with him," he ordered.

I was shoved and pushed, then finally lifted and carried to the entryway and dumped over the side. I came up coughing and choking, gasping for air. I started swimming for West Harbor, not knowing it would become my prison.

Chapter 29

Borrowed Time

Swift and I made our way out to the road. I didn't want to look back at the water, but like a loose tooth, I couldn't help myself. I stared at the shadows. *Well at least they didn't drown me*, I thought, as they disappeared with the setting sun.

"You get used to them after a while. All they can do is wait there. They can't cause too much trouble." Swift said.

I thought about my newspapers. "Except when they get you fired."

"What's that?" Swift asked.

"Nothing, but this is all insane." Did I actually say that out loud?

Swift shrugged his shoulders, "You don't have to believe it. Maybe I'm mad. I could've dreamt it all up."

For a moment I thought of Miss Webster's advice, 'ignore it, pretend like it's not real.' I shook my head no. I didn't want to do that. "What happened next?" I asked.

West Harbor, 1718

The pirates were busy on both ships, making ready to sail with the morning tide. They split themselves between the two with the intention of selling the Madeline *in the islands. It didn't matter to me. That chapter of my life was done.*

I watched till they sailed away, then I started walking. Sprowls's last words echoed in my head. 'Be here Swift when we return, or the Summerlee clan and this whole town will regret your going.'

I knew he'd spoken to James, assuring him business would go on as usual whether he wanted it to or not. Sprowls probably wouldn't say why they dropped me on the shore, not wanting to risk the Summerlees fleeing. He would lose his leverage over me if they did.

Sprowls assumed I'd be too much of a coward to tell them the truth. That my lust for gold put the whole town at risk. He was right, and in a year's time, I would find that island for him. Not long after I'd be dead.

I went to the door and knocked. James answered, walking with a cane and a strange gait. "I thought from your last voyage you'd part on better terms. Those villains weren't fond of you I gather?" he asked.

I could find nothing to say, still wondering what Sprowls had told him.

James sighed. "I suppose if men like that don't care for your company it's not a bad thing." He stepped aside, waving me in.

"It's good to be amongst decent folk," I answered, stepping through his door while thinking, 'James you fool, I'm the worst of them, a man even pirates can't trust.'

What things I owned and any money I had aboard went with the Freedom's Fortune, *taken by the crew. Luckily the Summerlees had held onto much of what I'd earned. It was enough to purchase some land and build a simple house and stable. The month of August I spent building a home.*

To the people in town, I was a friend come down from the north, a sailor by way of Boston with a bit of money who was ready to try working the land. This simple sailor I claimed to be was my third identity and my latest lie, but I was practiced at that.

What happiness I had in this world came from the Summerlees. Each night I ate dinner at their table with James, Sarah, her mother, and her youngest brother. They were kind to me, not treating me as the criminal I was. They kept my secret and sold me my first horse. I began to believe the lie.

Sarah picked the horse for me and delivered it herself. She rode to the top of my hill overlooking the water. I was dirty and sweaty, still in the process of building my home. It was the same land that I've lived on for the better part of three centuries. My new horse was behind her, held by a lead. She climbed down and came over. "He's thick enough to be a workhorse and slow enough for a child to ride," she said, getting down.

I looked at it nervously. "I'm sure he'll be just fine." I took the lead and asked, "This is what farmers do? Own horses, ride them and what not, right?"

"You've never been on a horse?" she asked.

"I've spent nearly two-thirds of my life at sea and before that..." I stopped, not feeling like giving her my whole history. "Well let's just say I didn't have much use for the equestrian arts."

She touched my arm gently. "It wasn't my intention to insult you." Her concern pulled at my heart. It would've been a simple thing to lean in and kiss her, but I stepped away.

In the past month, we'd grown closer. She'd been soft towards me and kinder than I deserved. We shared books with each other and talked for hours. We'd taken up the habit of going for walks alone. I knew it was wrong, but I was selfish, and the happiness I felt around her was intoxicating. I could never say no when she requested my company, even though I was a dead man with only a year to live. It wasn't fair to make her think there could be anything between us. Still, she pushed, with little touches and soft smiles. Her every gesture tortured me.

"You gave no insult," I answered, unwilling to push her hand away.

"I'll teach you to ride. I'll teach you everything you need to know," she said quickly.

"Thank you, Sarah," I said, looking at the big horse.

"You know Nathanial, I may be a colonial girl, but I know life can be hard in the poorest of England's colonies. You try to hide who you are, the way you speak, but still that lilt comes through. Certainly when you read poetry, it's impossible to disguise. I want to know who you are."

"There's not much to tell." I tried taking my arm away but she wouldn't let go.

Looking at me intently she said, "Please." It was almost too soft to be heard.

I shook my head in frustration while she led me to the footpath, to the stony beach my land sat on. She walked next to me. Her hand closed around mine.

I told her my entire story, all the things that led to my life at sea, who I was and the crime I committed, my father dying, my mother sending me off, the whole tale.

We went around the water's edge to a sandy strip of land, where small waves lapped at the shore. I took her right up to the moment I met her father. The trees blocked *all sight of us. She came forward, facing me, still holding my hand but saying nothing. I waited in fear for her response and felt relief as she leaned in and, with the softest lips, kissed me gently.*

I knew it was wrong, but I'd spent my whole life pursuing what I wanted without fear. What was it to me to do it once more? Sarah was no different than the gold I'd spent my days stealing. From that day forward she was mine, even if I was never truly hers. How could I be when my life belonged the Sprowls?

My house was finished by the end of the summer, and to my great surprise, I was a married man. Sarah and I began a life together. The leaves had hardly begun to change when we learned she was pregnant. Nine months before the summer solstice we had a child on the way.

Chapter 30

Mom Stuff

I was late again. In fact, this was probably the latest I'd been since all this stuff started. I wasn't half-drowned at least, but I was still shocked.

According to Swift, way back when, he'd been married into my family. Ghosts, magic islands, pirates; I could deal with all that, sort of, but being related to that crack pot? If he was like my great-great-great-great-great-granduncle (is that enough greats?) then I didn't know what to think.

It was a lot, and it distracted me from what I knew was coming. My mom hadn't been happy before. Coming home late again wasn't going to make it any better, especially on a school night. Luckily it was our last week. So when we weren't having exams, the rules were a little looser.

Maybe she'd take it in stride. I was getting older after all.

"Yeah right," I said. I'd be grounded for sure. Good luck getting away on my boat when I couldn't leave the prison-condo.

I pulled into our parking lot and looked for her car. It wasn't there yet. That was either really good, if she was late coming home from work, or really bad, if she'd gone out looking for me. I opened the door, going in slowly. Then I turned and looked back to see a car pulling in. It was my mom's. Moment of truth.

When she got out she was holding a pizza. "Sorry I'm late," she said.

Yay! Silent cheer, silent cheer! I thought while saying, "It's cool Mom. But you were starting to worry me."

"I tried calling, but you didn't pick up." She handed me the box. "I was trying to get some more work done."

"Must've missed it," I said. This would've been the perfect time to have the cellphone argument again, but I let that slide, not wanting a GPS tracker on my person.

She looked around the apartment. Not a single light was on. "What were you doing? Sitting in the dark?"

"I was meditating," I said.

She looked back at me, waiting for me to explain.

"Yum, pizza." I held the box up to my nose. "Can we eat? I'm starving."

She shook her head and went in, not willing to play detective. We ate dinner together and then watched some TV. I went to bed first. In the morning I left my room and was surprised to find I wasn't alone. She was sitting at the kitchen table, eating her cereal and reading the paper. This may seem normal, but I assure you it isn't.

Usually, my mom ate breakfast in the car, and she certainly never stayed in her bathrobe in the morning.

"Hey," I said, certain the universe was out of alignment.

"Morning," she greeted me between bites of corn-flakes.

"Aren't you going to be late for work?"

"No," she answered, "I took the day off."

'What?' I couldn't believe it.

"I've got some things to do."

"Oh, okay," I said, as if she needed my approval. Then I made a bowl and sat across the table from her, eating in silence. Usually, I ate alone. This felt strange, but not terrible.

In the afternoon I got off the bus at my normal stop, which was near my grandparents' house. I haven't explained this yet because it's not really that important, but while I live outside West Harbor, just over the line, I go to school in town and my bus stop is at my grandparents' house.

According to my school records, that's also my primary residence. Yes, my mother is a lawyer, and yes, this isn't exactly legal, but when she sold our house, which was in West Harbor, she didn't want to take me away from all my friends. Oh, how things have changed. West Harbor also has the highest rated schools in the state.

Like I said, none of this is really important. I only say it because every afternoon, when the bus drops me off, it's in front of my grandparents' house. I leave my bike, well-hidden so the bus driver doesn't get wise.

I don't always stop in at their house, but I always look over. This time I was surprised to see my mother's car pulling into the driveway. She had my grandmother with her.

I went over and asked. "Hey Mom, whatcha up to?"

She was helping my grandma out of the car, who looked back at me strangely. Grandma seemed tired. I'm fairly certain she didn't know who I was.

"I took my mother to the doctor." My mom held a large folder in her hand.

Wow, she actually listened to me, I thought. *That's awesome*. That was right before everything went bad. There was a sound. Another car was pulling up behind me. It was my grandfather.

He closed the car door a little harder than he needed to and I knew right then something ugly was about to happen.

"What's going on?" he demanded.

My mom stepped out in front of him. "Dad, I don't want you to get angry, but I was a little concerned about Mom—"

"Oh I'm fine dear, just a little tired," my grandmother interrupted.

"We went to a doctor, a specialist, and had some tests done," my mother said.

"You did what?" he growled.

My grandmother was wandering toward the porch. I helped her, taking her to the bench seat. She thanked me then stared at me for a long moment. I could tell she was struggling, trying to remember who I was.

I heard my mother say, "We need to talk about what they found."

"We don't need to talk," my grandfather insisted. "There's nothing wrong with your mother. And even if there were, she and I will handle it."

"But Dad—"

"I don't need your help with my wife! You couldn't even keep your own marriage together. What do you think you can tell me about mine?"

I watched all the fight go out of my mom. She walked over and laid the stack of papers on the porch.

"Everything they found is in there. Read it if you want," she said. Then she looked up at me and said, "Let's go Tom."

I wasn't about to point out that my bike was still there. I'd get it later, I thought as I got in the car, staying as quiet as humanly possible. It's not that I didn't have a lot to say. I wanted to tell her how glad I was she took Grandma to get tested, and I wanted to call my grandfather a jerk. But one look at my mom, and I knew she didn't want to hear any of it.

We walked into the condo. She looked at me and said, "It wasn't my fault he left." Then she went into her bedroom and closed the door.

Chapter 31

Promises Made

eah, so, yesterday wasn't great. In the morning my mom was already gone and I had to walk to my grandparents' house since my bike was there. I saw my grandfather's car and felt an urge to tell him off.

I didn't of course. I was raised better than that. Isn't that a funny thing to say? As if me telling him he'd been a jerk was the wrong thing to do. Respect can be a strange idea, especially when it's used to protect bullies.

I had my last few exams at school, but the rest of the day my class spent watching movies, killing time before summer break. There was only one more day of school and a pizza party ahead of me, then Friday was supposed to be our 'graduation,' leaving middle school. If things went the way I planned I wouldn't be here for any of it.

I rode home in the afternoon, cutting through the condo and heading straight out the glass slider to the deck. Don't worry, I left the bike outside.

We had an outdoor closet on the deck. Inside it was a pile of camping gear that'd been in the same spot since we moved in. There was a tent, some sleeping bags, foam mats, a lantern, and a propane burner. I loaded the whole mess on my back and got on my bike. I made it ten feet before I had to stop and put half of it back.

I rode past Swift's place and looked in the yard. Liam was there. He didn't even get up though, and I didn't see the old man anywhere. I was grateful for that. Officially the catboat wasn't mine, not till I took that trip and brought back his gold. I wasn't giving great odds that that was going to happen.

Swift was crazy, and he was trying to make me the same way. The things I'd seen had to be my imagination. I don't know why I woke up this morning certain of that. Maybe it was seeing my mom broken. Let's face it, there's enough baloney in this world. We don't need ghost-pirates to make things worse, not when we've got guys like my grandfather.

I was sailing out tomorrow and my destination was Florida. Swift would probably think I stole his imaginary gold, but there wasn't anything I could do about it.

I turned into the public boat launch. I was going to drop my supplies and try to get away without being noticed.

The only problem was that Swift was standing right there, by the water. I breathed out as the shock set in.

Swift's back was to me, but I knew he could see me. It was a well-known fact that crazy people have eyes in the back of their heads. I thought of running but instead, I went right up to him. I was scared, but I knew it was time we had a conversation. I try to make sure I only avoid one old man per day and I was already at my limit.

"Looks like you're packing for a longer trip," Swift said.

"Well you've got your plans, and I've got mine," I answered. Wow, right? I even said that without my voice shaking.

"But we both have our agreement," he shot back. He didn't look crazy or angry, but he did look dangerous. He stood rigid, and his eyes were sharp.

I hesitated to climb off my bike. "I'm going to look for your island, but…"

"But what?" he asked.

"If it's not there, I'm not coming back."

He stared out at the water. "You don't believe me?"

I didn't answer him. I just shrugged my shoulders and took off my pack.

"I guess it doesn't matter," he said.

"Look, I'm going out there like you want. But if I don't find anything, just don't expect me back here." Then

I added, "But if the island does show, and everything happens the way you say, I promise I'll return your treasure."

"How do I know you're not going to take it for yourself?" he asked.

The question seemed silly to me. I answered anyway. "You know me better than that. I wouldn't even steal one of the papers I deliver. Besides, if everything you told me is true and you are a three-hundred-year-old pirate, well that would pretty much make you immortal and the last person I'd want holding a grudge against me."

He shook his head and said softly, "It's not a lie. I have trouble believing myself sometimes…It was so long ago, but it happened." The frustrated look on his face was familiar. I'd seen it just yesterday on my grandmother when she tried to remember who I was.

"I'll look for your island," I promised.

"Your word?" he asked.

"Of course."

"Careful Tom," he warned, "promises can be dangerous, especially the ones not kept. If there's one thing I've learned in this long life, it's that."

"What do you mean?"

"What do you care? You think it's just a story anyway."

"I'd still like to hear it," I said honestly.

He sat down on the stone wall with his feet dangling over the dark, still water. He patted the spot next to him.

I hesitated for a moment, looking down. Yes, I didn't buy the magic island thing, but the ghosts—well, I'd seen them. *It's your imagination, remember that,* I tried convincing myself.

"It's alright Tom, it's all just a story after all." Swift pointed to a dark spot in the water. "There's nothing there but a captive audience."

I sat down next to him, crossing my legs so they wouldn't dangle too close to the surface. Then he told me the next part of his story.

West Harbor, 1718

Sarah and I married in September. The whole town attended to see the man who gained her hand. Most didn't care for the look of me, but it didn't matter. I only cared about how she saw me, with such compassion in her eyes. This woman knew my past and loved me still. Of course, she didn't know the whole story. She didn't know how it would end. But I knew it was coming. I would stay here and die, or a horrible fate would fall on her and her family.

By October she'd told me something I never expected to hear. There were many things I'd thought I'd be in this world, but for some reason a parent was never one of them. It's not that I didn't want children, it's just with the life I lived, always away, never having a home; I couldn't picture being a husband or a father. By the end of my year in West Harbor, I'd be both, if only for a little while.

"I've already seen the midwife, and she's confirmed it," Sarah told me as we sat on a bench near the hearth.

There were ways that women could tell when they were pregnant, but still, it was hard to know till she started to show, and that could take months. Midwives, these women, often elders of a town, could give a more accurate answer.

After the surprise ebbed away, I stammered out, "How long? I mean how soon?"

My wife looked at me, trying to gauge what my response meant. I knew what she wanted, pure joy, not fear. "The midwife said we should expect the baby in the early part of the summer, sometime in June."

I would know my child for only a few days. What sort of father could I be in such a short time? I forced myself to smile, hugged her close and tried to speak as little as possible, afraid I wouldn't be able to hide the tremble in my voice.

That winter was a happy and sad time, where only sometimes anxiety and anger intruded. It was the days when I'd walk by the water, considering strategies and trying to imagine some way out of this trouble that problems arose. Each time I saw my future play out, it ended in death and failure.

Sprowls would send as many men as he could to collect the treasure. I knew as soon as that gold was on deck, a noose would be around my neck. It wasn't only my death that bothered me. It was the idea of being bested. Those ingrates, my crew, they would have my treasure, and I'd die defeated.

Sarah sat by the window, watching me. She wanted to know my thoughts. Was I longing for the ocean, for the life I once led? She asked more than once. I told her nothing. With a raised voice she'd demand to know what concerned me so. I'd tell her to leave me be.

Those were the bad times, for the rest we were happy, huddled together through the long New England winter. I watched with amazement as her body changed and her belly grew. It was hard to the touch, rigid from the precious cargo inside.

On New Year's Eve, I saw the strangest and most amazing thing. My wife's stomach, of its own volition, moved. We were lying beside each other in our bed, and I was about to blow out the light when I saw it. Sarah was nearly asleep. She awoke to see me staring in amazement. She took my hand, placing it where the kick had come.

"My God, what a wonder," I said.

"Our little wonder," she answered.

I'd never felt more conflicted about winter ending. The days ran longer and longer. Spring came to summer and I thought for sure to see his sail, but the weeks passed *and there was no sign on the horizon. I tried to stifle the hope I felt.*

In the fine weather I helped the Summerlees plant barley and other grains, and learned what it meant to be a farmer. James asked me if I'd try planting on my own land. "I don't have much," I said to him, "I doubt I could put enough in the ground to make any profit."

"You could always buy more land, there's plenty to be had, and if I remember right, you have more money left over."

"Enough to avoid honest work for at least another year," I said, while getting my hands dirty in his field.

James shook his head, not understanding. In truth, if I were to be dead come June, I'd rather leave the small fortune I'd hidden to Sarah and my child. It'd be better than leaving her fields she'd have to tend.

June came, and Sarah's belly grew larger. She was swollen and uncomfortable in the heat, moving slowly but still getting around. I tried not to show the tension I was feeling, tried to smile as often as I could.

It was somewhere in the middle of that hot month that her pains came. It was in the evening. I'd just returned from one of my walks, a longer one than usual. "Fetch the midwife, Nathanial, our child is on the way," she said as I came through the door. She was standing above a puddle of water that soaked the bottom of her dress. I helped her to bed then took my leave.

The midwife lived only a short distance from the Summerlee home. I ran up the hill and pounded on her door. A thin slip of a woman answered. She was tall, and her hair was black as an evening tide, trussed up tight in her bonnet. At first, I thought she was far too young to be a midwife, her pale complexion showing no signs of aging, but as I looked in her eyes, there was no doubt of her maturity.

"Please come quick, my wife has gone into labor."

The midwife grabbed a bag and followed me. We entered my home to the sound of Sarah roaring in pain. I came to her side and took her hand. It was warm and soaked in sweat. The midwife went to the other side of the bed and reached beneath Sarah's dress. She looked concerned.

"What is it?" I asked.

She ignored my question, "We'll need clean linens. If you have spare sheets about, boil them in the hearth and be quick about it."

I went to follow her orders, but Sarah wouldn't let me go. She held my hand and pulled me back to her. "Does my father know? Someone should tell him." She sounded delirious.

"I'll tell him as soon as I've done what the midwife asked."

"Good," she said, breathing hard as another contraction came. Her grip tightened. She held fast even after. "Nathanial I want you to promise me something."

I touched her sweat soaked brow. "Anything for you, my love."

"Promise me that if something happens to me, if something goes wrong, you'll be here for our child. You'll stay here in our home and be a father to him."

She was looking at me so intently. My answer came without thinking. "Yes, of course. I'll be here. Don't worry my love. Everything will be fine. You'll be fine."

The midwife took her hand out from beneath Sarah's dress. It was bright red. Sarah's grip tightened, "Promise me, Nathanial. Give me your word."

Amazed at my audacity, I said, "You have it, I promise." And I knew it was a lie.

Sarah smiled, then groaned in pain as her eyes rolled back. Her grip loosened and fell away from me. I touched her face, felt the air moving in and out of her lips. I called her name and shook her, but she wouldn't respond.

"Sarah, Sarah wake up!" I yelled.

The midwife reached that bloody hand across to me and touched me on the arm. "Foolish man," she said. "Don't you know a promise like that given here with a lie in your heart could damn you for all of your days? And to do it in my sight, what an idiot you are. Hold your tongue and get me those linens." In the light of the candles, the midwife's eyes were glowing.

I backed out of the room, wondering what I'd done, hoping that the last thing I'd said to Sarah wasn't a lie. There was just so much blood. I didn't think for a moment it was normal. I boiled the linens. Then I left the house, running up the hill to get James and his wife. By the time I returned, I heard my child crying in the bedroom with my wife's now cooling body. Sarah was gone, leaving me behind with a promise I couldn't possibly keep.

Chapter 32

Selfish Man

"So the midwife cursed you?" I asked Swift. For some reason, I was thinking of Miss Webster. Swift's description of the midwife reminded me of her.

"No Tom. I don't think so. It was my own flawed nature that cursed me. I made a promise and broke a bond, but that was only a symptom of who I am, a selfish man."

I stayed quiet as Swift collected his thoughts then continued…

West Harbor, 1719
A week passed and on an afternoon tide, the Freedom's Fortune *came round the point and into the mouth of*

Purgatory Cove. Sprowls had come close to missing our deadline. It was only a day before the summer solstice.

I buried my wife and gave my son a name, James for his grandfather. The child and I spent that week at the Summerlee home so Sarah's stepmother could aid me with the newborn. I was in no shape to care for a child. The few times I held my boy I couldn't shake my numbness.

"Your compatriots are back," James said, joining me in front of his house.

"I'd hoped they wouldn't return," I said, staring at the water.

"I as well," he answered.

We stood there in silence, watching them come about. Finally, I said, "They're here for me."

James looked at me, unsure what I meant.

"I made a mistake and now I must pay for it. I have to go with them."

"What have you done?" he asked.

I couldn't bring myself to look at him. "They can't hurt Sarah anymore; at least I'm assured of that."

James grabbed my arm, forcing me to turn towards him. "Tell me what you did."

I told him everything; that I'd stopped trusting my crew. That they'd tried to oust me and that I took prize money to keep for myself. "It's hidden. Only I can find it," I said. "I'm certain once I do, they'll kill me—I'm not concerned about that, though. In fact, I wish they'd finished *me a year ago. But I had to protect you and your family. I had to stay here, or they'd murder you all."*

"You've known this whole time? You've known they were coming to take you and that everyone here was under threat? Why wouldn't you say anything? Why wouldn't you warn us?"

"It's why I stayed," I offered weakly.

He looked out at the Freedom's Fortune *then turned on me again. "And knowing this you wed my daughter, had a child with her?"*

"We were in love. It just happened."

Summerlee was tightening his fists. In a way I wanted him to hit me. "You are a fool and a wretched man Swift. That you would keep this a secret—We could have been ready. A garrison would have been here waiting for them if you'd only said something."

"A garrison? Are you mad? They would've hung us first. We are as guilty as the men aboard that ship," I said, pointing towards the water.

"Fine then, we would have left, or at least been better prepared," Summerlee said.

"Where could we go that they wouldn't have found us?" Summerlee had a tough time coming up with an answer. The colonies were small and returning to England would've cost him everything he'd built.

I turned back to the house, ready to say goodbye to my son, but before I took a step I added, "I said nothing because till this very moment I thought for certain that I'd escape this. I've always been lucky in that way."

"You should be ashamed," he said to my back as I went up the path.

I did feel shame, not for my crimes, but for my failures. It was more than I could take. I wanted it over with.

Something occurred to me, and I turned back to Summerlee, "The boy will have to be taken care of. Can I count on you?"

Summerlee's face, already locked in anger, turned darker. "What sort of question is that?" he breathed out through clenched teeth. "He's my daughter's son, who I doubt has ever really had a father. I'd like to think you've been mourning Sarah, but I think you've only been preparing for your own death."

"I'll find a way out of this and return if I can," I said, knowing it was another lie.

Summerlee scoffed, finally seeing through me.

I went into the house. My boy was sleeping. I left him that way, kissing him on the forehead. I went down the footpath to the water, where I had a small tender waiting on the shore. I pushed it into the cove and rowed out to the Freedom's Fortune.

The ship looked like it'd fallen on hard times. The men seemed to take no pride in the vessel. Barnacles clung to its sides, and in more than one spot I could see rotten wood begging to be replaced or repaired. On deck, *nothing was neat or tidy, and all about was the stink of human flesh and rum. Perhaps it was no different before, but I'd gotten used to the clean house that Sarah kept. Sprowls greeted me warmly at the entryway, satisfied that no matter what happened, he'd won.*

I stood before him, unafraid, "I'll need my sword and a compass," I told him, "and for you to drop anchor in the bay, where I can see open water."

Sprowls held his hands on his hips, towering over me. "You mean that little iron pig sticker with the fancy writing? I'd thought of selling it with the rest of your stuff, but I couldn't find anyone willing to drop a penny on it. It was tossed in with the ballast. We'll have to see if someone can find it." Sprowls was lying. He knew right where the sword was. He'd stowed it in his cabin, knowing how important it was to me.

"If you can't find the sword, then you've lost the island and the treasure," I warned. Sprowls just smiled, guiding me to his cabin, my old cabin. There was shouting and cursing as the men watched me cross the deck. Some of the pirates were enraged, barely held in check by their fellows, while others looked amused. All of them wished me dead.

Sprowls entered the cabin, going to his shelf. He took down the leather bundle and laid it on his desk. I hadn't realized how much I missed the weapon. I went to untie the bundle, but Sprowls stopped me, grabbing my wrist and pulling my hand away. "You won't do anything foolish with this will you Nathanial?"

"I've already done all my foolish things," I said, trying not to grimace from the pain.

He let go of my arm. I stared, wanting to kill him where he stood. The sword was right before me. I could have it in his gut quickly. But what about the others? They'd burn West Harbor to the ground. "It's time I left my rash behavior behind," I said, opening the bundle slowly.

"Time to leave everything behind," Sprowls agreed.

I nodded my head and pointed to the chart of Narragansett Bay on his desk. "I need to see open water at sunset to fix the island's position. It won't be far east of Block Island."

He dropped a compass next to the sword. "Get ready to make your magic," he said before turning to leave the cabin.

They turned the capstan and raised the anchor. Sails were lowered and set, and the rudder turned tightly to bring us away from the narrow headland of the point. I stayed in the cabin, listening to my old crew work.

Going on deck wasn't going to be pleasant, but that wasn't the reason I stayed below. I was leaving West Harbor behind, leaving the place where I buried my wife. I was breaking my promise.

We left before the flood tide waned, beating across the cove and out into the bay, sailing down the eastern shore of Aquidneck Island. The open ocean was before us. Currents pushed against the Freedom's Fortune. The ship tilted and swayed like the branches of a tree in the wind. The air was heavy and humid, but the skies were blue with the summer sun, shining down through a slight haze.

We sailed a little closer to land and dropped anchor. Then Sprowls had his men place a basin on deck. It was barely large enough for my sword.

The crew, these men who wanted nothing more than to see me dead, gathered around as I watched the sun reach the horizon. I looked about for Sampson's men, not that I thought they'd help me, but they'd seen this before. I wondered if they'd be brave enough to watch it again. It wasn't till then that I noticed none of them were left on the ship. After the Madeline was sold they must've taken their pay and gone. Given what happened next I was glad for this.

I dropped my sword in the water and said the ancient words my mother had taught me. The sword floated. Then it started to spin while the pirates stepped back in fear.

These men, so brave in battle, could think of nothing more terrible than magic. The sword stopped and I took out my compass, checking it against the blade's point. I looked up, trying to find the first stars of the evening, but they weren't there.

The sky had been clear a moment before, but now the failing light was covered in dark clouds. They'd rolled in quickly from the south. A gust was building. I'd only seen clouds move so fast, at an unnatural pace, once before.

The wind blew harder, and the water beneath us turned rough, rising and falling as waves hit us from both sides. The currents turned violent as rain began to fall in heavy blinding sheets. The men panicked, convinced this sudden change in weather was sorcery.

Sprowls grabbed me by the shirt, demanding, "What trickery is this? What have you done?"

"The anchor's let loose!" someone called. "We're being pushed back!"

The wind was coming off the land, blowing at our bare masts and hull. It was enough force to shove us towards the islands. The anchor may have broken from the ground, but it was still dragging along the bottom, causing the Freedom's Fortune *to list, putting us at a sharp angle to the ocean. The rough seas swelled over the rail.*

"You've captured a cursed man," I said to Sprowls, thinking of my promise. He didn't care for this, and he showed it by tossing me across the deck. I slid on the wet, tilting planks till my back smashed into the rail.

He turned and looked at my sword. It was in the basin, still defying gravity, floating rigid in the water. The basin was the only thing not moving on the deck. It was held fast by some unseen force. Sprowls reached down to try and grab it, but recoiled in pain as if he were burnt.

He held his hand and looked around at his men, scurrying in fear. "Cut that bloody anchor free! And set sail, turn us about so we can try and run from this weather."

He looked at me again. I still hadn't picked myself up from the ground, feeling as if my back was broken. I turned and glanced over the gunwale. In the distance, I could see the mouth of the cove. A southerly wind was pushing us towards it. I was being carried back home to West Harbor.

Sprowls stormed past me to where men were trying to cut the anchor line. They were taking whacks at it with axes, but in panicked fear, their swings went wide. Sprowls took one of the axes and with a single blow severed the thick line. The Freedom's Fortune swung back. The line snapped like a bullwhip while the ship rocked, swamping on the other side. Men tumbled and fell. I was sent sliding myself, barely able to get my hand on a line.

Our bow, once held roughly to the southeast by the anchor line, almost directly into the raging storm, was turned, putting our port side into the wind. It wouldn't be long before one of these waves rolled us completely. Sprowls, who held onto the rail, was making his way to the command deck, shouting orders above the screaming wind. "Turn us about, turn us about!" But the men were spooked and undisciplined.

Those that followed orders, trying to raise the sails, failed and lost their lives in the effort. The squall was so sudden and violent that anyone climbing the ratlines was tossed off or sent swinging, crashing into the ocean or the deck.

Sprowls got to the wheel. He shoved the helmsman who'd been unable to turn the ship and locked his brawny hands around the spokes. Slowly, but surely, he turned the wheel and the rudder with it. The wind and waves still smashed at us from the southeast, but now our stern took the beating. We were racing along without a single sail, just the wind on our transom.

I looked over the side again and saw the mouth of Purgatory Cove. The shallows on its north shore were darker beneath the swelling white caps. In the failing light, I could see those waves beat against the rocky beaches, uprooting trees and burying boulders. In a short time, we'd been pushed back.

As I watched us approach the mouth of the cove, I thought of all the hazards there, the hidden rocks that could destroy a ship even in good weather. Sprowls wanted shelter, but turning here was destruction. I got to my feet and made my way across the slick and pitching deck. I was thinking of the island where I'd hidden the treasure, the closest I'd ever come to magic. I knew I had to recover my sword.

The violence of the wind grew stronger with each step I took, and the rain and spray felt like it would drown me. I reached the basin and dipped my hand into the water, closing my fist around the pommel. The water, charged with mystical energy, washed up my arm with heat and terror. I held on and pulled the blade out.

No matter what happened to the men around me, as long as I had the sword I knew I had the treasure.

At that moment I heard a sound that I, and I'm sure Sprowls, had hoped never to hear again: the sound of a ship running aground.

We were at the mouth of Purgatory Cove when we collided with Fisherman's Rock, a wide, flat stone sub-merged under the tide. Every sailor from this area knew to avoid it, but we weren't given a choice. The wind forced us to where the rock sat in the deep of the channel.

The Freedom's Fortune *rose up on a wave and came slamming down, smashing her keel, snapping her back and breaking in half. Her weak seams splintered. On deck, it was a far different scene from when the* Mayfair *ran aground. There we'd had time; we'd hit the reef and the ship held together.*

The Freedom's Fortune *was not nearly as lucky. In a moment she dissolved before my eyes, ripped apart and torn down to the planks and nails. The ship became a swirling death trap for any on her. Most didn't even have time to scream the destruction was so sudden. The ship exploded from the fierceness of the impact.*

The boards beneath my feet came apart and I fell through to the water, while the broken wood crushed and suffocated the men around me, twisting and breaking their bones. I swam down through the wreckage while lumber swarmed over and on me.

I stayed alive, still struggling, but I couldn't surface for air. There was no space in which to bring my head up. The more buoyant timber of the ship kept men buried beneath the waves. Like having a house built on top of you. I held my breath till my lungs burnt. There was nothing to do but open my mouth.

That's when I saw her...

"Saw who?" I asked Swift. I was leaning over, pulling the line to the boat closer. I needed to load my things, but for some reason, I didn't want to wade out into the cove. The water was dark again.

"Does it matter Tom? If you haven't believed a single word I've said, what chance is there that you'll believe what happened next? I'm not certain I believe it myself."

"Please," I said.

He nodded.

Narragansett Bay, 1719

In the dark of the water, trapped below the wreckage with all those men dying, I saw my wife. She was glowing like a beacon, the one good thing in that moment of destruction. She came to me and took my hand, and led me across the water to the little beach that once sat below my home.

I stepped out of the water, coughing and choking, looking back at her. She wouldn't follow me. She stayed with the waves, though I could tell it pained her.

She spoke. "Because I love you," she said, "I've saved you from the damned and the ocean. But you've called on ancient powers and used them for selfish reasons." She pointed to my sword. "These things come with a price. They will test you."

"I'm sorry I lied. I'm sorry I broke my promise," I said.

"Are you?" she asked with a sadness a living person isn't capable of. I had to look away, unable to answer.

Then she continued, "Age will not kill you, nor any device of man, for as long as your desires remain impure." She reached out her hand to me in farewell, saying "I love you Nathanial," then she disappeared.

"I didn't understand her message, but I knew my time on the ocean was done. If I tried to cross it, my soul would be claimed by the men I sent to the bottom, those shadows waiting for me." He pointed to the cove. "My gold goes unclaimed since I can't return to the island."

He motioned back toward town. "I can't wander from this place. When I do, I grow weak, but I don't die. I have to stay here just as I promised her."

"And now I've promised you something," I said.

Swift was quiet, but it looked like he had more to say.

"So what happened in West Harbor when you returned?" I asked.

"For the longest time, I tried to stay away. I lived in the forest as a hermit, but I grew frail, weak and sickly. I thought I had a disease and that it would eventually kill me. Like you, I didn't believe, not completely. I thought my wife was an illusion brought on by nearly drowning. The island, my cursed crew; those things I was willing to accept, but living forever seemed too strange. I thought I'd pass away, but as time went on and I lived, I knew it was true. I aged but I didn't die," he motioned to himself.

"What did you do?" I asked.

"I eventually returned to town, to my land, and watched my boy from a distance. By then he was a man. Summerlee raised him as his son."

"You didn't tell him who you are?"

"No, he was better off believing James was his father. And besides, I knew something, something I've never spoken aloud."

I waited for him to continue.

He bent down and placed his hand on my shoulder. It made me uncomfortable staring into his intense blue eyes. "No matter what I've told you Tom, or told myself, no matter how much it seems like I had no choice, I didn't wait here to protect the Summerlees. I may have believed that at one time, but my best lies are to myself. I wasn't protecting anyone. I was here for greed and pride. I waited here for Sprowls because the man had my sword, my only way back to the island and my treasure."

Swift let go of my shoulder and stood up. "It's mine I tell you, and I won't be bested," he said firmly. I felt a shiver of fear, believing this was the most honest Swift had ever been with me.

Chapter 33

Family Matters

I left Swift and hit the grocery store, making a supply run for the boat. I made sure I was home before Mom and hid the canned food in the closet. She came in around six to find me already in bed. I'd jumped in when I heard her car pull up. I'd been standing close to a lamp with the shade off to make my skin feel warm. I heard the door close then started coughing, really working myself into a full-on, chest-rattling fit. She stuck her head in my room. "Why are you in bed already?"

"I'm a little tired. I thought I'd get some rest," I said.

"Have you been coughing like that all day?" she asked.

"Since this morning. It wouldn't be so bad if my head and throat didn't hurt so much."

She came into the room and touched my forehead. "You are warm. I'll go get the thermometer."

"Okay," I said. "Do you think you could get me a drink too?"

She nodded and I worked myself into another coughing fit. As she left the room, I wondered if she'd go so far as to buy another thermometer. You see, the one in the medicine cabinet had somehow managed to fall into the trash, then silly me, I took the trash out.

Okay, maybe I did that on purpose, but defeating the device was too tricky. I tried using a cup of hot water, but it was tough to get to the perfect, 'I'm sick' temperature. Cooking around 115 degrees kind of destroys your credibility. I decided to remove it from the playing field altogether.

"I don't know where that thermometer is," she said, coming back into the room and handing me a drink, "but if you're really not feeling that well maybe you should stay home tomorrow."

"If you think so," I said, rolling over. "I just want to get some rest."

"I'll let you do that then," she said, starting to leave.

"Hey, mom?" She paused in the doorway. *This is so not the best time for this,* I thought, but I wanted to check one more time. By tomorrow it'd be too late to change my plans. "You remember the letter Dad wrote?"

"Sure," she answered.

"You know how he asked me to come down and see him. I was wondering, is there any chance of that happening?" I tried to sound as pitiful as I could, hoping it might help change her mind.

"Tom, we already talked about this. You're going into that summer program. There's no way you could take such a long break," she pleaded for me to understand.

"Okay, okay," I said. "I just miss him, that's all."

"I'm sorry," she said lamely.

I am too, I thought, knowing tomorrow I'd be leaving.

Chapter 34

Navigation

There was no reason to get up in the morning. I wasn't going to school, but my eyes popped open with the sun anyway. I stared at the ceiling and listened to my mom in the shower. Then listened to her blow-drying and fumbling with the coffee pot. It was slow torture. Finally, I heard the door close. I got out of bed and started gathering my things.

I was going to meet Swift early, but I couldn't just run out the door, I had to leave a note. I had to let her know what I was doing…Well, not exactly what I was doing.

> *Dear Mom,*
> *I'm sorry, but I had to get away.*
> *I love you, and I'll write,*
> *Tom*

It was all I could come up with.

I rode my bike to Swift's yard. He was up on the bow of his tugboat, sipping a hot cup of tea and staring out at the cove. He waved me up.

"Are you nervous?" he asked.

"Should I be?" I came up the ladder.

He shrugged, finishing his drink in a long swallow. "We should get started." He put his cup on the stern rail and wiped his beard. "We need to go over your trip. Plan it so you can make your way out and back. You'll need to learn some landmarks since you're returning in the dark.

"We'll rig up some marker lights. I've got some battery operated ones that should do. How are you with a compass and a chart?"

"I've used a compass before, and I've been studying a few charts on my own." I showed him the maps in the ICW guidebook.

He flipped through the book. "This isn't what I meant. A good chart will give you things like water depth, lights, buoys, hazards, things to fix your position on. Come in, I'll show you."

As I followed him into his cabin, he said, "Luckily you won't be going far from Narragansett Bay."

Sunlight streamed through the dirt-stained windows into his little room. His rough wool blanket was thrown on the floor, half-covering a mountain of old books. He pulled a chart from a long plastic tube. "We'll take it outside," he said, after looking for a place to set it down in the messy cabin.

At the bow, he held it open with some discarded tools. Narragansett Bay was laid out with the land a sandy-yellow and the water a baby-blue, carved up by deep trenches of white showing where the water's depth fell below twenty feet.

"It'll be easier coming down the West Passage," Swift said, pointing at Conanicut Island, "Go under the bridge and head for the light at Beavertail." He handed me the compass and pointed to its face. "Once you can sight the light around 40 degrees off magnetic north, I want you to turn west, putting your heading at 120 degrees."

He saw the confusion on my face. "You said you know how to use a compass?"

"Well yeah, I get the whole thing where it always points north and that you can figure the other directions from that."

"And that'd be enough for anything but sailing. You're looking for a specific point in the middle of the ocean. Accuracy counts. Do you know what I meant by magnetic north?"

I held my hands up.

He rubbed his head. "What makes a compass work is the magnetic pull of the northernmost point of the Earth, the North Pole. However, there are two north poles; the geographic one, which is the point the Earth rotates on, and the magnetic one, which is the northern end of Earth's magnetic core. It moves about a bit. That's what compasses are set to, and that's what you have to steer by." He motioned to the face of the compass. "You see the inner ring with the numbers around it?" I nodded. "Those degrees are set by magnetic north. In my day we'd call them points."

He put his thumb on the edge and pointed out a hash mark. "This at the front is the lubber line. That'll be your heading. It should always be pointing in the direction of your bow, the direction the boat is going in.

"It'll look like the face of the compass is turning, but it's your boat that changes direction. These degrees let you know just how far off north you're moving."

"I think I get it. So when you say 40 degrees, the light'll be to my left um, port side and behind me."

"That's right, and when I tell you to turn on a heading of 120 degrees, you're now heading east and a little south." He went back to the chart and motioned to Brenton Point, the most southern tip of Aquidneck Island, home to the city of Newport. "Here I'll have you start to the south, towards open water and Rhode Island Sound. You'll set your course at 190 degrees then just keep going. It'll be a long stretch without much around you to get a fix on."

He looked at me again, hopeful that I knew what a fix was. I had that same blank look.

"A fix is the nautical term for being able to tell where you are." He explained.

I'll summarize the rest because it required a ruler and a long explanation by Swift. See you got a fix by figuring where you were in relation to landmarks; by seeing how far in degrees those landmarks were from magnetic north.

Knowing where you were in relation, you could get the line that your boat is on. If you could figure out a few of these lines of position and see where they crossed on the chart, you could come close to finding your actual location.

"Straight lines can only do what Tom?" Swift asked.

I remembered one of my geometry lessons. "They can only cross at one point," I answered.

"And that's where you'll be," Swift said before going back over the course. He drew it out on the chart with a pencil and a funny set of double rulers. Then he rolled up the chart and handed it and the compass over. We walked down to the water. Using points around the cove I 'fixed' our position several times on the shoreline.

"You'll be returning in the dark, so it's important you pay attention to your compass and the lights in the bay. It'd be easy to become confused and head in the wrong direction," Swift warned.

"You really believe I'll find it don't you?" I asked.

"Of course I do. I've been there. You'll see it at sunset this very day. It'll appear as if it had always been there. Point your bow right at it. Don't worry about moving with haste. I think once the island knows your intention it takes care of the rest.

"The dock will be glistening white. My treasure will be waiting there. You can climb up, but pay no attention to anything on the island itself. Don't listen to the music it sings or look at the sights it shows you. They're all seductions meant to pull you in."

"When the treasure is aboard, head back to the bay, the light at Point Judith will probably be the first landmark you see. If you can't find that, follow the fishing boats, they'll be heading there for the night."

I looked at the chart and found Point Judith. Not far from it was Galilee and Jerusalem; in-between was the entrance to Point Judith Pond, a wide, safe body of water to wait out the night.

Swift was still talking, his finger pointing at the course he wanted me to take home. "Follow the lights on land. We'll meet here, at Bishop's Point. Got it?" His hand touched the spot I first saw him use the sword.

"I've got it." I nodded my head. "If I find the island—"

"And if you don't?" he asked.

"Then don't expect me back. If the only thing I find out there is more ocean, then I'm gone."

I expected Swift to argue with me, to make me promise again or something. Instead, he asked, "Where is that you want to go so badly?"

It took me a moment to answer. "I'm going to see my dad. He's in Florida."

"Florida?" Swift asked. It was the first time I'd seen him surprised. "You're planning to sail all the way to Florida?"

"It can be done," I said.

"Oh I know," Swift said. "But it's also dangerous."

"More dangerous than your island?"

"I suppose not." He rolled up the chart and handed it to me.

We left his yard and walked to the water, to the wall where my boat waited.

I loaded supplies while he tried to impart as much knowledge as he could, rambling on and repeating many of the things he'd said before, "Now be careful coming about…. Remember to keep those lines neat…. If you lose the wind, let the sail out…." He seemed more nervous than me.

When my supplies were stowed, I came back ashore. We sat on the wall. "So all the way to Florida?" Swift asked again.

I nodded my head. "I want to see my dad," I said, then I filled him in on the whole thing. How it'd been a trip he wanted to take. "Just imagine the look on his face when I show up in this." I told him a little bit about my parents' divorce. Swift listened quietly.

Eventually, 2 o'clock came and it was time for me to leave. Swift took the little boat's line and pulled it in close to the wall so I could get aboard. "Thank you for fixing the boat, and you know, for everything you've shown me," I said.

He stayed quiet as I stepped onto the bow. I pulled up the anchor and placed the oars in their locks, rowing out into the cove and raising my sails. I looked back to find Swift, but he'd left, going up the road. I thought he was going back to his yard.

I pulled on the mainsheet, looking over at the docks. I found Swift there, his wild hair puffing out like a cloud around his head. His blue eyes were pointed at me, so I gave him a wave.

He didn't move, didn't respond. The wind took up my sail, demanding my attention. By the time I looked back, Swift's eyes were on the water directly below him. His mouth moved, and his finger pointed down, arguing with the surface of the cove. Crazy, I thought, knowing there was nothing out there waiting for me.

Chapter 35

A Little Trip

At the mouth of the cove, I found a good strong wind. I passed Conanicut point and looked south towards the Jamestown Bridge and Dutch Island. They grew slowly in the distance as the land, the houses, and the beach moved past. I kept my eyes forward, not wishing to see what was in my wake, knowing I had no intention of returning.

I passed under the Jamestown Bridge. Its shadow cast a long line in the bay, darkening the water around me. Above, I could just barely hear the cars speed by. It was quiet, and the wind felt stronger in the shade.

The afternoon sun beat on me, and the relief under the bridge felt good. A little over an hour out and my neck and arms were starting to burn. I hadn't thought of sunscreen. My ball cap was pulled down tight, protecting my head and most of my face, but my cheeks and ears were starting to get warm. I dipped my hand in the salt water and tried using it to cool off, but when the water dried the salt made me feel worse.

Dutch Island came and went. My hand felt frozen on the rudder holding the course. Occasionally a motorboat raced past leaving a bouncy wake.

I came to the light at Beavertail and fixed my course, heading east towards Brenton Point. Crossing the east passage, between Jamestown and Newport, I was shocked to see how many more boats were on this side of the island. Small ones and massive ones with white sails, too numerous to count.

I watched them as I crossed the passage, only a few were running down this far. Mostly they stayed in close to the harbor and the Newport Bridge, which stood even taller than Jamestown's.

Using a mansion on one island and a hotel on the other I found my position, steering towards Brenton Point. People were out flying kites at the small park on the Point. I came across it and corrected course again, turning out towards the open water. Hours passed and the afternoon wore on. From time to time I'd turn and watch the land behind me getting smaller. The number of boats decreased.

To my right, in the west, the sun was getting lower in the sky. The mainland was fading into the horizon, a blurry gray line. Block Island was coming into focus, its cliffs rising from the water, large and solid. There was nothing for me to do but hold this course till dark. *When the sun goes down, I'll turn around*, I thought, *head back to the light at Point Judith.*

Safe harbor for the night then back at it in the morning. A few weeks of this, then I'd see my dad again. I imagined us out on his boat, fishing and chasing around the islands of the Florida Keys.

The rocking of the waves was peaceful as I pictured his face, seeing me arrive in this sailboat, the work done with my own hands, mine and Swift's that is.

I felt bad for Swift, a lonely old man making up stories to get attention. He'd be waiting for me, waiting for his treasure. Maybe he could join us down there fishing. My father would like his stories…I was daydreaming of course. But all those people, Sampson, Sarah, James, Burnaby, and Sprowls and those shadows, I couldn't stop thinking about them. My own dreams slipped into mind, those pirates out in the cove, the shadows of men standing on water, that hand on the deck.

I thought about the day Swift tied the boat to the wall, something had pulled him down. It'd been right around this time of day. I pictured the dark water, the way it seemed to hold him. A shiver ran down my spine.

Open ocean was the only thing in front of me, going on forever, dark and vast. I looked back at the land. It made me feel more alone. It was so far behind me now.

The water moved across the hull, small waves slapping against it. The block and tackle creaked a little, and the wind moved across my ears, touching those small sensitive hairs. There was nothing for me to do but watch the sunset in the west, nothing to do but wait, breathe as if I didn't feel something creeping up on me.

The sun fell and fell. I had my hat pulled low over my eyes, watching the outer edges of its glow as it closed the distance to the ocean. Inches or miles, it didn't matter; the pace was slow, incredibly slow. I held the rudder, the most firm, real thing I could put my hand on.

There was a change in the air that had nothing to do with the wind. Though that had been becoming more erratic, gusting from every direction it seemed. I waited and watched with a heaviness in my chest. The sun seemed to be hovering rather than falling. I realized I was holding my breath.

The sail loosened and flapped wildly. I let out my lines a bit and played with them, trying to trim the cloth, but it refused to cooperate. I turned my rudder a bit and felt the sail catch. The swirling wind calmed as the sun touched the water. Slowly it was eaten by the curve of the earth. It was time, I realized as I pulled the main sheet tight, trimming my sail. I looked at the sun, expecting to see the island there.

Of course, it wasn't. I felt relieved.

I turned my eyes back to my sail, hoping that this change in the wind hadn't thrown me too far off course, when beyond my mast something happened.

As large and real as any piece of land it was suddenly there. It was in front of me like it'd always been, the island.

It was just as Swift had described it, tropical and beautiful, green and lush, with mountains inland that seemed to shine in the sun almost like the towers of a lost city. Sandy beaches surrounded its whole coast. The dock jutted out into the water, welcoming me.

There was something else. Something Swift hadn't told me about. On shore just inside the shadows of the forest, there were people. I could hardly see them with my eyes, but my head filled in the details, the way a sleeper remembers a dream.

They were amazing, slim and tall, beautiful beyond imagining as they danced to music both familiar and strange, like wisps of clouds in a blue sky. They moved in and out of the tree line, painfully inviting.

I wanted to land my little sailboat on that beach. I wanted to join those people. Then I remembered Swift's warning. 'Go only to the dock and do not leave it despite anything you see.'

I thought of my father, how much I wanted to see him. I was frightened by how much more I wanted to land on this magical place.

My voice cracked, "Oh boy," it was the only thing I could think to say. I set my course and trimmed my sail, running with the wind behind me.

Chapter 36
A Waiting Place

While I was out looking for magical islands, something happened back in town. I didn't get the whole story till later, but as it directly affects me and my trip, I'll fill in the details here. See, about an hour before I was faced with Tír-Na-Nóg, there was a theft.

Pete Barlson, who worked at the gas dock at the marina, witnessed the crime. He told the story to the police, who were trying to find out as much as they could about the hermit on the hill. Everybody else in town would hear through the usual lines of gossip. Apparently, Captain Swift had committed one final act of piracy.

Pete told the police, "There was a thirty-two footer pulled up to the dock, a real monsta. It was pretty, with these wicked powerful inboard engines. I tried making conversation with the owner, but he was Uppity. Anyway, I saw the nutter from up the way, sitting down on Dock E."

Apparently Swift had been in the same spot since I'd left that afternoon. "He was there by himself, but it sounded like he was arguing with someone." Pete said, "I saw him pointing his finger at the water and saying something like, 'What do you want me to do? He's already gone and you blackguards won't let me help him anyway.' Then the guy waits like he's listening." Pete said. "Then he starts yelling, 'Don't blame me! You were going to go in a bad way anyway. The boy will be fine.'"

Pete said he missed something after that because he took the boat owner's credit card, and walked into the little shack by the pumps. "I was looking down, punching the numbers into the card machine when I heard a ruckus. I looked up and saw the crazy guy come flying down the dock. He jumped into the boat and was holding this big weird knife on the owner.

"He says to him, 'I'll be having this boat now. I'm raising the flag on her. Off you go.' Nuttiest thing I ever heard.

"Anyway, the owner just stares at that knife, like he didn't know what to do. It didn't look very sharp, but it's huge, and the guy holding it was as crazy as a loon.

"'Walk or swim it's up to you,' he tells him.

"When he moved the blade away, the boat's owner jumps over the side, scared as can be. Then the old guy takes that knife, whacks the lines, cuts right through them. That's when I came out of the shack to help the owner up. I watched the old guy go tearing out of the cove. He brought the bow straight up and blew out of the no-wake zone, tossing people around on every dock."

"That was the last thing you saw," the police had asked Pete.

"No, there was something else, something kind of odd," Pete said. "I'd never seen anything like it before. There was this dark spot in the water, following the boat. It looked like a school of fish only darker, like pitch black. The motorboat left it behind, like way behind. But that black spot was following him. Tracking the boat like a dog."

That's what Pete saw while I was staring at a magical island. I was miles from home with the sun hanging on the horizon and the first stars of the evening in the sky. All I wanted was to land my little boat on the sand and run off into that forest.

It was the music that had me. If there were words, they weren't in any language I understood. Sampson, who had been taken from his home when he was a child, heard his mother's voice in the island's song. I don't know if it was singing or instruments playing, but they soothed me.

The ancient marble dock jutted out into the sea, a safe place to land, but I held my course straight for the sandy beach, not sure why. The sun was frozen above the horizon, and the waves lapping against my hull were muffled. The whole world was still. Time stopped. Only the music from the island moved. I was in a dream, sailing on.

Then something broke through the peace. A loud, unpleasant noise tore into the silence, smashing it to pieces. Buzzing just above the island's song, it was getting louder, coming from behind me.

I turned to see a powerboat bearing down on me, skipping across the waves, bouncing and jumping, closing the distance between us. *Someone must've seen the island and was heading for it too*, I thought. Swift said this was the closest it had come to the mainland in years. Maybe I wasn't the only one seeing it. I was angry as my head began to clear.

I looked at the dock again, remembering Swift saying it was the only place I should land. It took all my will to turn my rudder and change course. I was so close now. The water beneath me turned a different color. It was lighter, sparkling and shimmering in the fading light. With the spell finally broken I tried not to look at the island.

Swift and I had an agreement. I'd return his treasure to him. Then this boat would be mine free and clear, and I could sail away. I could see my dad. That's what I really wanted. I was afraid, though, frightened that as soon as I pulled up to the dock, I wouldn't be able to fight the urge to run down it to the beach.

The engines of the motorboat were getting even louder. I turned to see it nearly on top of me. *Sailboats have the right of way*, I thought while trying to predict his course. He was going to run straight across my bow.

The boat was coming down hard. "Turn away!" I screamed, waving my arms.

He wasn't going to turn. He was putting himself directly in front of me. The only way to avoid a collision was to twist the rudder hard over and break my sail loose. I did it quickly, and the wind dumped as the bow came about. All forward speed was lost.

The motorboat cut back its engines and turned in hard. It'd been moving like a bullet across the water, but it suddenly became more like a shovel as its momentum slammed it against the surface of the ocean.

The waves slapped hard on its hull, tipping and tilting it like a cork. The engines complained as they were pushed into reverse. Foam sprayed from below the transom till the boat stopped rocking enough for the screws to grab hold of the water. It was coming back towards me.

I looked at my sail, ready to pull the mainsheet in and take up another heading, but now I could see the motorboat's deck. I could see a head of wild, white hair and a bearded face whipped pink by the ocean air. It was Swift, and he was waving to me.

Why was he here? I had a tough time caring with the island in front of me.

He saw me fixing my sail and called over the engines, "No Tom!"

I looked at him then looked at the island. This was the reason he sent me. Why would he want me to stop?

The island felt like a bubble held on the end of a wand, as if it was going to pop at any moment.

"Please Tom," he pleaded after cutting his engines and letting the boats come slowly together. I looked at him, then let the halyard loose. The gaff came down with the sail, landing in a pile.

"Why!" I demanded.

He shook his head. "That island is no place for a boy. I've been guilty of many things, but I won't allow this."

"But it's real. And we had a bargain," I said.

"Of course it's real. But of all the things you're supposed to do in your life, I don't think this is included," he said, pointing over his shoulder. "Not yet anyway."

"I don't understand."

Swift reached across to hold my boat steady. He motioned for me to come closer. "Look there? On the beach, can you see them?"

There were people wandering down to the surf. "Yes," I said.

"Do you know any of them?"

I looked hard, there was something familiar about all of them, but none of the individual faces were clear. "I don't think so," I answered.

"Well, I do. See the woman in white, the one closest to the surf. She's waving to us now." I could see her. She was beautiful. "That's Sarah, who I lost so many years ago. She's there waiting for me, and she's never looked lovelier. I only hope I'm worthy of her."

Swift put his hand on my shoulder, "I think that's what this place is, somewhere where people wait. I've got to go, but you boy, you've got your whole life to live and you've risked enough today."

"But what about our deal?"

Swift smiled and nodded his head, "I'm changing the bargain. I have a different task for you."

I couldn't imagine what he wanted. I was scared, but still, I asked.

He pulled at his beard and looked at the little sail-boat. "You can keep this and take it anywhere in the world under one condition." His voice was stern and serious. "You have to take a trip, out into the cove, and take your mother with you as a passenger. You can take her any-where you wish, but until you do, this boat will still be mine and to sail off with it would be stealing, an act of piracy. If you've learned anything from my life, you'll see the weight of such sins."

I thought about it, thought about all my plans, the trip to Florida to see my father. Then I pictured my mom finding that note. I imagined what her life would be like during the month that I'd be sailing south, the fear and worry she'd go through. I nodded my head to Swift. "I'll do it," I said, feeling a heaviness lift.

"Good, Tom, but now it's time for me to go. The island won't wait, and there's others who'd take me somewhere worse." He reached below the gunwale and came up with his leather bundle, the one that held his sword, the sword of Oisín, the only way a mortal could find Tír-Na-Nóg

"Keep it safe," he said, before going back to the helm.

He looked toward the mainland. Something was approaching.

Swift pushed the throttle up, and the engines roared loudly as the boat lifted its bow. He turned and sped toward the island. The water turned dark behind him. It was moving, following him.

I watched the darkness close in. Swift saw it too. He was going full speed towards the beach. The blackness was creeping up over the side, covering the hull, reaching for Swift where he stood at the helm. In a moment the whole boat was covered. I stared in horror waiting to see if he'd collide first or be dragged off.

His boat slammed into the sand, flying apart. *He has to be dead or badly hurt*, I thought, looking at the wreckage. However, Swift wasn't on the boat when it hit. Just before it crashed, he'd tucked himself into a ball and jumped off the back, dropping like a sack into the water.

Sarah ran out into the waves, taking him by the hand and helping him to his feet. I watched Swift step out of the surf and onto the sand. With each step, he changed.

He was no longer an old man. Like Sarah, he was a truer form of himself, young and healthy.

The black shadow had held onto the boat as it crashed. It broke on the beach then spread and disappeared. It may have been pulled apart by the waves or sent to the bottom, or it may have clung to the island.

I couldn't be sure, because in another moment all the answers were gone. To my right, the sun dropped from view. The evening star shined bright to the north and the island, Tír-Na-Nóg was gone. I was alone.

Epilogue

It was past midnight by the time I returned to West Harbor and even later when I tied up the boat and started for home. The trip wasn't easy. I had to find my way through the bay in the dark. I followed the lights on the shore like bread crumbs, staying just off the coast.

I had a chart and a flashlight. I tried using them to figure my location, but mostly I was just guessing. When I sailed into the cove, I looked at the condos where I lived. It was easy to find ours because the light was still on.

I tied up the boat in the usual spot and took my bike from Swift's yard. I wondered what would happen to all these old boats now that Swift had left. Liam came out of the dark, like a shadow. He didn't wag his tail, but he didn't growl either. I bent down and petted him. It didn't dawn on me till later, that was the first time I'd ever done that. "We're going to have to do something with you, aren't we boy?" I asked, but that could wait till morning.

I rode home, secured my bike, and then went in the door.

"Tom," my mom called as my keys turned in the lock.

I didn't know what to expect. My mom was standing there, halfway between worry and anger. She grabbed me, pulled me close, and hugged me tight. "What were you thinking?" she asked.

"I just wanted to see Dad," I said, hearing her swallow back tears.

She looked at me, not sure what to say. I was beyond exhausted.

"I was just so worried. I just…" she choked up again, holding me. I was falling asleep standing there. She guided me to my room. "Get some rest. We have a lot to talk about in the morning."

I said to her, "I'm sorry Mom."

"It's okay Tom, we'll talk about it the morning."

"Hey, Mom?"

"Yeah?" she asked.

"Do you think Grandma and Grandpa would like a dog?"

I was asleep before I heard her answer.

Friday morning came, and my mom was at the breakfast table sipping her coffee. I was still exhausted when I came out of my room fully clothed. She looked up at me expectantly, calmer than she'd been the night before and ready to talk, but before she could even say good morning, I spoke up. "Mom, I know there's stuff we need to discuss, but there's something I have to show you first, something we need to do."

She, of course, asked me what it was, and she re-minded me of the graduation at school. "It'll be quick," I said.

I told her to put on some comfortable clothes. She asked again what it was while we drove down Main Street, turning toward the water. She also asked why my face was so sunburned. I didn't give her any answers, not until we were at Swift's yard where I had her park. She was nervous when Liam came out from the barn. He grumbled at us a little, but when I put my hand out he placed his head under it, letting me pet him.

"Oh, he's friendly," my mom said.

"That's a matter of some debate," I mumbled. Then I added, "I'm just going to feed him before I show you why we're here."

"You mean it's not the dog?" she asked as I ran off.

When Liam's bowl was full I came and grabbed her hand. I led her down the hill to the boat launch and the wall. "That's mine," I said, pointing at the little wooden craft.

"What, how did you…?" she started to ask.

"Well it's not mine yet," I interrupted her. "I prom-ised someone I'd take you sailing before it'll actually belong to me. Maybe I can tell you while we're out there."

She looked at her watch.

"Mom, it's more important to me than my middle school graduation."

She wanted to argue, I'd could tell but then she surprised me. "Fine," she said, shaking her head.

The two of us went down to the water. I helped her into the boat and rowed us out till I had enough wind to get underway. I tried not to show the pride I felt as I trimmed the sail, keeping my lines neat as I set us on an easy course.

My mom sat on the side bench and I had the rudder as we left the cove. We started to talk and we didn't stop till we returned home several hours later. I told her about Swift, but I didn't mention the island, only that he was gone now.

We talked about the academy, her reasons for wanting me to go, my reasons for wanting to stay. She talked about my father and how she understood how much I wanted to see him, and we talked about my grandparents, how maybe now my grandfather saw that my grandma needed help. We talked about what she wanted for me and about what I wanted for myself and how we weren't going to solve any problems between the two of us by running away.

When we got out of the boat, we talked about what a lovely day it was and how we'd have to make more time to do this again. No real decisions were made, nothing was settled, but by the time we were driving home, things felt better.

We each had our own thoughts. I couldn't tell you where my mother's head was, but I can tell you mine was in another world, another place called Tír-Na-Nóg.

About the Author

Pete A O'Donnell is the creator of the children's story website Illadvisedstories.com, where kids can listen to free and funny adventures. He is a graduate of Queens University with a degree in Journalism and Creative Writing. He works as firefighter and EMT, and has a deep interest in history. The Curse of Purgatory Cove is his first book. It started as a short story when he was a kid, but after reading about the pirate ship Whydah, recovered with its treasure off of Cape Cod, the little story about a paperboy became something more.

If you'd like to Contact the author you can reach him at:
Email: Pete@Illadivsedstories.com
https://twitter.com/PeteODonnell057
https://www.instagram.com/peteodinri/
https://www.facebook.com/illadvisedstories/
Snail Mail: PO Box 6072, Warwick, Rhode Island 02887
Or listen to free stories at
Illadvisedstories.com

Illadvisedstories.com